'IT WAS—AWFUL. AWFUL. OH GOD—'

She put her hands to her face, trying to shut the persistent images of blood and dark hair and white splintered bone, of green glass and bruised, splayed limbs.

'I panicked and ran away, out into the garden. I screamed, I can remember that...'

'All right, love. Last question: have you any idea why anyone would want to kill your employer?'

'*Want* to kill her? How *could* anyone want to kill Jasmine? It must have been done by someone who was trying to steal from her.'

'Um,' commented WPC Knowles. 'You don't know of anyone who hated her?'

'No! No, of course not. That's absurd, no one could possibly have hated Jasmine. Some people disliked her books, and some envied her money, but no one actually hated her. How could they?'

THE CHIEF INSPECTOR'S DAUGHTER
by
Sheila Radley

Bantam Books offers the finest in classic and modern English murder mysteries. Ask your bookseller for the books you have missed.

THE CHIEF INSPECTOR'S DAUGHTER

Sheila Radley

BANTAM BOOKS

TORONTO · NEW YORK · LONDON · SYDNEY · AUCKLAND

*This low-priced Bantam Book
has been completely reset in a type face
designed for easy reading, and was printed
from new plates. It contains the complete
text of the original hard-cover edition.*
NOT ONE WORD HAS BEEN OMITTED.

THE CHIEF INSPECTOR'S DAUGHTER
*A Bantam Book / published by arrangement with
Charles Scribner's Sons*

PRINTING HISTORY
Scribner's edition published December 1980

Bantam edition / January 1988

ISBN 0-553-26942-9

Published simultaneously in the United States and Canada

Bantam Books are published by Bantam Books, Inc. Its trademark, consisting of the words "Bantam Books" and the por-
trayal of a rooster, is Registered in U.S. Patent and Trademark
Office and in other countries. Marca Registrada. Bantam
Books, Inc., 666 Fifth Avenue, New York, New York 10103.

PRINTED IN THE UNITED STATES OF AMERICA

O   0 9 8 7 6 5 4 3 2 1

For Grace

Extract from the *East Anglian Daily Press*, Tuesday 7 April:

LOCAL AUTHOR MURDERED

Jasmine Woods, the well-known novelist, was found dead yesterday morning in her isolated Suffolk home, Yeoman's, near Breckham Market. The body was discovered by Miss Alison Quantrill, who has for the past six weeks been working as the novelist's secretary. Miss Quantrill, younger daughter of Chief Inspector Douglas Quantrill, head of Breckham Market CID, was not available yesterday for comment. A police spokesman has confirmed that the incident is being treated as murder. A man was at divisional headquarters last night, helping the police with their enquiries.

THE CHIEF INSPECTOR'S DAUGHTER

1

'Anthrax,' thought Douglas Quantrill gloomily as he watched his daughter step down from the London train, wearing a coat of shaggy hide that looked as though it had been transferred half-cured from a particularly unsavoury Afghan goat.

Alison, the younger of his daughters, had always been Quantrill's favourite. Knowing that she needed a new winter coat, he had given her part of an income-tax rebate as an unusually generous combined birthday and Christmas present, with instructions to buy herself a sheepskin. What he had had in mind was the kind of sensibly English fleece-lined suede jacket that he had recently bought his wife; he might have known, he sighed to himself as he turned up his raincoat collar against the February sleet and began to tramp down the long platform, that Alison would go for something more outlandish and impractical. It was unbecoming, too: she was small, and the combination of the over-long shaggily lined coat with the straight hair that fell over her downcast face gave her the sad appearance of a neglected Skye terrier.

A male fellow-passenger helped her with her luggage, and Quantrill saw her push aside her dark hair and dredge up a smile of thanks with obvious difficulty. Now she stood waiting for her father, forlorn, surrounded by the suitcased remains of her bid for independence.

Quantrill sent his heart out to her, and hurried after it. From behind him he heard the thump of footsteps, and a fit-looking middle-aged man passed him in a burst of speed, one hand hoisting an umbrella, the other outstretched. A fair

1

girl of Alison's age came running up the platform to meet the man, and they embraced enthusiastically.

'Daddy!'

'Darling—lovely to see you!'

'Great to be home again. Are you and Mummy well? You look well—oh, it's good to come home!'

They moved past him towards the exit, beaming fondly at each other under the umbrella, arms entwined, and Quantrill felt a touch of irritable envy: greetings were less ostentatious in his family.

He came up to his daughter, smiled at her, and bent to press his mouth shyly and awkwardly on her cold cheek. 'Hallo, Alison.'

She returned an equally unpractised filial kiss: 'Hallo, Dad.'

He was shocked by the thinness of her face and by the huge melancholy of the eyes that were green as his own. He longed to be able to hug his daughter as that other father had done—as he himself had done when his children were small. But as the girls had grown, so a reserve had grown up on both sides; on their mother's side, too, because Molly was from a family as traditionally undemonstrative as the Quantrills. Embraces and endearments between adults, he reflected, seemed to come more naturally to established middle-class families than to uneasily indeterminate ones like his own. A pity, but there it was; too late to try to do anything about it now.

He seized the two large suitcases and set off down the platform, turning his head to make a conventional enquiry. Breckham Market station is on the main line from Liverpool Street to Yarchester and the journey from London takes less than two hours, but Quantrill was so firmly rooted in Suffolk that he could never rid himself of his childhood impression that London was a distant foreign country.

'Did you have a good journey?'

Alison pushed a strand of damp hair out of her eyes. 'Yes, thanks,' she murmured listlessly. Her coat had a single inadequate fastening and she clutched the edges together, shivering in the stinging wet wind.

'Good!' Quantrill heard the false heartiness in his voice and moderated it slightly. 'Well, we'll soon have you home.'

He nodded to the ticket collector at the exit—''Evening, Jack'; ''Evening, Mr. Quantrill'—and hurried down the station steps and across the coal sidings to the car-park. Alison trailed behind, burdened less by a bulging hessian bag that carried a fin de siècle advertisement for French bicycles than by her own unhappiness.

As he drove off, with the wipers working overtime, Quantrill turned up the car heater. Then he glanced sideways at as much as he could see of his daughter's profile behind the dark fall of her hair. 'I'm glad you've come home,' he said gently.

She closed her eyes and nodded, not trusting herself to speak until she had pressed the side of her knuckle hard against her set lips. Then she said in a taut voice, 'I suppose Mum thinks the worst?'

Her supposition was right, but Quantrill temporized loyally. 'Your mother's been very worried,' he said. 'It's only natural—we both were. We could tell from your letters that something was amiss, but we didn't know what . . . We'd have liked to help, if only we'd known how . . .'

Alison gave a small, bitter laugh. 'There was no way you could do that, either of you.' She turned towards her father, lifting her chin proudly. 'I'm not pregnant, you know. Haven't ever been. There are no . . . complications for Mum to have hysterics about. If the neighbours ask, I've decided to come home for a bit—that's all anyone needs to know.'

'That's all anyone will know,' Quantrill assured her, trying to disguise his relief. 'And your Mother and I are both very pleased to have you back.' He opened the window of the car a little to disperse the rank smell that was rising from Alison's wet coat. 'A quiet rest at home will do you the world of good.'

She shook her head. 'No—I don't want to hang about brooding. I'd like to get a job as soon as possible. Any chance, do you think?'

'Sure to be.' Quantrill was proud of his younger daughter's five 'O' and one 'A' levels, her ability to audio-type with conscientious accuracy, and the secretarial job she had had at the BBC ever since she first went to London, eighteen months ago. 'Any local employer will jump at the chance of

3

having a secretary with your qualifications and experience. Not that you're going just anywhere, mind—I'm not having you in one of those factory offices up on the industrial estate. I'll make a few inquiries in the town first: the district council offices, perhaps, or one of the banks...'

Now that Alison was safely beside him, neither aborted nor pregnant, Quantrill felt almost lighthearted. He had, during the last few weeks, worked up such a hatred against the unknown man who was causing his daughter's unhappiness that he had been shocked by the realization of his own capacity for violence. It was one thing to acknowledge, as he did freely and frequently, that policemen are human beings and as prone to criminal impulses as anyone else; quite another to realize that if he were ever to meet this man, he would almost certainly want to inflict grievous bodily harm on him. And Quantrill was afraid of violence. Not of getting hurt, because that was an occupational hazard, but of losing his temper; of losing control and lashing out blindly, ferociously. That was one of the ways that could lead to murder.

But now, with Alison home, he felt that his double burden—an uneasy conscience as well as concern for her welfare—had been lifted. True, the poor girl seemed heartbroken; but nineteen-year-old hearts, he thought confidently, mend with surprising speed.

'And you'll soon be able to pick up your social life again,' he said. 'All those old school friends—'

She shrugged. 'Most of the ones I'm in touch with are away, at college or in London or nursing or something. Anyone who's still in Breckham seems to be either engaged or married already, and in the circumstances—'

'Ah, yes,' said Quantrill hastily. And then he had an idea: 'I don't think you've met my sergeant yet, have you? Martin Tait—one of the bright boys, university and police college and all that; twenty-five, and he'll probably make superintendent by the time he's thirty. Pushy, of course, and a bit too pleased with himself, but he's a good detective: doesn't miss much. You must meet him, and see whether you like him.'

Alison shook her head. 'No, thanks,' she said bleakly. 'I've gone off men.'

4

The Chief Inspector's Daughter

* * *

For his part, Detective Sergeant Tait was very much in favour of women. He was talking to one now, in the course of his duties; a duty that entailed sitting in an armchair in front of a log fire, watching an attractive unattached woman refill a china cup with China tea must, he thought, be one of the best available.

'You were lucky, of course,' he said, referring to the subject of his visit, while his sharp blue eyes missed nothing at all. About five foot four, he estimated, a height that made his own five eight and a half comparatively tall; slim-hipped in dark-blue cord trousers, but with an interestingly feminine outline under her sweater and a dramatic confusion of Victorian rings on her small, square hands. Thick dark hair curved and swung against her high-boned cheeks as she moved her head, and from under strongly marked eyebrows her grey eyes assessed him in return, without embarrassment, as she handed him his tea. Thirtyish, he guessed; a good age for a woman. Young enough not to have lost any of her attractiveness, but experienced enough to enjoy an affair without getting emotionally involved. A very promising discovery, late on a cold, wet February afternoon.

He took his cup fom her. 'Thank you. As I was saying, you were lucky not to have been bashed on the head when you heard the noise and came downstairs to investigate. Not many burglars are gentlemanly enough to clear off empty-handed once they've broken in—and I see from the report the constable made this morning that you keep a number of small valuables in the house.'

She smiled with pride and pleasure: 'My two collections—jade and netsuke. Would you like to see them?'

She had a good voice, too: warm and slightly husky, as though from cigarette smoke, although she was a non-smoker. 'Watch your head on the beams,' she advised him as she led the way across the large low-ceilinged room.

The house, which she called Yeoman's, had obviously been converted at considerable expense from a many-roomed sixteenth-century farmhouse. The major part of the ground floor had been gutted, leaving lines of three or four timber uprights standing exposed in unexpected places, like well-scraped spare ribs. One end of the long room was occupied by a massive chimneypiece of soft rose-red local brick, and the log fire burned deep in its centre. The room was furnished with antiques, a great many books and a comfortable variety of chairs. On the oak floorboards was a cream double-knot Bokhara carpet. There were some modern paintings, one a rural primitive, one a stylized early Hockney; a stereo recordplayer occupied one area, a Bechstein upright another. The affluence of the owner was evident, but deliberately understated. The predominant impression was one of casual comfort. The only flowers were from the garden; a few snowdrops, standing on a desk in a pottery egg-cup, their white petals arching over the writing paper like miniature art-nouveau table lamps.

In an alcove was an illuminated display cabinet. Tait stood at her shoulder while she unlocked it with a key she took from her trouser pocket. There were no more than twenty pieces in the cabinet, all small, some tiny; he bent his head to look with wonder at an intricately carved ivory monkey, five centimetres long.

'These are my netsuke,' she said. 'Incredible, isn't it, that they should have been so completely undervalued as works of art?'

'Incredible,' agreed Tait knowledgeably, brushing an irritatingly boyish wedge of fair hair off his forehead with his fingers. He knew nothing at all about netsuke and was completely unfamiliar with the word as she pronounced it—something Russian, he surmised. He was always ready to absorb new information, but he preferred to do so without revealing his ignorance; and enthusiasts, he knew, once prompted, could always be relied on to tell him as much if not more than he wished to learn. His eyes flicked over the illustrated books on the nearest table and found a useful title: *Netsuke, the Miniature Sculpture of Japan*. He shrugged. 'But then, I imagine that the Japanese simply took them for granted,' he murmured.

'Very much so. After all, they were functional pieces, and it seems that the craftsmen who made them ranked very low in eighteenth- and nineteenth-century Japanese society.' She placed on the palm of her hand a tiny wooden tortoise, every scale on its neck and toes distinct, and stroked it lovingly with the tip of her finger. 'Just imagine, though—

6

how could a man regard something as beautiful as this as nothing more than a toggle to hold his purse and tobacco pouch onto the sash of his kimono? And then simply to throw it out, when it became fashionable to wear Western dress at the end of the last century? . . . Apparently netsuke could be bought by the bucketful in bric-a-brac shops in Tokyo before the last war.'

'Rather more pricey now,' Tait suggested.

'And rapidly increasing in value,' she said with satisfaction. 'I started my collection—oh, ten years ago. These are particularly good examples, but I paid less than ten pounds for most of them, sometimes less than five. Now they're collected all over the world, and they're fetching four-figure sums in salerooms. I started the collection simply because I loved them, but—' she looked up at him with a grin '—I have to admit to a nasty streak of commercialism. It's comforting to know that my accountant reckons they're a much more interesting financial reserve than Krugerrands.'

Impressed, Tait did a rapid assessment of the contents of the cabinet. 'And these?' he asked, pointing to some small carved stones on the second shelf.

'That's my Chinese jade—purely decorative pieces, and correspondingly more valuable. I had to pay a few hundred for each of these, and now they're worth several thousands. But aren't they beautiful?' She touched a cream-coloured pendant, carved with a three-clawed dragon among clouds.

Tait blinked at what he estimated to be twenty or thirty thousand pounds' worth of Oriental handicraft. 'I thought jade was green,' he commented, trying to sound off-hand.

'Only some of it. Emerald green like this—' she picked up a tiny pendant carved with gourds, bamboo and plum blossom '—was one of the favourite colours, but jade goes from almost pure white—like this kitten with a butterfly on its back—to this mottled amber horse.'

She replaced the pieces with loving care. 'I suppose I ought really to keep them at the bank,' she said, 'but there are limits to my commercial instincts. I love looking at them, and touching them; and then, they're an incentive to keep me at work. Ever since I started writing, I've bought myself something special and beautiful with the advance on each book. Then, when I get depressed because I write

7

romantic fiction instead of straight novels—I did write one, but couldn't get it published—I can tell myself that something good comes out of my work, apart from the money to pay the bills.'

Tait, the divisional crime prevention officer, gave her his official frown. 'I take your point, of course; naturally you want to keep the pieces where you can see them. But you must realize that a collection like this makes your house an obvious target for burglars. One of them got in easily enough last night. You were lucky this time, but with the pubicity you'll get when that magazine article appears—'

He gave her a friendly lecture and she listened meekly, nodding with contrition as he took her on a tour of her inadequately secured windows and doors. She promised to call in a reputable locksmith; Tait told her that he would come again to make sure that she had done so. She offered him a drink and Tait—remembering that he had officially gone off duty half an hour earlier—accepted. Another half-hour passed rapidly and agreeably before he rose reluctantly from his armchair.

'I hope we meet again,' he said. 'Socially, of course.'

She stood back and considered him, an incipient smile denting the corners of her mouth. Making up her mind how far she intended to go? Tait grinned at her in return, quietly confident.

'Why not?' she said pleasantly. And then: 'As a matter of fact, I'm having a party next Friday evening, to celebrate the publication of my new book. Would you like to come? Any time after nine.'

She was eager, then; so much the better. But she must have sensed his complacency, because she added quickly, 'Bring a girl, if you'd like to. There'll be too many men anyway, there always are at my parties. Yes, do bring a girl.'

Not a bad idea at that, Tait thought: a useful way of entertaining one of his local girl-friends at no expense, combined with an opportunity of becoming better acquainted with an attractive older woman. What more could a man ask for?

He thanked her and followed her to the door. 'And remember,' he added, 'from now on, if you hear any suspicious noises in the night, dial 999 from you bedroom. *Don't* come down to investigate. You could get yourself killed doing that, you know.'

2

In his office at Breckham Market Divisional Police Headquarters, Detective Chief Inspector Quantrill looked through his sergeant's report on the previous day's work.

'This woman,' he said, skimming the last page. 'You'd think she'd have more sense. Doesn't she know that it's asking for trouble to have her house described in a magazine article? It's an open invitation to any villain who wants easy pickings.'

'She realizes that now,' said Tait. 'The abortive break-in on Monday night really shook her, and the article hasn't even been published yet. She showed me an advance copy. No address given, of course: just the information that she lives alone in a delightful country cottage set in a big garden in unspoiled North Suffolk, not far from sleepy little Breckham Market... you've read the sort of thing.'

'Squit,' agreed the Chief Inspector with Suffolk dismissiveness. He knew too much about country life to have any time for people who imagined it to be idyllic. 'And I suppose there's a photograph, to make the place easily identifiable?'

'Of course. But because there's no address in the article, and because her telephone number's ex-directory, she thought that no one would be able to trace her.'

Quantrill sighed over the folly of it. 'She's not just inviting trouble, she's begging for it... How come she's featured in a magazine, anyway?'

'Publicity. She's a romantic novelist.'

'Hah!' said Quantrill, who had no time for romantic

novelists either. 'Jasmine Woods . . . that's not her real name, then?'

'Yes, it is. She married a man named Potter, but preferred to use her unmarried name for her books.'

'Hmm. Yes, well, that's understandable. What happened to Mr Potter?'

'They're divorced.'

'Very romantic,' observed Quantrill censoriously. He had been brought up to believe that it is morally wrong for married couples to admit that they have made a mistake; a marriage, he thought, was something you were stuck with and had to make the best of. 'And does this magazine article make it clear that she's got a houseful of valuables?'

'Clear enough—it mentions her love of jade and netsuke, and that'll draw the intelligent professionals.'

'Jade and what?' Quantrill asked.

'Netsuke—they're miniature Japanese sculptures in wood and ivory,' Tait explained authoritatively, without a flicker of shame from his stiff fair eyelashes. 'They were used in the eighteenth and nineteenth centuries as toggles to fasten the men's purses to the sashes of their kimonos. They've been completely undervalued until recently, but now they're fetching a packet.'

'Ah,' said Quantrill, accepting it as a fact that there was no limit to the breadth of his sergeant's knowledge; that, he assumed enviously, was what a good education did for you. 'Well, we shall have to keep an eye on that particular patch of unspoiled North Suffolk in the near future.'

'I intend to,' said Tait.

'Oh yes? Attractive, is she?'

'Very. And she's invited me to a party on Friday.'

'She's probably planning to have you for supper afterwards. You want to watch out with older women, boy,' Quantrill advised him kindly, from hearsay not personal experience. 'They can get their hooks into a young man and ruin his career.'

Tait smiled confidently. 'Don't worry about that, sir, I can look after my own interests. Anyway,' he added fairly, 'she's nowhere near old enough to be my mother, you know. And she did say that I could take a girl with me to the party.'

'Generous of her. Jasmine Woods...' Quantrill scratched his chin. 'I'm sure I've heard the name.'

'Two romantic novels a year for the past ten years, and every one a best seller, apparently. Perhaps Mrs Quantrill reads them?'

'More than likely,' said her husband disparagingly. 'It must pay, then, this writing business?'

'According to Jasmine Woods, it certainly does.'

Quantrill fumbled in his trouser pocket, looked at his small change, and found that he would have to break into a pound note to buy them a pint of lunch-time bitter apiece at the Coney and Thistle.

'We're in the wrong job, Martin,' he said.

3

The Quantrills lived at Number 5 Benidorm Avenue, a road built in Breckham Market by a local developer in the late 1960s and named after his favourite holiday resort.

The houses were semi-detached. Quantrill had been a sergeant when he had first taken out his mortgage, and a semi was all he could afford; a step up, anyway, from a police house. He and Molly had been so proud of their status as owner-occupiers of a brand new house that he had had great difficulty in preventing her from giving their property a name, instead of using the number. The prevailing fashion had been to concoct house names from the abbreviated names of the owners, or of their children. Quantrill, with apprehensive guesses at what his wife might suggest if she put her mind to it—*Doug-Moll? Jen-Al-Pete?*—insisted that they lived at Number 5, and fixed the numeral to both front door and gate to prove it.

On the day after Alison's return, four of the family sat at supper, trying to think of something to say to each other. It was a meal from which Quantrill was frequently absent, because of the irregular hours he worked. Left to themselves, he knew, Molly and fourteen-year-old Peter ate sandwiches in front of the television set. He preferred to fry bacon and egg for himself when he came in, and to eat it in peace in the kitchen.

But Alison was home, for the first time—apart from quick weekends—for eighteen months, and so a display of family solidarity was called for. As on the previous evening, the meal had been set in the dining area of the main room, under the supervisory stare of a herd of wild elephants, one of Boots' best-selling framed prints. To Peter's chagrin the television set had been turned off. Conversation was required, but with Alison melancholic and Molly fretting over her and trying to coax her to eat, it was hard going.

They had all, Alison included, made a special effort to be bright the previous evening; fortunately there had been Jennifer, her elder sister, a nurse at Guy's Hospital, to talk about. But now the topic of Jennifer was exhausted: Peter was sulking over a missed television programme; Quantrill and his wife had nothing to say to each other; and Alison had resumed the desolate air of a space traveller who has landed on an uninhabited planet. Quantrill wondered guiltily how long it would be before they could all stop pretending to togetherness and revert to their usual practices; a fried egg in the kitchen, with the *East Anglian Daily Press* for company, had never seemed so desirable.

'Are you warm enough, Alison?' Molly asked. The houses had been built when electricity was a relatively cheap fuel, and the room was heated by a system of ducted air. There was a fireplace, but it had been designed merely as a decorative feature to house an electric appliance disguised as a blazing log. Quantrill hated the phoney fire, disliked ducted air heating, and was appalled by the running costs of the system; but as he could not afford to move, this seemed to be yet another part of his life that he was stuck with.

Molly, on the other hand, enjoyed the trouble-free cleanliness of electric heating. She worked part-time as the local doctor's receptionist, and was on the committee of the Women's Institute as well as being an active member of the

Breckham Market and District amateur operatic society, and she had quite enough to do without coping with a real fire. She enjoyed the sight of the simulated flames flickering over the simulated log; cosy, and with no messy grate to clear up afterwards.

'Alison,' she repeated patiently, the skin at the outer corners of her mild brown eyes puckering with concern, 'are you warm enough, dear?'

The girl continued to stare down at her unwanted food, absently pushing a long strand of hair behind her ear when it threatened to dip into her plate. 'Yes, thank you,' she murmured.

Molly gave a bright, uncertain smile. 'That's good,' she said.

She longed to know the reason for her daughter's sudden homecoming. An unhappy love affair, that was obvious; but Molly would have liked the detail, the who-with and the how-far and the what-next. Douglas had assured her that there was nothing to worry about and had instructed her not to plague the girl with questions, but it was not his edict that deterred Molly. She had asked Alison nothing because she knew perfectly well that her daughter would not confide in her.

Molly Quantrill very much regretted the lack of closeness in her family. She blamed it, to a large extent, on the influence of the grammar school; she was proud that her daughters had gone there, but at the same time she resented the fact that the girls had grown so far away from her. What with that and with Douglas's rapid promotion from sergeant to chief inspector in four years, she felt left behind, unregarded. Even Peter, her favourite child—now making bored one-handed inroads into his food, with surreptitious contributions to the cat—had grown secretive. Perhaps that was to be expected with an adolescent boy, but a girl ought to be closer to her mother; she herself had told her mother everything—

Well, not everything, of course. Molly glanced at Alison and then at her husband. The girl had such a look of her father about her, and Douggie as a young man had been darkly handsome; still was, despite the scattering of grey hairs and the weight he had put on. Molly remembered the irresistible way he had gazed at her soon after they had first met, the pleading look in his green eyes, the persuasiveness of his tongue . . . no, she hadn't told her mother everything, not by a long way. Perhaps she had no right to expect her own daughter's confidence.

'Eat your supper while it's hot, Alison,' she said. 'And, Peter, do sit up and use your knife and fork properly. And stop encouraging that cat, or it'll have to go outside.'

Quantrill cleared his throat and prepared to contribute to the conversation. Ordinarily he made a point of never mentioning any aspect of his work at home, but anything that seemed likely to divert his wife's attention from Alison was worth a try.

'Tell you who young Martin Tait went to see yesterday, Molly. A woman writer who lives out at Thirling—Jasmine Woods.'

Molly's mouth fell open with excitement. 'Jasmine Woods! She's my favourite author.' Her eyes shone at her husband over a poised, pallid forkful of cauliflower and mashed potato and Birds Eye cod-in-butter-sauce. 'I never knew she lived in Suffolk, never mind three miles from here! She's not in any trouble, is she?'

'No, of course not,' said Quantrill. 'Martin was just making routine enquiries. He seems to have made a good impression on Jasmine Woods, though. She's invited him to go to a party and to take one of his girl-friends.'

'The lucky boy!' Molly's plump face looked dewily maternal, envious of her husband's sergeant's good fortune. 'Oh, if only we could go instead, Douggie . . .'

'It's not me she fancies,' pointed out Quantrill, who hated being called Douggie.

Molly straightened her back. 'I should think not,' she said primly. 'After all, you're a married man—'

Quantrill would have liked to comment that even married men are human, and that fancying—or loving, come to that—takes no account of marital status on either side, but he prudently filled his mouth with overdone cauliflower instead. No point now, when last year's love for another woman had finally dulled to an intermittent ache, in arousing his wife's suspicions. Her gullibility was a permanent reproach to him. Apparently it had never occurred to her, when he offered to buy the sheepskin coat that she coveted, that he was making a belated attempt to ease his conscience.

Molly turned to her daughter, glad of something to talk about. 'You like Jasmine Woods, too, don't you, Alison? I'm reading her latest now—well, not her very latest, there's such a long waiting list at the library. This one's called *The English Governess*. It's one of her best. It's all about this girl who goes to St Petersburg before the Russian Revolution—' her face was pink with animation, and for a moment Quantrill thought that they were going to hear every convolution of the plot; but Molly, whose contribution to the amateur operatic society was confined to the outer fringe of the chorus and helping with the costumes, suddenly felt that she was making herself conspicuous. 'Well, anyway,' she finished lamely, 'I'm just on the last chapter. I'll pass it on to you, if you like.'

To Quantrill's pleasure, Alison assented with what sounded almost like enthusiasm. She had actually been taking an interest in what her mother was saying, and he congratulated himself on having introduced a topic that had taken her mind off her problems, if only for a few moments. A pity that she had said so decisively that she didn't want to meet young Tait, though; Quantrill was confident that, with a little persuasion, his sergeant would have made a point of inviting his daughter to Jasmine Woods's party.

Molly Quantrill's mind was moving in the same direction. She had seen Martin Tait several times and had found him charming—well-spoken, flatteringly attentive and just a little awe-inspiring: a very clever and attractive young man, and just the right age for Alison.

She exercised her tact, waiting until she had served her family with canned pears and cream before saying casually to her husband, 'Isn't it about time we had Martin Tait to supper again? I'm sure he doesn't feed himself properly in that flat of his. What about one day this week?'

Quantrill looked at her with surprised approval, and agreed to pass on the invitation. 'But don't go to a lot of fuss and bother,' he instructed his wife. 'Nothing fancy—the boy's not a senior officer yet, you know. Something homemade,' he added wistfully. Since Molly had taken on a part-time job she had made it an excuse to give up baking, and he had a weakness for pastry. 'How about one of your juicy steak and kidney pies?'

But Molly, whose married life had encompassed a num-

ber of humiliations, known as well as unguessed-at, enjoyed
the exercise of what limited power she possessed. No conscientious wife, she declared with virtuous relish, would feed
pastry to a man of Douglas's age and weight; and wasn't it
time that he went on a diet again?

Her husband remembered that he had brought some
paperwork home and strode out of the room, scowling. But as
he closed the door behind him he rejoiced in the fact that he
could hear, for the first time since her return, his daughter's
cheerful giggle.

Douglas Quantrill finished reading the local newspaper,
tossed it onto the bedroom floor, yawned, scratched the back
of his head and slid a little further down the pillow. Beside
him in their double bed, in pink sleeping net and pink frilly
nightie, with her reading glasses halfway down her nose and
her mouth slightly open, Molly was ingurgitating the final
chapter of Jasmine Woods's *The English Governess*.

It was unusual for the Quantrills to go to bed at the same
time, and particularly unusual for Molly to go on reading
after her husband had switched off his bedside light. Often his
work kept him out late, but even when he was at home for
the evening Molly made a point of going upstairs before he
did, so that when he went up she was asleep; or feigning
sleep. Tonight, Jasmine Woods was keeping her awake, and
not only awake but excited.

Quantrill watched his wife with a mixture of amused
tolerance and irritation. Incredible, he thought, that a middle-
aged woman could be aroused by a rubbishy book. Her
plump cheeks were patched wih colour, and the ample frills
over her breasts were rising and falling more rapidly then
they had done in response to his own attentions for a very
long time. He didn't know whether to laugh at his wife or to
snatch the book from her in a fit of jealousy and fling it across
the room.

The fact was, he acknowledged, that Molly was still
attractive. He propped himself on one Marks and Spencer
paisley pattern pyjama'd elbow and looked past the hideous
net and the ageing glasses; yes, the pretty girl was still there.
Her soft brown hair hadn't a touch of grey, the tilt of her nose
still beckoned him, and the fullness of her cheeks suited her

far better than the deep vertical lines her face acquired every time she went on one of her wretched diets. When she looked flushed, as she did now, Molly was definitely desirable.

Quantrill cautiously inched himself nearer. His wife was very rarely in a cooperative mood; keen enough in their younger days, but for the past few years she'd gone off it, or him, almost completely. He didn't know why because they had never been able to discuss the subject of sex. When they had first gone out together, he had been tongue-tied and she was far too prudish; then, in the early days of their marriage, they had hidden their mutual embarrassment behind lovers' baby-talk. Later, discussion had seemed superfluous. Now it was impossible, because they had no common adult vocabulary.

Here, then, was an unlooked-for revival of her interest. The fact that it was Jasmine Woods's contriving rather than his own was immaterial; Molly was in the right mood, and that was enough. He reached out a hand and spread it experimentally on her plump thigh.

Molly's muscles twitched absently, like those of a grazing mare plagued by flies in summer.

Quantrill edged closer, and explored a little further.

'Give over,' Molly muttered, closing her legs and crossing her ankles and continuing to read.

Quantrill, with the finesse of a salesman who keeps his foot in the door, left his hand in place and pressed his shoulders against his wife's. She was a page or two from the end of the book, and he began to read with her.

'Nicolai,' *she whispered. She could not look at him, but she was overwhelmingly conscious of his presence beside her on the furs of the troika, of the length of his body, the turn of his head, the shape of his hands.* 'Nicolai,' *she said again, and he caught her to him, pressing his body against . . .*

Quantrill grinned expectantly at his wife. 'Hurry up,' he said with a lecherous nudge, 'turn the page!'

Molly sat up, exasperated. 'Ooh!' she cried, clutching the open book to the front of her nightdress like a chastity shield, 'mind your own business! Why can't you go to sleep?'

Her husband plucked tentatively at one of her rounded

pink frills and tried a revival of the boyish grin that had rarely failed to work in the distant past. 'You know why not,' he pleaded, half-laughing, half-intense. 'Come on, Molly...'

Typical, she thought bitterly. Just like her husband to start making demands when she was enjoying herself; just like him to go straight to one of the sexier passages in the book and want to put it into practice, ignoring the preliminaries of affection and tenderness that had been woven into the excitements of the story.

This was the difference of course, she told herself, between romantic novels and real life. Jasmine Woods understood and wrote about the importance of the smaller intimacies, the things that really mattered, like the entwining of hands and fingers and the exchange of words of reassurance and love; whereas in real life it was just a sudden 'Come on, Molly,' and a lot of heavy breathing and a clumsy tussle under the bedclothes, and the nothing but lying, disappointed, in the dark.

She glared at her husband through the gap between the pink elastic edging of her hair-net and her half-mast reading glasses. 'Leave me alone, do,' she snapped. 'I want to finish my book in peace. And it's no use your looking at me like that, Doug Quantrill, because I'm too tired.'

She turned away, hunching her shoulder against him: another small victory to help balance her account.

Quantrill sighed and rolled back to his own side of the bed and counted the unsolved crimes in the division until eventually he fell asleep.

4

With a little persuasion from Quantrill, Martin Tait made up his mind to invite the Chief Inspector's daughter to accompany him to Jasmine Woods's party.

Like any other agile bachelor, Tait was equipped with an inbuilt early warning system. It had bleeped loudly when Quantrill asked him to supper and mentioned that his daughter would be at home. 'Oh, yes...' Tait had told himself cynically, assuming that Mrs Quantrill—an embarrassingly fussy woman, he thought, who had been married for years to an ordinary police constable and found it difficult in middle age to adjust to being a senior officer's wife—was angling for a likely son-in-law. While Tait had no objection at all to meeting girls, he had his priorities absolutely clear: senior—very senior—rank first, marriage later; and to a girl who would be capable, early in her marriage, of playing the part of the wife of one of the country's youngest assistant chief constables.

Meanwhile, he was conscious of being only a sergeant. When his Chief Inspector issued a summons to supper he thought it politic to accept, and to look glad at the prospect of being introduced to the old man's daughter.

Quantrill, however, wanted no misunderstandings. 'Alison has plenty of friends in Breckham Market when she wants to pick up her social life again,' he had said firmly. 'She's not in any need of a regular escort, or short of parties to go to, but she does happen to be a particular fan of this Jasmine Woods woman. So I'd appreciate it if you'd invite her to go with you, Martin—unless of course you've already asked the Mayor's daughter... or the girl from the Shell garage?'

The lobes of Tait's ears had reddened. His social life was less successful than the old man imagined, because the Mayor's plain daughter Fiona was given to drinking too much and making embarrassingly randy remarks in public, whereas Sally from the garage, who looked so promisingly sexy when they set out on their private excursions, drank nothing but Coca-Cola and had frequently proved herself to be rather more difficult of access than Fort Knox.

In the circumstances—and especially as the Chief Inspector didn't expect him to make a habit of it—Tait was agreeable to escorting Alison Quantrill. 'There's one snag, though, sir. You did say that you wanted me on observation on the industrial estate from eleven on Friday night, after that tip-off we had about a warehouse raid. So I'll have to bring your daughter home early from Jasmine Woods's party. I hope that won't spoil the evening for her.'

Quantrill scratched his chin. 'Ah, yes, I'd forgotten. Pity. Well, tell you what, I'll come to the house in time to relieve you, and then I can take Alison home as soon as she's ready. I'd quite like to have a look at this Jasmine Woods myself.'

'Did you discover whether Mrs Quantrill is a fan, too?' asked Tait, pretending innocence. He had not failed to notice that the Chief Inspector's voice had taken on an edge when he mentioned the writer's name.

'Yes . . . hanged if I know what the women see in that rubbish,' said Quantrill with savage gloom. He stared at a paperclip that he had picked up a few seconds before; it had, quite suddenly, snapped into two pieces in his fingers.

Tait had noticed that, too. The Chief Inspector, he surmised with an inward grin, was someone else who was at present suffering from frustration.

But at least he himself had hopes of Jasmine Woods. He remembered that horizontally ridged sweater, the frank assessment in those large grey eyes. With Jasmine Woods available, he would have no need of Fiona and Sally—nor yet of the Chief Inspector's daughter.

5

Alison Quantrill had, as she had told her father, gone off men.

Specifically, she had gone off a man called Gavin Jackson, who had made use of her and then moved on. More generally, she wanted nothing further to do with men who, like Gavin, were tall and dark, soft-bearded and soft-voiced. About slight, sharp, fair men like Martin Tait she had no views at all, except that she could manage perfectly well without them.

Tait, however, had one point in his favour: he knew Jasmine Woods, and for that reason alone he was worth being civil to. Alison was aware that the invitation to go with him to the party had been prompted by her father, and that suited her very well; so did the knowledge that it would be her father who would bring her home. She could make the most of the opportunity to meet one of her favourite writers without feeling especially beholden to Martin Tait.

Alison dressed for the party with care, although not for her escort's pleasure. Her mother had talked about Jasmine Woods's probable appearance in some detail. Molly was convinced that a romantic novelist ought to be middle-aged, tall and beautifully dressed, with a blue rinse and damson fingernails and a good many teeth and diamonds; as glamourous as Danny la Rue, but exuding sensibility rather than sauce. Alison, who had inherited her father's pessimism, had thought it more likely that the writer would turn out to be ordinary if not dowdy, until she saw the look in Martin Tait's eye.

When he had visited the Quantrill family for an unnecessarily elaborate meal of roast chicken with all the trimmings, followed by sherry trifle, Tait had made it clear that Jasmine Woods was attractive. Alison, who was anxious not to make a bad impression on her, had begun to feel nervous. On the evening of the party she took more trouble over her appearance than she had done since the ending of her affair with Gavin.

Martin Tait took note of the shyness, and of the shining hair and the long flowery dress with the demurely high neckline, and naturally assumed that it was for his personal benefit. A pity in some ways, he thought, as he drove to the party, that he wouldn't be taking her home afterwards; Alison was pretty, and it would do no harm to add her to his list.

But then they reached Yeoman's, and Jasmine Woods met them at the door, and he lost interest in anyone else.

Jasmine looked stunning. She wore a long black velvet

skirt and a peacock-coloured top with a mandarin collar, and her eyes seemed bluer than grey and her dark hair swung forward against her cheeks, and the selection of rings on her hands was more dramatic than ever. She greeted Tait like an old acquaintance, and was reassuringly friendly to Alison.

A good deal of noise was coming from the direction of the sitting-room. Jasmine Woods showed Alison a side room where she could leave her coat, and while they waited she and Tait looked each other over with approving smiles.

'So now I know what the well-dressed young man is wearing for parties,' she said lightly. 'A pale grey suit, an open-necked dark blue shirt and a silver chain, casual but elegant—thank you, I must make use of that in a short story I'm writing. One gets a little out of touch here. I see plenty of men, of course, but very few of them seem to measure up to my heroines' exacting standards.'

Tait rose several inches in his own estimation. 'I'm here simply for your research, is that it?' he mocked her.

She laughed. 'Of course. Why else?'

'Why indeed. Will you do a complete portrait while you're at it, warts and all?'

'Certainly not,' she said promptly. 'All my fictional characters are composite, and any resemblance to any person living or dead is purely coincidental.'

'I've never really believed that one," said Tait.

'That's what comes of being a detective and having a suspicious mind. But it's true, as far as I'm concerned. I need to understand my characters completely, and real people are so very difficult to get to know. They're always far more complicated than characters in fiction. I imagine that this is one of the problems of detective work. Real human beings erect barriers to hide behind, and then put up façades in front of the barriers. When you question suspects, I suppose what you're doing is breaking the barriers down... Fascinating. I'd love to talk to you about it some time.' She changed the subject, glancing towards Alison. 'That's a very attractive girl-friend you have.'

Tait looked, too. The girl stood in profile in the open doorway of the room where she had left her coat, with both hands raised to flick her long hair away from the neck of her dress. It was a feminine stance that always aroused his interest. 'Yes, isn't she?' he agreed, accepting the implied compliment on his taste.

'She looks sad though,' Jasmine Woods commented quietly. 'You must take care of her this evening—most of the people here are my relations and neighbours, rather than personal friends, and I'm afraid that some of them get a bit loud-voiced and opinionated after they've had a drink or two. I imagine that she must be feeling vulnerable at the moment, so don't let any of them intimidate her.' She smiled at the girl. 'Ready Alison? I do like your dress—'

The low-ceilinged sitting-room was already hazy with smoke, and loud with talk and laughter and the plangent warmth of Cleo Laine's recorded voice. Most of the other guests seemed to be in their late thirties or older, and there was a preponderance of men. Alison kept close to Martin Tait as the introductions began.

'This is my brother-in-law, Paul Pardoe. He's a surveyor in Yarchester, and he found this house for me, so I'm eternally grateful to him. He's also very good at pouring drinks—'

'Have some wine,' said Paul Pardoe in a lugubrious voice, offering two filled glasses. He was tall and grievously thin, with deep-set eyes and greying, fly-away fair hair. 'When Jasmine says "drinks" at one of her new-book parties, all she means is Anjou rosé.'

'But only to make it easier for you, Paul dear,' his sister-in-law apologized. 'I don't want you to spend the entire evening mixing drinks for everyone else. Besides, you know I'm superstitious. I celebrated the publication of my first book with Anjou rosé, and I don't like to break the pattern. And you must admit that you find it drinkable, or you wouldn't be here.'

Paul Pardoe shrugged and refilled his glass from one of the many tall long-necked bottles of the Loire wine that stood on the table near his elbow. 'Oh, you're right of course,' he said. His voice was already slightly slurred. 'I'll go anywhere for a free drink.'

'It's very drinkable indeed,' said Tait quickly. He had always avoided rosé on masculine principle and was agreeably surprised to find that it could taste fruity and at the same time dry.

Alison found her voice. 'It's a lovely colour,' she said.

Jasmine Woods stared at her glass doubtfully, as though she herself might have chosen a different adjective, but she let it pass. 'The wine's more potent than it looks,' she advised with a smile. 'Ah, this is my sister Heather, Paul's wife.'

Heather Pardoe wandered towards them, so busily transferring food from a heaped plate to her mouth that she did not at first hear her name. She was as short as her sister Jasmine, but older and fatter, coarser featured and considerably worse dressed; her bulk was draped in layers of what looked like curtaining material. When her husband repeated her name sharply she looked up from her plate, dropped a half-eaten miniature sausage roll back into a greasy nest of coleslaw, swallowed with haste and wiped her fingers guiltily on her bodice. Then she produced a dazed smile and acknowledged the introduction.

'How do you do—so sorry; I didn't have time to eat before we came out, you see. We've five children, and it takes so long to get them to bed and to explain things to the baby-sitter... and with another on the way, I don't seem able to stop eating.' She wolfed the remains of her sausage roll and licked her fingers compulsively. Her husband looked away, and swallowed some more wine.

'Help yourself to whatever you want, Heather—you know where the kitchen is,' said Jasmine Woods affectionately. Then she gave her elder sister a sudden, cheeky grin: 'Only I hope it's not coal you're craving for, love, because I've nothing but logs... Excuse me, I think there's someone else at the door.'

She hurried away, and Paul Pardoe stared after her morosely. 'Bitch,' he commented.

Alison Quantrill felt as shocked and hurt as though the word had been applied to herself. She covered her embarrassment by asking his wife the names and ages of her children.

Heather Pardoe gave an eager recital. 'They keep us poor, of course,' she added, 'but we wouldn't have it any other way. Would we, Paul?' Her husband, who had been peering into the emptiness of his glass, did not at first bother to reply; but then he seemed to remember that there was plenty more wine where that came from and poured himself a refill. 'No,' he answered her.

'Besides,' Heather went on defiantly, 'money isn't everything.' She glanced round the room at the evidence of her sister's wealth, and tried to refuse to be impressed by it, but her eyes gave her away. 'I mean, look at Jasmine.'

Martin Tait had been doing little else for the past five minutes. Jasmine Woods—laughing, poised, well-groomed, self-assured—was standing at the centre of a small group of interested men. The contrast between her and her sister needed no emphasis, but Heather obviously felt a compulsion to draw attention to it.

'Jasmine may have money,' she said, 'but it can't buy happiness. After all, she's on her own. She married eleven years ago, but they separated after about eighteen months together. She never had a child, poor dear. Oh, she says she's a natural loner, but I don't believe it. I feel sorry for her, really I do. It must be so painful for her to write about love and happy endings when her own life is so unfulfilled.' She bit into another sausage roll and left some strands of coleslaw adhering to her upper lip like a lop-sided yellow moustache.

Her husband gave an abrupt laugh. 'Don't waste your time,' he jeered. 'Jasmine doesn't need any sympathy; she's got it made, we all know that.' His wife frowned at him and retired to replenish her plate. Paul Pardoe looked at his glass, finding it half-empty again. 'Anjou rosé,' he muttered contemptuously.

'A romantically pretty drink,' observed a horn-rimmed man with thin, flat dark hair who had pushed his way forward to reach the bottles. He was Tait's height; rotund, but fashionably dressed with a silk scarf filling the open neck of his shirt. He poured himself a generous glassful of wine, held it up to the light and shrugged. 'Hardly a man's drink,' he continued in a plumply patronizing voice, 'but appropriate for a romantic novelist, eh, Paul? An ideal drink for the ladies, bless them.'

He bestowed a salacious smile on Alison. Tait, who had

been hoping to leave her and ease himself into Jasmine Woods's orbit, thought that it might perhaps be advisable to stay put.

The newcomer introduced himself as George Hussey; dear Jasmine, he said, switching his leer in her direction, was positively one of his favourite customers.

'Antiques,' explained Paul Pardoe without enthusiasm. 'George has a shop in Thirling.'

'An out-of-the-way village for an antique shop,' commented Tait.

Hussey gave him a pitying glance. 'I am known,' he stated. 'Customers come to me from all over the Eastern counties, and from Holland, Belgium and Germany. When one is known, one's location is immaterial. Customers beat a path to my door.'

Tait twitched an eyebrow in acknowledgement. Alison, emboldened by half a glass of wine, commented that Jasmine Woods, at least, had a very short journey.

'Dear Jasmine,' said George Hussey. He leaned forward, extracted a cheese straw from a dish, ate it in small neat bites and dabbed his lips fastidiously with a handkerchief that matched his silk scarf. 'She used to visit my shop when she lived in Essex. I was one of the first dealers in this country to see the potential of netsuke, and I was able to encourage her to start her collection. My prices were ridiculously low, of course—this is the trouble with antiques, one so often ends up enriching one's friends at one's own expense. But as soon as Jasmine left Thaxted and came to this house she sought my help to furnish it, so I feel amply repaid; by that and of course by her friendship. A charming woman, don't you think?'

Alison nodded, wondering whether there was going to be an opportunity to speak to Jasmine Woods during the course of the evening. Paul Pardoe looked sceptical, and chomped an untidy handful of cheese straws with large yellow teeth, scattering flakes of pastry about him.

Tait put one hand under Alison's elbow and steered her away. 'Let's find someone more congenial to talk to,' he muttered, impatient to join his hostess. 'Like dear Jasmine herself...'

6

Jasmine Woods was still surrounded by men, and the girl hung back, letting Tait join the group. On a side table there stood a pile of copies of a brand-new romantic novel, presumably her hostess's latest. Alison opened the top copy, after a slightly guilty glance over her shoulder to make sure that she was unobserved, and began to read.

Once again, Jasmine Woods had set her story in the early years of the twentieth century. This time the location was a mountainous Balkan kingdom, and the heroine was an English girl who had gone out as companion to the wife of the British ambassador just before the start of the First World War... and there, on the first page, was a description of the girl, as vivid as if she were alive: shading herself from the fierce Balkan sun with her parasol as she walked in her elegant long white dress and magnificent hat across the dusty main street of the half-barbaric, half-feudal capital city, with its veneer of early twentieth-century manners and modernity that—according to the blurb—concealed but could not suppress the surging revolutionary spirit of the people and in particular of Constantine, the half-English bastard son of the king himself...

'Enjoying it?' said a friendly, amused voice beside her. Alison looked up, two-thirds of the way through the first chapter, and blushed to find herself eye-to-eye with the author. 'Keep it, if you'd like to,' Jasmine Woods went on. 'My publisher sends me a pile of complimentary copies, and I'm often hard put to it to find willing recipients. This is supposed to be a party to celebrate its publication, but I doubt if anyone except my sister will deign to accept a copy, so you'll be doing me a favour.'

Alison stammered her thanks, asked if she might have

the book autographed and followed Jasmine Woods to a writing table. She was disappointed that there was no evidence there of the novels in production, but only some sheets of writing paper with the Yeoman's heading, a pottery trough of purple crocus, and a framed photograph of Jasmine Woods and a girl in her mid-twenties standing together in long dresses at some formal function. In the photograph the writer was holding a silver bowl, which Alison recognized as the one which stood on a shelf above the desk.

'The trophy's on loan for a year,' explained Jasmine Woods. 'I belong to a writers' association, and they very kindly presented me with it at a dinner last autumn.' She gave a deprecating laugh. 'A sort of long service and good conduct prize, I think. The photograph was taken at the dinner. That's Anne Downing, my secretary—or at least she was my secretary, until last month. She was invaluable. She'd been with me for two years, and I hated letting her go, but she felt that she needed a change. I must admit that I miss her even more than I thought I would.'

For a moment, Jasmine Woods looked unusually downcast. Then she shrugged, and her face brightened. 'Ah well, that's the way it goes. I'll get a replacement eventually. I've advertised, and interviewed one or two girls, but unfortunately their spelling wasn't good enough. My secretary must be able to spell impeccably, you see—one of us has to, and I certainly can't!'

Alison met her hostess's eye for the first time, saw the laughter in it and began to giggle. They were still chuckling together when a tall man with dark curly hair, greying sideburns and a long pointed nose ambled up to join them. He wore a leather jacket and a white silky polo-necked sweater, and held a half-full glass of wine negligently in a long thin hand.

'The new "novel," Jasmine?' he said, glancing with amused disdain at the book she had just handed Alison. His voice was classless, but his vowel sounds unmistakably originated from somewhere north of Trent Bridge: there was no mistaking, either, the inverted commas that he chose to place round the word 'novel,' and his opinion of his hostess's work. His loftiness was emphasized by the fact that he kept his heavy-lidded brown eyes fixed on some point in the middle distance six inches above her head, as though she were completely beneath his notice. 'Which one's this, then?' he went on. 'Number twenty-five? Your silver jubilee already? You turn them out at such a rate that I get confused.' He gave the 'con' a tell-tale north-country emphasis.

'It's number nineteen, actually,' said Jasmine Woods smoothly. 'I've barely come of age... Alison, this is Jonathan Elliott, who lives in Thirling. My famous neighbour—a *real* novelist, as I'm sure you know. *Three Point Turn* was short-listed for the Ford Prize last year, wasn't it, Jonathan? I really must read it again.'

When it came to inflection Jasmine Woods was no amateur either. She delicately inserted a barely perceptible pause between the last two words. Elliott stiffened. For all his relaxed appearance, there was a tension about him; an intensity, despite his throw-away style. Alison looked uncertainly from one to the other, sensing that she was a spectator at some long-playing needle match, and would have edged away if Martin Tait had not appeared at her side with friendly words for her and eyes only for Jasmine.

Their hostess introduced the two men. 'I was just going to say to Alison that Jonathan is best known as a television critic. Have you seen him hosting the late night Books and Writers programme? I believe he does it splendidly, but unfortunately it's on ITV. I know it's stuffy of me, but I do so much prefer the BBC. Don't you find, Jonathan, that it inhibits serious discussion when you know that your viewers are going to be distracted in the middle of your programme by dog-food commercials?'

'Not at all,' Jonathan Elliott informed the air above her head. 'I'm grateful to the dog-food manufacturers for the generous fees they enable the television company to pay me, but the source of my income doesn't mean that I have to pander to my audience. The quality of discussion on the programme isn't affected by what goes on during commercial breaks. We may be hemmed in by exhortations to buy Doggo and Woof, but we still keep our intellectual integrity.' He glanced down for a moment at his hostess, his eyes flicking over her face and her clothes: 'Which is more than can be said of anyone who deliberately writes to please a mass market—wouldn't you say so, Jasmine?'

'Ouch!' protested Martin Tait on her behalf. She shook her head, refusing his support; her eyes were lively with the enjoyment of battle.

'Jonathan is a novelist, too,' she told Tait, 'but unlike me, he has intellectual aspirations, so his books have only a limited appeal. They're elitist. I believe there isn't much demand for them outside university campuses and the trendier districts of London.'

Jonathan Elliott scowled. He lowered his eyes to look directly at her, jerking his head to toss the dark curls off his high forehead.

'My novels are *not* elitist,' he said stiffly. 'If anything they're too easy to read—you've said yourself that they're hilariously funny. What I'm afraid of is that the ordinary reader may enjoy the humour and fail to realize that the books are satirical. I am fundamentally a serious writer, and my aim is to inform my readers about themselves and contemporary society. I am concerned with the human condition—unlike you, Jasmine, with your romantic fantasies for bored housewives.'

Jasmine Woods smiled at him. 'Your pretensions are showing, Jonathan,' she chided him gently. 'It's precisely because I'm concerned with the human condition that I write as I do. You have no "ordinary" readers, as you call them, because your books are neither about nor for ordinary people. The society you describe is too esoteric. You've grown so far away from your north-country-working-class-lad background that you forget what the human condition really is. What you write are narrowly introspective books about and for extraordinary people like yourself—the kind of books you praise on your own television programme. Reviewers rave about your books, and I admit that I enjoy their wit, but they're meaningless to the general public. Contemporary society is chiefly composed of the people you dismiss as "ordinary" readers. They neither know nor care about the complicated professional and sexual relationships of fashionable media people in Hampstead, or trendy academics at the new universities. They can't identify with any of your characters. They know from experience that real life is unfashionable, hardworking, uneventful and often ultimately sad—and so what they look for in a novel is an absorbing story that leaves them with a feeling either of satisfaction or of hope.'

Jonathan Elliott was staring over her head again. '*Your* readers, perhaps. But, then, I had no sense of being part of the same profession as you romantic novelists.' He lifted his glass as though he were about to drain it, remembered that the wine was rosé, lowered the glass with disdain and wandered away.

Alison glared at his back and then looked at Jasmine Woods with admiration. 'I think you won,' she said, expressing feminine loyalty. 'After all, he retreated.'

Her hostess shrugged. 'He always does.' She met Alison's eyes, they began to laugh together again, and the girl suddenly made up her mind that she could not let slip a wonderful opportunity.

'Miss—er—Mrs Woods—' she began nervously.

'Jasmine.'

'Jasmine . . . Look, I'm a secretary you know, and I need a job—' She gave a hurried account of herself. 'The only thing is,' she finished lamely, 'that my spelling's nowhere near impeccable. It's not all that bad, honestly, but I can't pretend—'

Jasmine Woods looked at the girl with interest. 'Who am I to demand perfection?' she said. 'As long as we get on well together we could always look up the difficult words. There's a problem about getting here, though—no public transport from anywhere. Anne solved that by living in, but what would you do?'

'Oh—I could cycle,' said Alison eagerly. 'It's only three or four miles from home.'

'Good. Come and see me tomorrow afternoon about four, then, and we'll discuss it.'

She smiled and left to talk to some other guests. Alison turned to Tait, dazed by her good fortune. The sadness had vanished from her eyes. 'I may get a job, Martin! Secretary to Jasmine Woods . . . wouldn't that be wonderful?'

'Wonderful,' said Tait, a touch sourly. He had been following Jasmine Woods hopefully all evening, and had hardly had a word from her.

'I say,' said Alison, who had become suddenly animated,

'wasn't Jonathan Elliott *awful*? He was so rude. He must hate Jasmine, though I can't imagine why."

Tait scoffed at the girl's innocence. 'Don't be silly, of course he doesn't hate her! He's after her, and she's not interested, so he's trying to get rid of his frustrations verbally.'

Alison blinked. 'How do you know all that?'

'I'm a detective,' he said. 'I notice these things.'

7

Martin Tait looked at his watch. 'I'll have to go in half an hour. I'm on obbo tonight.'

The Chief Inspector's daughter knew all about obbo. She had frequently, in her youth, heard her mother's bitter opinion about a job which took a married man from the bosom of his family and left him sitting all night in the police car on observation duty, waiting for a crime to happen. But her father was a policeman through and through, a man who had no other training and to whom no other career was open. Martin Tait was a different calibre.

'Do you like being a detective?' she asked.

'Of course. I wouldn't do it otherwise.'

'That's what I thought. Isn't it depressing, though, dealing with the unpleasant side of life all the time? Always analysing people's motives, and thinking the worst of them?'

Tait gave her an indulgent smile. 'Try thinking of it in terms of keeping the Queen's peace,' he advised. 'It's much more picturesque that way.'

She shook her head. 'It makes you cynical,' she said.

'Some of us were born cynical.'

'That's a pity,' said a gentle masculine voice. A man who had been easing his way through the noisy crush near the bottle table paused beside them with a vague, amiable smile. He wore a denim jacket over a T-shirt, and jeans that were pale with wear at the knees and on the seams. He was taller than Tait, but stooping, with long fine light brown hair that flowed and mingled with his long fine beard. His eyelids were puffy, his eyeballs reddened, his eyes distant, dream-faded blue.

'I'm Jasmine's gardener.' He spoke slowly, and his smile lingered as though he were enjoying some private vision. 'If she were here, she'd introduce me as an old friend, so perhaps I can lay claim to being both. But cynical I'm not . . . I have too great an awareness of the harmony and rhythms of nature for that.'

Tait gave him a long cool look. 'Oh, yes?' he said. He was about to draw Alison away from the man's company, but she had begun to ask about the garden. Tait listened for a moment, heard him rambling innocuously about organic methods, saw that Jasmine Woods had gone to change a record, and took the opportunity to join her.

She looked glad to see him. She had just put on a Lloyd Webber record, full of electronic vitality and contrasting woodwind lyricism, and one of her guests, a thick-set dark-bearded man, tried to persuade her to dance. She laughed and shook her head and answered Tait's question instead.

'My gardener? Oh, that's Gilbert—Gilbert Smith, an old friend. We were at university together, until he dropped out. Gardening suits him much better. He's a nice, gentle soul—a poet.'

Tait was neither surprised nor impressed. 'He lives locally, I imagine?'

'At the end of my garden, actually—we converted a loft over the garage into living quarters for him. I saw him quite by chance last year, trying to sell leather belts and purses at Oxlip Fair—you know, the Easter holiday medieval junket. I went out of curiosity, and it was enormous fun anyway, but seeing Gilbert again was a real bonus. He was living in a slummy part of Yarchester at the time, so I offered him a roof in return for help with my two acres, and the arrangement has worked beautifully.'

'Hmm,' said Tait. He had heard about Oxlip Fair. There was more than one thick file on it at Divisional Headquarters, and preparations were already underway for the policing of the next fair. Beginning a few years previously as a small open-air crafts market, it had established itself as a major regional Bank Holiday event with a distinctive pseudo-medieval flavour. It attracted great crowds of spectators, to the harassment of the traffic division. It also, Tait had been told by his jaundiced colleagues, attracted every druggy, drop-out and weirdo in eastern England; so many of them openly smoked pot at the fair that the police couldn't hope to pick up more that a token number.

'I see—' said Tait.

Jasmine Woods's smile faded. 'You're not going to go all official on Gilbert, I hope?' she said warily.

'Not at a private party, of course not. But I've seen enough of the effects of cannabis to be fairly sure that he's on it, and I can hardly socialize with a man I suspect of committing a criminal offence. I'm sorry, Jasmine, but I'll have to pass his name to the drug squad, and I'm afraid that the fact that he's living on your premises could put you in a difficult position. He's probably growing cannabis in your greenhouse, have you thought of that?'

'He's doing nothing of the kind,' she said with some asperity. 'Not that I'd recognize a cannabis plant if I saw one, but I'm interested in gardening and I do know what tomatoes and courgettes look like!'

'But can you guarantee that he *isn't* growing it, in some quiet corner of your garden? Don't risk it, Jasmine, your name's too well-known; if Smith's picked up and charged, the fact that he lives here will put the report of the case on the front page of the local paper, and probably some of the national dailies as well.'

'*Romantic novelist harbours drug user*?' she suggested wryly.

'Something like that. If I were you, I'd tell him that if he can't kick the habit, he'll have to go. And I'd do it soon.'

She looked at him squarely, thoughtfully. 'I'd hoped that we were going to become friends, Martin,' she said, 'but I see now that you really don't know what friendship is. For me, it entails loyalty. Like you, I suspect that Gilbert smokes pot; I don't know for sure, because I don't enquire. I'm fond of him, and I'd much prefer it if he didn't feel the need for drugs, but it was precisely because I was worried about him that I brought him here in the first place. He was adrift, insecure—inadequate, I suppose. And some of the people he knew in Yarchester were junkies, he told me that. I was afraid that if he stayed with them, he would be tempted to turn to hard drugs himself. As it is, he's busy and useful and happy here, and I certainly wouldn't dream of throwing him out and putting him at risk again. After all, smoking pot is acknowledged to be a relatively harmless pastime, and we're all entitled to our private pleasure. If Gilbert chooses to smoke it occasionally, in the privacy of his own flat, then I don't consider that it's any of my business.'

'It happens to be against the law,' pointed out Tait.

'Then perhaps it's time that particular law was amended. I'm sure that half the kick that kids get when they start experimenting with soft drugs comes from the knowledge that it's illegal. And there's nothing they enjoy more than an opportunity to flout authority.'

'Arguably. But my job is to enforce the law as it is, regardless of my personal opinion. As it happens, I disagree that pot smoking is harmless. Addiction to cannabis is known to inhibit the user's sense of responsibility. It makes it much harder for him to resist temptation—sooner or later he's almost certain to try hard drugs. And if you'd heard as much as I have about people who started on cannabis and ended as heroin addicts, you wouldn't take such an indulgent view—'

He'd blown his chances completely now, of course: impossible to argue about law and ethics with your hostess at a party, and to point an official finger at one of her friends, yet still expect her to be prepared to go to bed with you. Imprudent, anyway, for a future chief constable to establish a liaison with a woman knew to be harbouring a suspected criminal offender.

A great pity...Of course, there was now Alison as a possibility, but he'd have to go carefully there. It wouldn't do to upset the old man, or to let Mrs Quantrill imagine that she could hear wedding bells. Well, perhaps if he tried a different technique with Sally from the garage...

'Sorry about the lecture, Jasmine,' he apologized, 'but do

think about what I said, in Smith's interests as well as your own.' He looked at his watch. 'Actually I'll have to go now— I'm on duty tonight. My boss, Alison's father, will be calling to take her home.' He looked for the girl across the room, saw with relief that she had left Smith and was now sharing a bowl of peanuts with Heather Pardoe, caught her eye, pointed to his watch and waved good-bye. 'Thank you for a splendid party,' he told his hostess.

She smiled, with only a little less warmth than when he had arrived. 'I'm glad you could come. And thank you for bringing Alison—I'm delighted to have met her.'

The doorbell rang, and Tait on his way out was able to introduce Quantrill on his way in. He would have liked to be able to drop a hint to the Chief Inspector about the potential awkwardness of the Gilbert Smith situation, but there was no opportunity. Well, if Quantrill met the man, he would draw his own conclusions.

But Quantrill was interested only in collecting his daughter, and incidentally taking stock of Jasmine Woods. He saw that Alison was talking happily to a motherly woman, and turned his attention to the writer. From the paragraph of her book that he had read over his wife's shoulder, he had expected Jasmine Woods to be foolishly soft and blonde and eager and cuddly, a pushover for a practised young man like Tait. He was surprised to find that she looked and sounded quite different.

She insisted on giving him a glass of wine. Quantrill, no wine drinker, commented gallantly on the attractiveness of its colour.

'Pretty pink plonk,' sneered a fierce deep voice at his shoulder. He looked down to see a small man with a large head helping himself from what appeared to be his personal bottle. It was two-thirds empty.

Jasmine Woods introduced her cousin, Rodney Gifford. He had a wrinkled forehead, a wide mouth and large ears that protruded through his long wavy gingerish hair, giving him the appearance of a middle-aged leprechaun. He was dressed in a badly fitting suit which, from the narrow cut of the lapels and trousers, must have been at least ten years old; the cuffs of his pale green drip-dry nylon shirt were discoloured with wear. 'Pretty pink plonk,' he repeated angrily, gulping it down.

Jasmine Woods raised her glass to the light, as she had done when Alison spoke favourably about the colour of the wine, but this time she gave her own opinion. 'Pretty, Rodney? Oh, no! Come, now, you're a writer—a better writer than I am. And you're too exact an observer to dismiss this pink as "pretty." It has too dark an undertone for that. It always reminds me of watered-down blood.'

Douglas Quantrill was surprised. It was not, he felt, a suitable comparison for a romantic novelist to make. Jasmine Woods saw his frown and smiled at him. 'Sorry,' she said, 'but that's the way my mind works. You mustn't be misled by the kind of books I write—they're not the real me at all. I'm not romantic, I'm a realist; that's why I write romance, because it pays.'

'Prostituting yourself to a genre,' growled Rodney Gifford fiercely. His cousin shrugged, smiled at Quantrill and moved away to talk to someone else. Gifford refilled his glass. 'Contemptible, don't you think,' he demanded of Quantrill, 'to write books she despises simply for the sake of money?'

Quantrill had come to the party prepared to dislike Jasmine Woods, but he found that his dislike was rapidly being transferred to her sozzled cousin. 'We all have to earn a living,' he pointed out, 'and a lot of us find ourselves doing it in ways that can be distasteful. I wouldn't dream of criticizing your cousin for what she does—and I most certainly wouldn't do so at her party. What's more—' he sipped his wine cautiously, found that it didn't mix with the half-pint of Adnams he'd had at the Plough and Gull on his way through Thirling, and crunched a couple of cheesy biscuits to take away the taste '—I'm damned if I'd drink her wine *and* sneer at it.'

But Rodney Gifford seemed not to hear. He waved his almost-empty bottle. 'It's deliberate, you know,' he said belligerently, 'giving us this pink swill. It's a calculated insult to our judgement, just like the new book she expects us to celebrate. After all, she could be a proper writer if she tried. She's got the ability to write real novels, but she doesn't because she knows they wouldn't make her enough money.

She's not prepared to write about real life because she's not prepared to be poor. She's a hedonist. She's never suffered, that's her trouble.' He made a sudden, vicious gesture with the bottle. 'A bit of suffering would do cousin Jasmine a world of good.'

Quantrill stared down at him with distaste. 'Do you live far away?' he demanded.

The man blinked and swayed. 'Yarchester. Why?'

'Because you're obviously not fit to drive home.'

Gifford laughed, with anger rather than amusement. 'Drive, me? How in heaven's name do you imagine I could afford to run a car? I'm the beggar of the family—a better writer than Jasmine, as she so kindly says, and an honest one. I always write what I believe in, and so I don't make money. I'm here only because Jasmine arranged for the Pardoes to give me a lift. Ducky of her, wasn't it?'

Quantrill looked at the long-necked bottle which Gifford was upending unsteadily above his glass. Jasmine Woods was right, he decided, as he watched the last few drops trickle out; the wine did look remarkably like watered-down blood.

'At least you'll get something out of the evening,' he said coldly, 'even if it's only a headache.' He turned away and accidentally jolted a woman's arm, spilling her wine over her hand; he began to apologize for his clumsiness and offered his handkerchief, but she declined it and flicked the wine off carelessly.

'No gallantry required,' advised Jasmine Woods, who had been talking to the woman. 'That's right, isn't it, Roz?'

She introduced him to Roz Elliott, a big square handsome woman in her late thirties with thick, rough-cut auburn hair. She wore shabby leather knee-boots, a billowing dun-coloured calf-length skirt, and a patterned blouse that looked like an Indian peasant's cast-off. Quantrill would not have been able, if asked, to define ethnic, but in terms of dress he recognized it when he saw it.

Alison, having heard her father's voice, joined the group. Jasmine Woods repeated the introduction.

'Are you Mrs Jonathan Elliott?' the girl asked. 'I met your husband a few moments ago.'

Roz Elliott's strong-boned unpainted face looked disapproving; her untrimmed eyebrows rose to conceal themselves under her wilting-chrysanthemum fringe. 'No,' she said firmly, 'I am not Mrs Jonathan Elliott.'

'Oh, come off it...' Jasmine Woods told her pleasantly. 'You're married to the man—that's all Alison wanted to know. Roz,' she explained to Quantrill and his daughter, 'is liberated. Aren't you, love?'

'Certainly.' She had a richly beautiful voice; a striking woman, Quantrill thought, if only she were not determined to make the worst of her appearance. 'And if I hadn't been a committed feminist before, I'd have become one as soon as I discovered that I had a romantic novelist as a neighbour.'

'You don't seem to mind coming round to see me, much as you dislike my books.'

'That's because I haven't entirely given up hope of persuading you to join the women's movement.'

'Never. I don't believe in quarrelling with the source of my income.'

'And *that's* what's so infuriating about you! If you were stupid enough to believe in what you write, I wouldn't mind so much; but you know perfectly well that it's rubbish. That means that you're deliberately exploiting your readers.'

Quantrill stared uneasily at Roz Elliott. He had never before been at a party where the guests seemed to regard it as a duty to insult their hostess. He thought that it was time he took his daughter home, but she was engrossed in the duologue; like a Wimbledon spectator at a Centre Court rally, she hardly dared to blink for fear of missing something.

It was apparent to Alison that, with the Elliotts as neighbours, Jasmine Woods must come under regular verbal attack. Her hostess seemed to enjoy it, and to be perfectly capable of defending herself, but on hearing Roz Elliott denounce the Jasmine Woods canon as rubbish, Alison intervened.

'The books aren't rubbish!' she said indignantly. 'They're interesting and colourful and exciting... I enjoy them.'

Jasmine Woods gave her a friendly smile. 'Thank you for

that unsolicited testimonial. You see, Roz? Alison doesn't feel in the least exploited.'

'Oh, for God's sake—' Roz Elliott pushed her hair off her forehead in a gesture of exasperation. She gave the girl a stern glance, but spoke to Jasmine Woods. 'Isn't this exactly the trouble with the great majority of women? They're so conditioned to accept their traditional role in society that they're incapable of questioning, let alone challenging, your kind of fiction. I loathe romantic novels because they perpetuate so many silly myths and give impressionable girls so many false expectations. It's completely cynical of you, Jasmine, to encourage girls to believe that love is the answer to everything, and that getting married solves problems by automatically ensuring a happy ending.'

The verbal battle continued, with Roz Elliott vigorously reinforcing her assertions about social conditioning, much of which she blamed on the influence of romantic novelists, and condemning the oppression of women, for which she appeared to hold Jasmine Woods personally responsible.

The writer defended herself with weary good humour, pointing out that the immemorial propensity of young people to fall in love and get married could hardly be blamed on romantic novels. People do, after all, she said, grow up in and among families; they see for themselves how difficult family relationships can be, and how many marriages fail. And yet they persist in getting married, because they believe that things will be different with them. Hope, she asserted, of an eventual happy ending is the supreme motivation without which life for many women might not seem worth living.

It was, quite clearly, ground which the two of them had covered before.

As soon as he could decently interrupt, Quantrill made getting-away noises. Jasmine Woods walked with him to the hall, explaining that she had arranged for Alison to see her the following day to discuss the possibility of a job. Quantrill was delighted. Having taken against Jasmine Woods sight unseen, he now found himself liking her; the more so as the other guests he had met had behaved so bitchily. She made him feel protective. Besides, he agreed with her about the importance of hope; in his job, he saw too often how the loss of it could ruin lives, and not just those of women.

While Alison was putting on her coat, the bell rang. Jasmine Woods opened the door. A couple stood on the step, an attractive fine-featured blonde girl in her mid-twenties, dressed in high boots and a long suede fur-lined coat, and a man a few years older.

'Hallo, Jasmine,' said the girl in a quick, light, slightly breathless voice.

Jasmine Woods looked completely surprised. 'Anne—my dear. How lovely to see you.'

Alison recognized the girl immediately as the writer's ex-secretary and felt, ridiculously, the pinch of jealousy. She had already begun to imagine herself in that role, and she was afraid that Anne Downing might have come to reclaim her job.

Jasmine Woods seemed to be equally unsure of the purpose of Anne's visit; she looked pleased to see her, but wary. She stepped back, inviting the couple in, and Anne drew her escort forward. He was tall and broad and tweedy, with a healthy red outdoor face. When he took off his flat cap he revealed a high, prematurely balding forehead that was in strangely white contrast to his weathered cheeks. A farmer, Quantrill guessed. He looked honest and shy and proud and pleased, and a little bewildered.

Anne Downing stood with her left hand tucked possessively through the crook of his arm, and the light from the hall winkled out flashes of brilliance from the half-hoop of diamonds and sapphires on her finger. Her cheeks were pink, her eyes shone. 'This,' she announced, 'is my fiancé, Oliver Buxton. We knew each other years ago, then lost touch. But we met again last month, and we're getting married at Easter.'

'Married—how wonderful for you!' Jasmine Woods stretched out her arms to take the girl by the shoulders and give her a warm, impulsive kiss. Anne released her fiancé for long enough to return her ex-employer's embrace, and then immediately seized his arm again as though it were a lifebelt.

'Oliver farms in Norfolk,' she said, 'and I'm staying with him and his parents at the moment, so I probably shan't see you again before the wedding. We drove over this evening to have dinner with Oliver's uncle in Breckham Market and as we were so near I simply had to call. You'll get a proper invitation to the wedding, of course, but I wanted to tell you about it in person. You'll come, I hope?'

'If I can, certainly. I do wish you both every happiness.' Jasmine Woods offered her congratulations to Buxton, then spoke again to his fiancée. 'I'd like you to meet Alison Quantrill and her father. Alison may well be taking your old job—'

Introduction over, the women began to talk to each other in rapid, heightened voices as women do, Quantrill thought, when discussing emotional subjects like weddings. He turned to Oliver Buxton, who stood tongue-tied, milking his cap with bucolic hands.

"Well, congratulations," said Quantrill heartily. Despite his own imperfectly rewarding experience, he was not cynical about marriage as an institution. 'She's a very attractive girl.'

'Isn't she?' Buxton's high-rise forehead had become pink and sweaty with joyful embarrassment. 'I can hardly believe my luck, I can tell you. I just hope that she'll be happy with me on the farm. I know that she misses her job here already, but it's much too far for her to travel every day.'

At that moment Alison, having said good-bye to her hostess, ran up and—unusually—caught at her father's arm. Her eyes, like Anne's, shone with happiness. 'I've got it!' she whispered exultantly. 'I'll still have to come and see Jasmine tomorrow to finalize it, but from what she's told Anne there isn't much doubt that I've got the job!'

8

On Monday 6 April, at approximately 9.25 a.m., Alison Quantrill arrived on her bicycle at Yeoman's, Thirling, near

Breckham Market, where she worked as secretary to the novelist, Jasmine Woods. Alison Quantrill had been employed in this capacity since the 20th February. She cycled daily from her home, 5 Benidorm Avenue, Breckham Market, and it was her usual practice to leave the bicycle in one of the outbuildings near the drive gate, and then to walk up to the house, ring the front-door bell twice, and go straight in.

On the 6th April she followed this practice, leaving her coat in the downstairs cloakroom and then going to the office, which was also on the ground floor. She was not aware of anything unusual. Sometimes her employer would already be at work in the office, but if she were not there, Alison Quantrill would continue with whatever audio-typing or proof-reading she had on hand.

At approximately 10.30 a.m., at which time Jasmine Woods usually made coffee for them both, Alison Quantrill became concerned that her employer had not appeared. She went into the hall, called and listened, but could hear no sounds from any other part of the house. She opened the door to the sitting-room, and found that the curtains were closed over the windows. This was unusual. She drew back the curtains and knew immediately, without consciously noting why, that the room had been disturbed in some way. Then she saw some clothing scattered on the floor. She went towards it, and saw the body of her employer.

Jasmine Woods was lying on the floor behind a sofa. The body was partly clothed and on its side, with one knee drawn up. The right side of the skull had been crushed, and a broken Loire wine bottle lay eighteen inches away. A further bottle, intact, had been used as an instrument of rape.

A 999 call was made from the Yeoman's number. The caller was male. He declined to identify himself. The call was logged by the police at 11.24 and a patrol car reached the house at 11.32.

When Chief Inspector Quantrill arrived at Yeoman's six minutes later he found his daughter crouched in the orchard, sobbing and retching among the daffodils, and the first thing he did was to take her home.

9

The narrow country road that passed the gate of Yeoman's was partially obstructed by police cars. Quantrill, returning after taking Alison home, edged his big Austin close to a hawthorn hedge that bristled with a four-day green beard. He nodded to the uniformed constable on traffic and gate duty, and strode past some brick outbuildings and on up the drive towards the house.

Yeoman's was of typically Suffolk construction: timber framed, with the timbers—unlike those of equally old houses in the more decadent Home Counties—decently covered by an all-over cladding of pink-washed plaster. Massive brick chimney stacks buttressed the house at either end. The roof was thatched with reed that rose—as the Suffolk voice rises at the end of each sentence—to form a snout of thatch above each gable.

Untypically, the property was in immaculate condition. Thatch and plaster are ruinously expensive to maintain, and neglect soon shows. The thatch becomes colonized by birds and rodents; the lime plaster cracks and peels to expose walls made of clay lump, that friable pudding mixture of rubble and horse hair and clay and straw which was for centuries the basic East Anglian building material. But at Yeoman's the thatch was thick and trim and the plaster—coloured a delicate magnolia pink rather than the commoner strawberry-ice-cream shade—unblemished.

Detective Sergeant Tait, who was examining the exterior of the window to the right of the front door, looked up as Quantrill approached.

'How's Alison, sir?' he asked sympathetically.

'Under sedation by now, I hope. She's thoroughly shocked, poor child.'

'No wonder, if she saw that body.' Tait looked paler and a good deal more subdued than usual. With reason, Quantrill remembered; Tait had at one time fancied his chances with Jasmine Woods. Seeing her murdered body must have shaken him up. It wasn't a duty that Quantrill himself was looking forward to, either.

Tait wiped his hand over his mouth and made an obvious effort to revert to his usual briskness. 'Was Alison able to tell you anything?'

'Nothing coherent. Understandably—she was fond of the woman. She used to talk at home about Jasmine Woods until we were sick of the sound of the name, so she's bound to be in a bad way. I've left a policewoman with her to take a statement as soon as she's up to giving it. Still, this is one case where we've plenty of information before we start.' The Chief Inspector peered at the window that Tait had been examining. 'A break-in, was it? Someone after her collection?'

'The display case is broken open and the jade and netsuke have gone,' Tait confirmed, 'but nothing else has been disturbed and there's no sign of a forced entry into the house. Presumably she opened the door to her killer, and the injuries suggest that it was a man. Rigor seems to be complete, by the way. Until the pathologist pins down the time of death, I'm working on the hypothesis that it was yesterday.'

'Sounds reasonable. Sunday... and it must have been someone she knew, or she wouldn't have let him in to the house.'

'One thing's for sure,' said Tait. 'It was done by someone who really hated her.'

'You can never be sure of that,' argued Quantrill. 'Murder's often done in blind panic—the first blow may be intended just to keep the victim quiet, but then the attacker loses his head completely. That's what's so terrifying about violence; it fuels itself. You can't assure that hatred is a motive.'

'You haven't seen the body yet,' Tait said grimly. 'Wait until you see what he did to her.'

Quantrill looked and was appalled. He had seen death—and death by violence—often enough in his career to think himself incapable of being shocked by it, but this one was different; more vicious than any murder he had ever seen. That the victim was a woman he knew compounded the horror. He blinked as the photographer's busy flash illuminated the corpse, and swallowed down his nausea. *God help her, poor woman . . . and that child Alison, who had seen her friend like this . . .*

'Nasty one, eh, Chief?' said an abominably cheerful voice.

Keith Pulham, the duty divisional scene-of-crime officer, was a blond round-cheeked young civilian whose teenage ambition to join the force had been frustrated by his failure—despite his surreptitious enrolment for a postal body-building course—to grow an extra two and a half inches in height. Now, after a period of training at a forensic science laboratory, he held an appointment that gave him all the immediate technical interest of detective work with none of the foot-slogging enquiry routine, and he was as happy and eager as a newly trained police dog. While he waited for the arrival of Inspector Colman and the serious crimes team from Yarchester, Pulham padded round the periphery noting the whereabouts of every one of the far-flung spots of blood on the walls and furniture.

Quantrill, glad that he could leave the detailed examination of the body to the experts, stood back and took note of the position of other objects in relation to it: the shoes and trousers that had been torn off and flung on the floor, the broken bottle glass, and the orange blob that looked at first glance like a fallen jelly-baby, but proved to be a small piece of amber jade.

'Seen anything useful yet, Soco?' he asked.

'This might come in handy.' Pulham pointed to something on the floor below the wrenched-open doors of the display cabinet, some yards from the edge of the great crimson lake of blood—still tacky—that spread over the hand-knotted cream Bokhara carpet below and about the place where the body lay. The Chief Inspector crouched beside him to peer at some brownish-white splinters that had been trodden into the carpet.

'I'm not sure what it was,' continued Pulham, leaving the fragments exactly where they were for his senior colleagues to see, 'but I imagine our villain must have trodden on it. Chances are that some of the bits will have stuck to his shoe.'

'It's probably ivory,' said Quantrill. 'She had a valuable collection of netsuke.'

Pulham's forehead puckered like that of a puzzled Doberman. 'Come again, Chief?'

Quantrill stood up and glanced round. Tait, talking to the photographer on the far side of the room, was out of earshot; even so, the Chief Inspector was reluctant to air his recently acquired knowledge. 'Ivory,' he repeated off-handedly. 'Japanese knick-knacks.'

Pulham nodded, pleased at the prospect of impressing his colleagues with the information. 'Ah.' He studied the corpse dispassionately. 'Doesn't look much like murder in furtherance of theft, though, does it? I mean—'

'No,' said Quantrill shortly, moving away. He had to suppress a completely unprofessional instinct to get the body decently covered.

The police surgeon came, pronounced the woman dead, agreed with Tait's hypothesis that the murder had been committed the previous day, and went. Inspector Colman and his team arrived and began their minutely detailed examination of the scene of the crime. Chief Inspector Quantrill sent for the mobile incident-room and sited it on the outskirts of the village, where it could be used as a centre for co-ordinating the activities of the enquiry team. He gave a briefing, and sent policemen along the winding road that ran from the village past the gates of Yeoman's, to enquire at the scattered dwellings whether anyone had noticed a vehicle parked outside Jasmine Woods's house the previous day. More policeman began to search the drive for tire marks or footprints.

As soon as Jasmine Woods's office had been checked over, Quantrill and Tait moved in to find out what they could about the dead woman. Quantrill had heard from his daughter that the room was called an office. He would have supposed that a romantic novelist might give it a cosier name, but having met this particular novelist, he knew that she had unromantic turn of mind. The room was, strictly, an office with two plain desks and swivel chairs, an electric typewriter, a tape recorder, filing cabinets and reference books. Only exotically flowered curtains and a large bowl of hyacinths saved it from austerity.

A blank sheet of paper was in the typewriter, and some completed work lay beside it. Quantrill glanced at a neatly typewritten sheet, blinked over the hair-raising event it described in breathless prose, and decided that it had to be fiction. 'Try the recorder,' he told Tait. 'There might be something relevant on it.'

The machine was not a model that Tait was familiar with. He talked to cover the fact that he was having to fiddle with it. 'I imagine that this is what Alison was using this morning, before she found the body. Presumably Jasmine dictated her novels, and her secretary typed them from the tapes—ah—' He picked up the earpiece and listened for a few moments, wide-eyed with amusement. 'It seems to be all about an intrepid heroine protecting her virginity with one hand while she clings to the gargoyle on a church tower with the other.'

'Typical,' grunted Quantrill. His sympathy with Jasmine Woods, alive and dead, did not extend to her works. 'Well, that's one book my wife will never get her head into. Pack up the tapes, anyway, we can run them through later if we're stuck for ideas. You know, I'm puzzled about what happened this morning, Martin. The anonymous three-nines call, for one thing.'

'I thought that might have been the man who looks after the garden,' said Tait. 'I met him at Jasmine's party. Gilbert Smith—he lives somewhere in the grounds.'

Quantrill looked up quickly. 'Does he? Yes, come to think of it, Alison did mention him once or twice. Very gentle, she said—won't even exterminate the greenfly.'

'Oh, he's a left-over from the flower-power era,' said Tait disparagingly. 'Hair down to his shoulders, and peace and love to all—you know the kind of thing.'

'You mean a druggy?' Quantrill demanded. His eyebrows rose fiercely. 'You knew this and you didn't do anything about it—even though Alison has been working here?'

'Certainly I did something,' said Tait, irritated that the Chief Inspector should underestimate his professionalism. 'I met Smith just once, at the party, and I spoke to Jasmine

48

about him. Apparently they were old friends. She suspected that he smoked pot, and thought it was harmless, but I advised her either to tell him to stop it or to throw him out. I told her I'd have to pass his name to the drug squad, and I did, but I had no evidence and they've probably been too busy to follow him up. Damn it all—sir—' he added, aggrieved, 'I spoiled my chances with Jasmine by giving her a semi-official warning, so there's no question of dereliction of duty. Besides, you were at the party too; for all I knew, you'd met Smith yourself. And Alison knew him and told you about him—'

'Yes, well . . . as it happens I didn't meet the man, and I don't always listen to everything my daughter says. She was happy in her job, and that's all I cared. What I'm concerned about is what happened this morning. Alison's time for starting work here was 9.30; the three-nines call is logged at 11.24. I wonder why it took so long to find the body? And if it was Smith who made the call, why didn't he give his name?'

'I've sent a PC to find him,' said Tait. 'We shall want a statement from him anyway, since he lived on the property.'

Quantrill agreed. 'Not that he's likely to be the murderer, if he's about the place this morning. Of course, the man who made the call might have been the first passerby that Alison could find, or that milkman or the postman—'

'Who did his duty but didn't want to be involved—?' said Tait doubtfully.

'Well, it's a possibility. We shall know as soon as we can get Alison's statement. Or we may get the answer from one of the nearby houses.'

'Did you meet any of her neighbours who were at Jasmine's party?' asked Tait. 'I did, and they interest me. I don't know what impression you got of the guests, but mine wasn't favourable.'

'Mine neither. I'm not much of a partygoer,' understated Quantrill, 'but I didn't think it was usual for guests to be deliberately rude to their hostess.' He recalled the people he had met at the party. 'Bloody rude. In fact,' he added, remembering Jasmine Woods's drunkenly belligerent cousin, 'I can think of one man I'd very much like to interview in connection with her murder.'

Tait took out his notebook. 'Between us,' he suggested, 'we can probably compile a list...'

They did, and compared their impressions, and looked at their findings with surprise and interest.

'Rum lot of friends, she had,' mused Quantrill.

'She did make a point of telling me that most of the guests were relations and neighbours rather than personal friends.'

'I should hope so. With relations and neighbours like that, she'd need a few good friends somewhere. Well, this list is going to come in useful. Can you find her address book? And an engagement diary?'

Tait found both and opened the diary at the page for Sunday 5 April.

'Sociable day,' he commented. *'J and R drinks here 12.* That could be Jonathan and Roz Elliott, she said they lived locally. Presumably she was alive at that time, or they'd have come in when she didn't open the door, and would have found the body. Then it says *Heather's, supper* query. Heather is her impoverished sister in Yarchester—the one with the envious husband. Why the query, I wonder? And did she keep the appointment? And if not—'

'Heather must be her nearest relation, to our knowledge,' said Quantrill. 'I'll go and break the news and find out what happened yesterday. And while I'm in Yarchester, it'll be interesting to go and have a word with Rodney—'

He broke off as a middle-aged constable, as heavily moustached as Kitchener in the First World War posters, hurried in to the office.

'Smith's hopped it, sir,' he reported, breathing hard. 'There was no sign of him in the garden, and there's a path of oil on the floor of the double garage, alongside the car. From the spares lying around, it looks as though a motor bike was kept there. I found his living quarters above the garage. The door was locked, so I forced an entry. There's almost nothing left in the way of clothes and personal gear except—'

The constable took a deep breath, brushed his moustache with his knuckle and tried not to sound too pleased with the importance of the news he brought: '—except a pair of jeans and a pair of shoes. And they're both soaked with blood.'

10

Alison Quantrill floundered up through layer after suffocating layer of sedation, heart pounding, limbs thrashing, voice crying out against the enormity of her nightmare. There was blood in it, and glass, and torn flesh, and the pain of what she saw ripped screaming through her skull: 'No! No!'

To Beth Knowles, the busty policewoman who sat patiently near her in the bedroom with the Laura Ashley wallpaper at Number 5 Benidorm Avenue, it seemed merely that the girl twitched and murmured for a moment in her sleep.

Two detectives and three uniformed policemen converged on a building at the end of Jasmine Woods's garden, near the gate. It was a two-storey red-brick structure that had presumably once been a stable; an exterior iron staircase led to the upper part, and the men clattered up it one after the other and burst into Gilbert Smith's flat.

The door opened immediately on to an all-purpose room, with sloping walls that were lined with white-painted board. In one corner was a sink unit and a small calor gas cooker, and near them a table on which were the remains of a meal, although it was difficult to decide exactly which meal cornflakes, baked beans spooned cold from their tin, brown bread and canned lager added up to.

The room smelled of stale smoke, and dust was thick everywhere. An unmade divan bed stood against the far wall. The room was generously supplied with built-in cupboards, but most of them were closed and unused. All that remained in the wardrobe was an army surplus great-coat and a holed T-shirt that looked as though it might have been used for cleaning purposes. On the T-shirt was a blazing-sun motif circled by the legend *A fair field full of folk*.

Of material possessions—other than the furniture, rugs and curtains, presumably supplied by Jasmine Woods—there was little evidence: a broken guitar, a few paperbacks, some posters stuck or pinned to the walls. Many of the posters were elderly, their edges curled and beginning to tear. Some were illustrations and maps of Tolkien's Middle Earth, leftovers from the cult of Gandalf and the Lord of the Rings. On a bench were some pieces of wood in process of being carved into weird animals, half men, half beasts.

Above the bed, handwritten on the sloping wall with a red felt-tip, was a statement: 'The higher you go, the more precise and intelligent must be your nagivation.'

A small shower-room led off the main room. The April sun, full on the window, filtered greenly through the leaves of the plants that flourished in pots on the sill. Hidden behind the shower curtain, where the constable had found them, were the gardener's bloodstained jeans and shoes.

'I thought you said *soaked*,' grumbled Quantrill. 'There's nowhere near enough blood here.'

'And anyway,' said Tait, 'fresh blood would saturate the fabric. Most of this is lying on the surface in clots.'

The two detectives stared accusingly at the constable, who shifted his weight from one foot to another and brushed at his moustache. 'It's significant evidence,' he asserted indignantly.

'So it is, Ron,' Quantrill agreed. 'Doesn't seem to point to the murderer, though, does it? If it was Smith who killed her, his clothes really would be soaked. These aren't. Still, this quantity of blood and the fact that Smith has gone is significant enough, as you say.' He jerked his head at his sergeant. 'Get him picked up, Martin.'

'I'm doing so,' said Tait, who had stopped to radio the instruction before racing up to Smith's flat. 'There are smears of blood on the doors and on the washbasin taps, so he must have had it on his hands as well. I'll get the fingerprints from this flat checked against the ones in the house, and send these clothes to forensic. Then I'll give this place a thorough going-over.'

'Right. I'll get the usual notice circulated to antique

dealers, asking them to report anyone who tries to sell them netsuke or Chinese jade. Then I'm off to Yarchester to find out what I can from Jasmine Woods's sister and her husband.'

'Better see if you can find a WPC to go with you,' advised Sergeant Tait. 'Heather Pardoe's got five kids and another on the way, and I'd hate to think of you being lumbered.' He turned away, grinning to himself, not hating the thought at all and betting that he knew which policewoman's company the Chief Inspector would prefer.

'We'll call on Jasmine Woods's brother-in-law first, Patsy,' explained Quantrill, driving along the main road towards Yarchester through a lashing of April rain that stopped as suddenly as it had started. 'She had an entry in her diary that suggested that she might be having supper with them last night, so I want to find out about that. And then we can take him home to break the news to his wife.'

'Good,' said WPC Patsy Hopkins. She had a brusque voice and a very firm chin that could give her a formidable, tough-as-a-pair-of-police-boots air; misleading, because nine years in the force had failed to blunt her natural sensitivity. 'I don't like having to tell women that their relatives have been murdered. Thank heaven,' she added frankly, enjoying the company of her favourite senior officer to whom she could talk much more freely than to her own uniformed Chief Inspector, 'for the Sex Discrimination Act—I really resented the old business of being stuck in a special policewomen's department, where we were dealing with nothing but women and juveniles. There was so much emotional wear and tear. Give me operational work every time.'

Quantrill grinned. He found her combination of competence and candour very attractive; her smartness in uniform, her smooth fair hair and the length of her legs had never, he told himself firmly, had any bearing upon his good opinion of her.

'Think yourself lucky you're in this force, then,' he said. 'In some cities, women aren't used on beat patrols at night anymore, for their own protection. And you know that the Federation want exemption from the Sex Discrimination Act, so that they can keep you out of harm's way.'

'Hah! It's not just our protection they're concerned about,' Patsy Hopkins said indignantly. 'That's an excuse to try to reduce women's recruitment. Good grief, if we were afraid of danger we wouldn't join. Once a woman is trained, she can do just as much as a policeman—more, sometimes. The Federation knows this perfectly well, but some of them are just a bunch of—"

WPC Hopkins made a liberated comment which showed her to be completely unappreciative of the chivalrous instincts of the male members of the Police Federation. Quantrill gave a snort of laughter.

'You're obviously not a reader of Jasmine Woods's romantic novels,' he said dryly, slowing to a crawl through a village whose ancient gabled houses confined vehicles to a street barely wide enough for one, let alone two lanes of traffic. Pedestrians went sideways, flattening themselves apprehensively against the buildings as massive container lorries, snorting past on their way between the industrial Midlands and the East Coast docks, mounted narrow pavements, gouged holes in plaster walls and sprayed both pedestrians and buildings with puddle dirt and diesel fumes.

'As a matter of fact,' admitted Patsy Hopkins, slightly shamefaced, 'I do read Jasmine Woods. Not that I find much time for reading at all, but when I do I want to get right away from reality; I see enough of that on the job. I like a book with an exotic setting, a fast-moving story and plenty of excitement—and a nice bit of True Love at the end,' she added, mocking herself defensively. Then she sighed. 'I wouldn't have thought it, but I suppose I must really be a romantic at heart. I felt quite upset when I heard that it was Jasmine Woods who'd been murdered—not that I'd ever met her, but I felt as though she was someone I knew.'

'I did meet her once, a few weeks ago,' Quantrill said. 'My daughter's been working for her, and it seems she found the body. Alison's shattered—she was really fond of Jasmine Woods. I liked her, too. Shocking that she should come to such a violent end.'

'Horrible. Symbolic rape, somebody at division said.'

'Possibly actual as well. We shan't know that until the pathologist has finished with her.'

'Oh, God . . .' said Patsy Hopkins soberly.

They drove the rest of the way into Yarchester without

speaking, listening to the radio as it put all patrol cars on watch for Gilbert Smith's motor cycle.

11

Paul Pardoe, Jasmine Woods's brother-in-law, worked for a firm of estate agents whose offices were near Yarchester cathedral. Quantrill parked his car on cobblestones under a row of pollarded lime trees just outside one of the gates that led into the lower end of the cathedral close. He left WPC Hopkins in the car on radio watch and took a short cut, between showers, across a corner of the close. Here, despite the fact that most of the Queen Anne houses once lived in by cathedral clergy had become the offices of solicitors or architects or accountants, there was still an ecclesiastical calm. Traffic was shut out. The great lawn in the centre of the lower close was ornamented by almond trees, whose rained-down pink blossom was spread over the wet grass like sugar icing on the sponge cakes at a mothers' union tea.

Once out of the main gateway, Quantrill re-entered the last quarter of the twentieth century and waited impatiently for the little green man on the traffic lights to allow him to cross the roaring road. The offices of Pardoe's firm were in a parallel street, once an early Victorian residential area but now the estate agents' quarter of the city. Nearly every ground floor plate-glass window displayed photographs of small modern houses that looked, and in many instances were, identical with those in the windows of rival firms.

Mr Pardoe was with a client, said the skinny girl at the reception desk. Quantrill took the opportunity of glancing through the firm's leaflets while he waited. Some of the estate agents in the city were old-established and distinctly up-market, offering country houses at prices that began at £50,000, but Paul Pardoe's firm appeared to concentrate on bread and butter properties. He was not named as one of the firm's principals. It was impossible to guess what his income might be, but any man with five children and another on the way would be bound to feel financially straitened. The death of his wife's affluent sister might well be of considerable advantage to him. It would be interesting, Quantrill thought, to see how he took the news, especially as he had not troubled to conceal from Tait the fact that he disliked Jasmine Woods.

Pardoe's 'Come in' was clogged with food and irritable with incipient dyspepsia. An open plastic container on his desk was filled with waxy white sandwiches, one hurriedly gnawed at.

Quantrill, introducing himself, remembered the long thin face, the dishevelled greyish-fair hair and the look of gloom and harassment. Pardoe, having swallowed what he was chewing, was staring at his visitor uneasily, his mouth partly open.

'I've seen you somewhere before, haven't I?' he demanded. A paste of masticated bread filled the interstices of his large yellow teeth.

'I believe so,' Quantrill agreed, 'though we didn't get a chance to speak. I called in on a party given by your sister-in-law at Thirling, about six weeks ago.'

Pardoe's frown deepened. 'I didn't realize you were in the police.'

'I wasn't on duty at the time—but I am now, I'm afraid. It's your wife's sister, Jasmine Woods, I've come to see you about.'

'Oh, yes?' Pardoe closed his sandwich box and looked at his watch. 'I've got a site meeting out in the country at three, so I can only spare a few minutes.'

'I think perhaps you'd better cancel the meeting, Mr Pardoe,' Quantrill advised him. 'Your wife is going to need you. Her sister was found dead this morning.'

Pardoe's mouth opened again. His face was so pinched, his eyes so deep set, that it would be difficult for him even at the best of times to appear anything but haggard. 'Jasmine?' he said hoarsely. 'Dead—how?'

'Her body was found in the sitting-room with fatal head injuries. I'm afraid that it was murder.'

'Oh, my God!' Pardoe rose from his chair in agitation. 'But that's . . . terrible. Why should anyone do such a thing?' His eyes evaded Quantrill's, flicking round the small room as though he sought the answer among his plans of cheek-by-jowl housing-estate properties, the first-time-buyer's dream world that he worked to create. 'It doesn't make sense. Jasmine, of all people—'

'Oh, come now, Mr Pardoe,' Quantrill pointed out briskly, reserving his sympathy for the man's wife. 'It was public knowledge that your sister-in-law was a wealthy young woman. She was known to have some small items of considerable value in her house. Her death is tragic, and of course it's a shock to you, but it's certainly not incredible.'

'Ah.' Pardoe let out a long breath. His eyes stilled. 'Yes, now I understand. You mean that she was murdered by someone who was trying to steal from her?'

'That's possible. We shan't know until we've completed our enquiries. At the moment I'm trying to trace her movements yesterday, Sunday. According to a note in her diary, she was coming to have supper with you and your wife. Did she come?'

'No.' Pardoe walked over to the window and stood there, tall and round-shouldered. He had a large frame, but he was so thin that the seat of his ready-made trousers hung in a slack fold below his jacket. 'No, Jasmine didn't show up. Apparently she'd told my wife that she might not be able to come—it wasn't a definite arrangement.'

'Did she telephone to let your wife know she couldn't come?'

'No. Heather tried to ring her, but there was no reply.'

'What time was that?'

Pardoe's shoulders twitched, declining commitment. He remained at the window, staring out at the huddle of roofs above which the sunlit spire of the cathedral rose to take a stab at the scudding flotilla of fleece-lined shower clouds.

'Mr Pardoe!' Quantrill spoke sharply, and the man turned with obvious reluctance. 'This is a murder enquiry, and I need an answer. At roughly what time yesterday did your wife try to telephone her sister?'

Pardoe kept his eyes lowered. 'I don't know,' he said. 'I was out on business yesterday.'

'On a Sunday?'

'It was a private commission, nothing to do with this firm.'

'I see. What time did you leave home?'

'Oh . . . about ten in the morning.' He moved to his desk, sat down and began to riffle absently through some papers. 'I had a meeting with an acquaintance who wanted me to do a survey of a house he'd inherited over near Newmarket. I was working out there all day.'

'And what time did you get home?'

The man hesitated. Quantrill stared hard at him from under his thick eyebrows. 'I shall need to see your wife, of course, but I don't want to question her any more than is necessary—'

'Just before eleven.'

'At night? You were out for over twelve hours?'

'It takes a long time to do a full survey—and then there was the journey.'

'It's an hour's drive from here to Newmarket. It might have taken you as much as an hour and a half to get back, allowing for the Sunday evening traffic returning from the coast. You mean that you were still surveying the house at half-past nine yesterday evening—in the dark?'

'I didn't say that. I stopped to have a drink.'

'With your client?'

'No—he left me after he'd shown me the house.'

'What time did he leave you?'

'About midday. I had a lot to do, it wasn't a social occasion. I worked until the early evening, and then took his keys back to him and started to drive home. But I was tired, so I stopped for a drink.'

'I see. Mr Pardoe, the direct route from Newmarket to Yarchester passes within eight or ten miles of Thirling. Did you by any chance call on your sister-in-law for that drink?'

Pardoe gave a bitter shout of laughter. 'Jasmine's? That's the last place I'd go to. I stopped at a pub on the main road. I didn't go nearer to Thirling than that.'

'Were you on your own?'

'Yes.'

'You must have had more than one drink, then, if you didn't reach home until just before eleven.'

The man's face was narrow as a nutmeg grater. 'Yes, I did have more than one drink! And at more than one pub. I can tell you which ones, if you're interested. Good God, I'd earned the drinks! I've no doubt that I was over the legal limit when I finally drove home, and you can book me for that if you want to, but I'm damned if I can see what any of this has to do with my sister-in-law's death.'

It was Quantrill's turn to move to the window. One of the clouds had opened and rain had begun to beat against the glass as noisily as flung gravel, but beyond the newly wet roofs the cathedral spire was still sunlit under the weather-cock sky.

'Tell me, Mr Pardoe,' he said, turning to face the man again, 'when did you last see your sister-in-law?'

'At that party, I suppose,' Pardoe said slowly. 'She called on my wife about once a month, but I didn't see her very often.'

'She didn't make a practice of coming to supper?'

'No, thank God.' Pardoe got up, in the manner of a wooden rule unfolding itself. He attempted to square his sloping shoulders. 'Look, Chief Inspector,' he said with grim frankness, 'you're bound to find this out, so I might as well tell you now. I didn't like my sister-in-law. I avoided her whenever I could. That's why I stayed out last night. There was a possibility that she'd be at my house for supper and I couldn't stand the prospect of her company, not after I'd been working all day. Do you blame me?'

Quantrill rubbed his chin and thought about his own sister-in-law, a fluffy woman who irritated him immeasurably.

'I can't say that I do,' he concurred. He gave Pardoe a brief, brothers-in-law-in-adversity grin, and the man relaxed visibly. 'Well, then,' Quantrill continued, 'we'd better go and break the news to your wife. There'll have to be an identification of the body—always a distressing formality.'

Pardoe nodded, brisk, businesslike and unmistakably relieved that he had confessed his ill-feelings toward the dead woman. 'Yes, of course, Heather will need me. I'll be with you in a moment—I must just rearrange my site meeting.' His hand went out to the telephone, but Quantrill interrupted.

'Of course, if there are any other close relatives, I could get them to do the identification. Are there any hereabouts?'

'There's an elderly aunt, Mrs Gifford, and her son Rodney. I saw you talking to him at the party.'

'Ah, yes, Rodney. Any relatives anywhere else? Parents, or other sisters or brothers?'

Pardoe caught the drift of the questioning. He flushed, and his eyes glittered. 'No,' he said, his voice taut again. 'My wife is Jasmine's nearest relative. But for all I know, she might have willed her money to someone else—'

Quantrill waved aside his protest. 'Just checking,' he said equably.

Molly Quantrill put her anxious face round the door of Alison's bedroom. 'Is she all right?' she demanded in a stage whisper as she brought a cup of tea for the attendant policewoman.

WPC Beth Knowles, startlingly golden-haired, five foot eight, thirteen stone and dying for a cigarette, raised her eyes from the volume she had borrowed from among the faded children's books lined up on the window sill. The two women looked at the girl, who lay on her side with flushed cheeks and parted lips.

Alison's eyelids were closed, but they twitched with the rapid movement of her eyes as she dreamed that she fled from blood, screaming a name. From blood and through blood, puddles of it that glued her feet to the double-knotted cream Bokhara that, incongruously, carpeted the garden path. Ahead of her she could recognize the figure of a man, and she reached out to him, crying for help. But when he approached, she saw that he was a stranger, and she was afraid. She turned and in despair tried to re-enter the house for safety, calling a name.

'I think she's trying to say something,' said Beth Knowles. She bent over the girl, hoping to obtain some useful information that would give her an excuse to go downstairs to telephone and light up.

Then she straightened, disappointed. 'It was just "Jasmine," I think. She's all right, Mrs Quantrill, don't worry, I'll call you as soon as she wakes. Thanks for the tea.'

Molly retreated. WPC Knowles helped herself generously to sugar and settled down again to read *Winnie the Pooh*.

12

Chief Inspector Quantrill and WPC Hopkins escaped from the Pardoes' sitting-room, where Heather was crying noisily on her husband's thin shoulder while the two youngest children wailed in sympathy, and conferred in the hall. The house was in a substantial mid-Victorian terrace. The hall was a long high passageway, and the coloured glass in the front door gave it the gloomy yellow light that Quantrill always associated with non-conformist chapels. He lowered his voice, and took the precaution of keeping his eyes down too; the hall was perilous with parked skateboards and twelve-wheeled juggernauts too small to be noticed by anyone above three feet in height.

'I'm anxious to see Jasmine Woods's cousin, Rodney Gifford, while we're in Yarchester,' he told the policewoman. 'While I'm doing that, will you arrange the identification of the body with the coroner's officer? And then I want you to—'

The sitting-room door opened and the toddler was forcibly ejected, his squeals rising like a whistling kettle on the boil. Paul Pardoe looked out into the hall, harassed and apologetic.

'Would you mind minding Ben?' he asked Patsy Hopkins. 'Just until my wife gets over the shock...' He withdrew his head, and she raised an exasperated eyebrow at the closed door.

'He wouldn't have dreamed of asking a policeman to do that,' she asserted. 'It's a ridiculous situation. Most of the boys in the force are married and have kids of their own, so they're a lot more used to dealing with them than policewomen are. Me, I've no personal experience with children at all. I don't particularly like them. I'm a professional police officer,

61

not a nanny in uniform. But neither the public nor the force can get this into their heads. To them I'm a woman, so I'm the one who's expected to hold the baby.'

Quantrill murmured deviously to indicate that she had his complete sympathy, and, mollified, she crouched down to try to soothe the child. Ben Pardoe, rising two, had his father's dishevelled hair, and a pair of unusually large front teeth. His sobs touched WPC Hopkins's vulnerable heart, and she sighed and bent to pick him up. He clutched at her immaculate collar with sticky, starfish hands.

'Yes, well, perhaps you can find a friendly neighbour who will cope with the children for a bit,' said Quantrill hastily. 'What I'd like you to do, when you've arranged the identification, is to ask Paul Pardoe for a detailed account of his movements last night. The coroner's officer will give you a lift back to the city police station, and I'll pick you up from there. All right?'

He made for the door but then, an undeniably experienced father, he remembered that howls are a prelude to dribbles, and that dribble stains are a devil of a job to clean from police uniforms. He fumbled in his pocket, racing the saliva as it gathered on the child's tremulous lower lip, and produced a large white handkerchief.

'Here—watch him.' He strode forward, fielded the toffee-tinted blob as it began to drool down the child's chin, and thrust his handkerchief into the policewoman's hand. 'Thanks, Patsy...'

He escaped, leaving WPC Hopkins to invoke the provisions of the Sex Discrimination Act while she finished mopping up.

Rodney Gifford lived with his mother, Jasmine Woods's aunt, in a 1930s semi-detached house in Rowan Road, on the northern outskirts of Yarchester. Their house boasted the three essential features of between-the-wars suburban ambition: a front garden with a privet hedge, a wooden gate with an art-deco sunburst design, and a bay window with green and amber leaves in the upper leaded lights.

The front door was opened by a featherweight old lady, sprightly in her late seventies. She peeked up at Quantrill. 'Mrs Thompson...?' she asked uncertainly.

The Chief Inspector managed to deny it with courtesy. 'I'd like to see Mr Rodney Gifford, please. Can you tell me where I can find him?'

She looked disappointed. 'Oh, dear—I thought you might be the new visiting chiropodist. Roddy's just gone round the corner to the shops. He'll be back in a few minutes. I'd ask you to come in and wait for him, but he says I must never let strange men into the house.'

'Quite right,' said Quantrill. He saw no reason to alarm her by saying that he was a policeman. 'I'll wait in my car until he comes back.'

'Oh, there's no need for that,' she said quickly. 'We don't have many visitors and I enjoy a little company. And if you stand under the porch, at least you'll be out of the rain.' She gave him an artless smile that revealed orange-coloured false gums above the top set of her false teeth. Her white hair was frizzed out on either side of her face, but it was insufficiently thick to conceal the fact that her ears, like those of her son, protruded at an unusual angle from her head. 'Roddy won't be long. He's such a good boy to do my shopping for me, now that I can't get about so well.'

'He's not working today?' Quantrill asked.

'Oh, no! Roddy doesn't work—that's to say, he doesn't go *out* to work. He does it here at home. He's a famous playwright, you know.'

'Is he?' Quantrill leaned against the arched brickwork of the porch, trying to convey that his interest was merely idle. 'I knew that he was a writer, but I didn't realize that he wrote plays. You must be very proud of him.'

She nodded, bright-eyed. '*Very*—both of us. His father was alive when Roddy first started writing, of course. I don't mind telling you that we'd been worried about the boy. He did so well at school and we thought that he'd settle down to a good career—in the bank like his father, perhaps, only with better prospects. But he *would* go off to London, living in an uncomfortable room and doing nothing but odd jobs, as far we could make out. Such a waste of his education, we thought. We didn't realize, you see, that he was busy writing his very first play.'

'Was it shown on television?' asked Quantrill whose acquaintance with live theatre had been limited to an annual visit to the pantomime in his own youth, and again when his children were young; and more recently to dutiful attendance in support of his wife at the performances of the Breckham Market and District amateur operatic society.

'Oh, no—at a London theatre,' she said impressively. 'Roddy's play was all the rage, you know. Everybody talked about it. Well, not everybody in Yarchester, but then as Roddy said, you couldn't expect them to. It was too advanced for the provinces. But everybody who knew about such things said that it was brilliant . . .' She looked a little wistful. 'I didn't quite understand it myself, I'm more of a film-goer. I used to be a real film fan in the old days . . . Robert Taylor, Clark Gable, Paulette Goddard, Bette Davis . . . they were lovely films, in the '30s. I'd love to go to a cinema again, but I can't persuade Roddy to take me. He doesn't like films. Not that it would ever be the same, of course; there'll never be another Clark Gable.'

Quantrill, whose own mother had been a film fan as a young woman—there had never before been a Douglas in the family, and he suspected her of having had Douglas Fairbanks in mind at his christening, or perhaps at his conception—brought Mrs Gifford back to the subject of her son. 'You were telling me about Rodney's play.'

'Well, I can't tell you very much about it. I'm afraid I'm not clever enough. I didn't really enjoy it, to be honest—some of the language wasn't at all nice. But Roddy explained that it was true to life. Not the sort of life he'd been brought up to, you know, but he said that it was life as most people have to live it.'

'And he's been writing plays ever since?'

'Oh, yes—a lot of them. I'll show you his press cuttings.' She hurried stiffly to the front room, where Quantrill could hear her muttering to herself and opening and closing drawers. Presently she emerged clutching a folder which she thrust proudly into his hands.

Quantrill glanced through the discoloured cuttings. Most of them dated from the late 1950s, and were play reviews fom the *Observer* and the *Manchester Guardian*. There was also a feature from the *News Chronicle* headed, 'The Angry Generation,' and another from the *Daily Express* demanding in thick type 'WHAT HAVE THEY GOT TO BE ANGRY ABOUT?' Both features linked the name of Rodney Gifford and those of John Osborne and Arnold Wesker.

The reviews were enthusiastic about the message Rodney Gifford had given to the theatre-going public: 'A savage indictment of the values of the established social order'; 'Modern life in a new perspective'; 'Gifford routs Aunt Edna from the theatre'; 'Gifford excoriates the Establishment.'

The pile of cuttings was impressively thick, but none was dated later than 1964.

'Extremely interesting,' said Quantrill. He smiled at the old lady. 'No wonder you're proud of your son. He's still writing, I believe you said?'

'Yes, of course. That's his work, you see—his work and his whole way of life, you might say. But there's a lot of jealousy in the theatre world, and new writers elbowing their way in, and Roddy's plays have been neglected recently. In London, that is. They're still performed, though—why, his first play was put on here in Yarchester last winter, by the students at the technical college. I didn't go myself—Roddy said that I would only be disappointed after the brilliant London performance—but it just shows how highly his plays are thought of. He's sure they're due for a London revival, and once that happens—'

She broke off her sentence. 'There he is,' she said eagerly, 'I've just seen him going past the hedge. He'll be able to tell you all about his plays himself.'

Quantrill turned. Rodney Gifford, one-time angry young man, avant-garde playwright and scourge of the Establishment, was pushing open the garden gate. He wore a felt hat that was a little too small for his large head, and a black nylon mackintosh that flapped loosely round his short legs. From his plastic mesh shopping bag there protruded half a dozen sticks of rhubarb roughly wrapped in newspaper. He looked preoccupied, so much absorbed in thought that he failed to notice the Chief Inspector.

'Rodney!' piped his mother from the doorway. She gave the Chief Inspector a conspiratorial pat on the sleeve. 'He doesn't like me to call him Roddy in front of others.' She raised her voice again, trying to compete with the noise of the traffic. 'Rodney dear, here's a visitor for you.'

Gifford raised his head, making a visible effort to adjust

to Quantrill's presence. He appeared dazed, but at the same time covertly elated.

'This gentleman,' his mother continued importantly, 'has come to talk about your plays.'

'My plays?' Gifford focused on his visitor and hurried forward to join him in the porch. 'Are you an agent?' he demanded with a look of sudden hope. 'A producer? A journalist, then?'

'None of them—and it isn't your plays I want to talk about. My name's Quantrill. We met about six weeks ago, at Jasmine Woods's party.'

Rodney Gifford's ears, protruding through the ginger camouflage of hair, went scarlet. His eyes dulled and slid away. 'Did we?' he growled. 'I don't remember.'

Quantrill wasn't surprised, considering the man's condition at the time. 'I'd like to have a word with you, please. In private, if you will excuse us, Mrs Gifford?'

The old lady had been following their conversation with eager incomprehension. 'Oh, I didn't realize that you knew my niece,' she apologized. 'If only you'd said! What will she think if she hears that I kept you on the doorstep?' She scolded herself busily as she beckoned him into the house. 'I'll go and make you some tea—yes, of course I will, it's no trouble at all.' She peered into the shopping bag that she had taken from her son. 'Rodney, didn't you get me the evening paper?'

Gifford shook his damp hat and mackintosh in the porch, then hung them on the hallstand. He tugged down the cuffs of his pullover, hand-knitted in the same sludge-green wool as his mother's neat cardigan. 'The paper hadn't come, Mother, it's too early. I'll go for one later.'

'Thank you, dear.' She led the Chief Inspector into a sitting-room crowded with drab furniture. 'He's a good boy,' she confided. 'Now, you have your discussion while I make the tea, and then you must tell me how you met Jasmine. Such a charming girl—a good deal younger than Rodney, of course, but there was a big age gap between me and her mother. Jasmine's a writer, too; it must run in the family. Her work is much more frivolous than Rodney's, but she's made quite a success of it in her own way. And although we don't often see her, she doesn't forget us. Jasmine always sends flowers for my birthday, and chocolates for me and whisky for Rodney at Christmas. Not that he really cares for alcohol...'

She hobbled away in the direction of the kitchen, and Quantrill and Gifford stood facing each other across a bulbous three-piece suite, still antimacassared in memory of the Brylcreem that men smeared on their hair in the days when the furniture was new.

Gifford shrugged away his mother's confidence in his sobriety. 'Jasmine won't send any more,' he said. 'That's the last bottle of whisky I've had from her.' He gave Quantrill a narrow look, as if assessing his relationship with Jasmine Woods. 'She's dead.'

'I know,' said Quantrill. 'I didn't want to mention it in front of your mother, but I'm a Detective Chief Inspector in the county police.'

Rodney Gifford sat down more quickly than he had apparently intended, his small body almost bouncing as it hit the metal sprung seat of the armchair. His ears paled; so did the tip of his nose.

'What are you doing here?' he demanded.

'I came to Yarchester to break the news to your cousin Heather. As we'd met, I thought I'd call on you on my way back. Tell me, Mr Gifford, how do you know about Jasmine's death?'

Gifford wriggled forward in his seat so as to be able to assume a small man's position of dignity, back straight, feet firmly planted on the floor. He pulled from his hip pocket a torn-off and folded front page of the early edition of the *Yarchester Evening News*, and handed it to Quantrill. 'Stop press,' he indicated.

Quantrill sat down and read the smudged type: *Jasmine Woods, famous local author, murdered.*

'I heard someone mention it when I got to the news-agent's,' said Gifford, 'otherwise I might not have noticed the stop press item. Mother would have seen it, though, she reads every word. That's why I had to lie to her about getting the paper—I must break the news to her gently, poor old dear. She thought the world of Jasmine.'

'But you were of a different opinion, if I remember,' commented Quantrill dryly.

Gifford reddened again. 'I've always been disappointed

by Jasmine's lack of literary integrity,' he said, obviously choosing his words with care, 'and I believe I had a drink or two at the party, so I might perhaps have expressed myself rather strongly. But I had nothing against Jasmine herself, nothing at all.' He bent forward to retie the double knot in his shoelaces. 'How was she murdered, may I ask?'

'She was struck on the head by a blunt instrument,' said Quantrill who, unlike Sergeant Tait, could use standard police phrases without self-consciousness.

'Death would have been immediate, I hope? I mean, my mother will want to know—'

'Quite so,' agreed the Chief Inspector with deliberate ambiguity.

Gifford sat up and nodded, apparently satisfied. 'A burglar, I suppose. Jasmine was mad to keep her collection in the house, I told her that.'

'You're familiar with her collection, Mr Gifford?'

'Of course. She is—she was my cousin.'

'Did you visit her house very often?'

'No.' Gifford's tongue flicked across his wide lips, but he kept his eyes on Quantrill's face. 'I hardly ever went there—I haven't any transport and it's all of seventeen miles. But she was showing off her jade and netsuke when I arrived with the Pardoes for her party. That was the last time I saw her. Six weeks ago.'

'I see. Can you tell me what you were doing yesterday?'

Gifford licked his lips again. 'Why?' he demanded. 'You surely don't imagine that I had anything to do with her death?'

'I need to interview everyone who knew your cousin,' said Quantrill with stolid patience. 'Is there any reason why you want to avoid telling me what you were doing?'

Gifford sprang up from his chair and made a stand on the hearthrug with his back to the embroidered fire-screen, feet slightly apart, hands in pockets, head up, ears blazing through his pale ginger hair.

'None at all,' he asserted fiercely. 'I'm avoiding nothing. Yesterday I followed my usual Sunday practice—my mother will confirm that. In the morning I sat in here reading the *Observer*; in the afternoon I took her by bus to the cemetery to put flowers on my father's grave, and in the evening I sat here with her watching television. Didn't I, Mother?'

He darted forward and helped the old lady manoeuvre a heavy wooden tea-trolley through the door. 'Didn't you what, dear?' she said.

'Didn't I sit in here with you yesterday evening, watching television?'

'Yes, of course, you always do on Sundays. He's a good boy,' she informed the Chief Inspector for the third time. 'He knows that I enjoy television more in his company, but he doesn't like to waste his time on frivolous programmes. He's very serious. He works up in his room every evening during the week, writing his plays, but on Sundays he joins me and we watch BBC2. Sunday afternoons and evenings are our times together, aren't they, Rodney?' She smiled at her son, then turned to the Chief Inspector. 'Now, Mr—er—do you take milk and sugar?'

Lunchless and thirsty, Quantrill moved to the door. 'Very kind of you, Mrs Gifford, but I'm afraid I can't stay. I have to get back to work.'

He glanced at her son, who had resumed his proprietorial stance on the hearthrug and was now looking smugly triumphant. He recalled the way Gifford, at the party, had gestured towards his cousin with the long-necked bottle of wine; the way he had looked when he said, '*A bit of suffering would do Jasmine a world of good.*'

But dislike and suspicion could never be enough. The Chief Inspector knew, regretfully, that he had no grounds at all for inviting Rodney Gifford to accompany him to the station to assist with his enquiries.

13

Alison sat on the edge of her bed, huddled in a pretty quilted cotton dressing-gown. Her eyes were wide, dark with the recollection of horror. Her mother had switched on an electric fire and the room was so warm that WPC Knowles had taken off her uniform jacket, but Alison was white-faced and shivering.

Molly had made a tentative gesture of support, but the Quantrill family were not accustomed to touch one another; Alison almost immediately flinched away from her mother's hesitantly encircling arm. Now Molly sat beside her daughter, trying not to feel redundant, listening with horrified fascination while the girl stumbled through an account of the events of the morning.

'I honestly don't know,' Alison said, trying to answer the supplementary questions that her father had given the policewoman to put to her. She spoke in a lifeless, husky, cried-out voice. 'I looked at my watch just before half-past ten, thinking that it was time for coffee. I went out of the office a few minutes later to call... to look for... But after that I just don't know what time anything was.'

'Well, never mind about times for the moment, love,' said WPC Knowles kindly, moderating her normally hearty tone to one suitable for soothing a small child. She turned a page of her notebook. 'Now, you've told me what happened up to the time when you found the—when you found her. Can you remember exactly what you did after that?'

Alison picked at a loose thread in the quilting of her dressing-gown. 'I don't know... I was too shocked... I was terrified. It was—*awful*. Awful. Oh, God—' She put her hands to her face, trying to shut out the persistent images of blood and dark hair and white splintered bone, of green glass and bruised, splayed limbs. Her mother murmured with sympathetic incomprehension, putting out a shy hand as if to touch the girl and then retracting it quickly.

'I know, love, I can imagine,' comforted the policewoman, glad—from what she'd heard at division—that she couldn't. 'Don't think about what you saw, just tell me what you did, I mean, did you try to telephone for help?'

'No.' Alison let her hands slide down her face and fall helplessly into her lap. She shook her head slowly. 'I never thought about telephoning—I couldn't think straight at all. I told you. I was terrified...'

Beth Knowles looked up from her notebook, round-

eyed, and asked a question of her own. 'Did you think that
the murderer was still somewhere about?'

Molly stiffened, put her fingertips to her mouth and
gasped.

'Oh, no.' Alison managed to focus her eyes on the
policewoman. She sounded surprised. 'No, as a matter of
fact, that didn't occur to me...I was just terrified of—of
her—of how she looked. Too terrified to stay in the house. I
panicked and ran away, out into the garden. I screamed, I can
remember that, once I got outside. I don't know what I was
screaming, but I know that I hoped Gil would come.'

'Gil?'

'Jasmine's friend, Gilbert Smith. He lives above the
garage and does the garden for her. He's nice. I knew that
he'd take care of things for me, if I could find him.'

'And did you find him?'

'Not at first. I couldn't run straight, any more than I
could think straight. I tried everywhere, the greenhouses,
and the outbuildings and the orchard, but I could hardly
see where I was going and I kept bumping into things and
falling down and crying. I went up to his flat, but there was
no answer the first time. Then I found that his motor bike
was still in the garage, so I knew he must be somewhere
about. After that I just hammered on his door until he
answered. He'd been asleep, so he hadn't heard me the
first time.'

The policewoman raised her eyebrows, which were several shades less golden than her hair. 'Asleep, at that time in
the morning?'

'Yes. Well, he was a friend more than a gardener. Jasmine didn't mind what hours he kept. Anyway, I told him
what had happened—what I'd found. He was very shocked
and upset, of course. But then he said he'd do what was
necessary.'

'You mean, telephone the police?'

'Well, he couldn't do that right away. There's no telephone in his flat. He wasn't properly awake at first, and I
don't suppose he could think straight either, but he put his
head under the tap and then he hurried up the drive to the
house.'

'What time would that be?'

'I've no idea...'

'Did you go up to the house with him?'

'No. No, I couldn't face it. I left it all to Gil.'

'And did you see anyone else? Any tradesmen, or passers-by on the road?'

'No. No one except Gil.'

'About how long was he in the house, would you say?'

'I don't know...I just wandered away into the garden. I was too upset to know where I was or what was happening. I didn't see Gil anymore, after he went down the stairs from his flat and up the drive. I think I heard his motor bike starting up, a bit later, so he must have gone to fetch help. Soon after that the police cars began to arrive, and then Dad came to find me.' The girl drew a long, shuddering breath. 'And that's all I know.'

WPC Knowles was disappointed. The Chief Inspector wasn't going to like this. He had most particularly wanted her to establish the timing of Alison's movements, and those of anyone she had spoken to. But there were limits to the amount of pushing you could do to a girl who had gone through such an ordeal.

'That's fine, love,' she said briskly sympathetic. 'Now there are three more things I have to ask, and then I'll leave you in peace. First, did Jasmine Woods say anything to you, when you last saw her, about what she intended to do yesterday?'

Alison shook her head. 'She didn't mention the weekend at all. She must have worked most of the time, because there were some tapes waiting for me to transcribe this morning.'

'I see. Second thing, then—can you recall anything about the house or the sitting-room that seemed unusual this morning? Anything that could possibly give us a lead to the murderer?'

'I've told you...I've told you as much as I can...'

'All right, love. Last question: have you any idea why anyone would want to kill your employer?'

'*Want* to kill her? How *could* anyone want to kill Jasmine? It must have been done by someone who was trying to steal from her.'

'Um,' commented WPC Knowles. 'You don't know of anyone who hated her?'

'No! No, of course not. That's absurd, no one could possibly have hated Jasmine. Some people disliked her books, and some envied her money, but no one actually hated her. How could they? She's—she was—'

'I know. I understand.' Beth Knowles put away her notebook and stood up, longingly anticipating the taste of cigarette smoke. 'Sorry I had to bother you—you've been a great help. And you'll probably remember a few more details later, when you've had time to get over the shock.'

Alison shuddered and hid her face in her hands again. Her mother gave her knee an uncertain pat.

'There, there...' Molly cast about for a more positive way of expressing her concern, and remembered the tea tray. She had brought it up as soon as the policewoman had called downstairs to tell her that Alison was awake, but the girl had left her cup untasted and the milk had formed a skin on the surface of the liquid. Molly lifted the knitted tea-cosy and touched the lukewarm pot with an expert hand.

'I'll go and make some fresh tea,' she said, glad to return to her proper element. 'And this time, dear, you must try to drink it while it's hot.'

14

'The man's certainly got green fingers,' pronounced Chief Inspector Quantrill. 'If he can get tomato plants to grow anywhere near the size of his cannabis plants, he must produce quite a crop.'

The two detectives were in Gilbert Smith's bathroom, looking at the cannabis that grew in pots on the window sill. The plants were luxuriant, flourishing like nettles on an old garbage dump, four or five feet tall; their feathery tips brushed the ceiling.

'We haven't found any other cannabis plants in the grounds, or anywhere on the property,' said Tait, 'so I very much doubt that Smith was growing enough to supply anyone else. He's a user himself, of course—we could all smell that as soon as we came in. And I found this in one of the cupboards.'

He showed the Chief Inspector a wooden box that contained an ordinary tobacco pipe. For the purpose of smoking cannabis resin, the bowl had been made much smaller by an insert of foil which would also serve to prevent the wood from burning. There were traces in the bowl of a brown powdery substance. In a plastic bag was the source of the powder: a thumbnail-sized piece of cannabis resin, a brittle brownish-black substance that smelled strongly of sage. Also in the box were some cigarette papers, a rolled cardboard filter and a handful of what looked like greenish hay, which both men recognised as marijuana, the dried flowering top of the cannabis plant. Some of it had been chopped up, and it looked and smelled like herbal tobacco.

Quantrill looked at the contents of the box with distaste. 'What we're concerned with at the moment is murder; the fact that he smokes this muck doesn't automatically put him at the top of our list of suspects. Any news of him yet?'

'None at all. But I've heard that WPC Knowles has got Alison's statement.'

'Good. Where's she taking it to, the station?' asked Quantrill. His stomach was rumbling a reminder that it had had nothing to occupy itself with since breakfast, and he had been vouchsafed a sudden and unusually alluring vision of the Breckham Market police canteen.

'No, she's bringing it to the incident-room.' But Tait had heard the rumbles. 'I've got the mobile canteen there, too,' he added.

It was one of the occasions when Quantrill regarded his sergeant with almost unqualified approval.

* * *

In the incident-room, the Chief Inspector passed his daughter's statement to Sergeant Tait. 'You can't blame her for running away,' he said defensively. 'I know that she ought to have reported the murder immediately, but it's understandable that she panicked, poor girl.' He bit into a crusty bread roll from which protruded an edge of corned beef supported by a pale green ruff of lettuce.

Tait agreed, and not merely as a matter of diplomacy. Horrifying enough for Alison to have found a body at all, let alone that of someone she knew and liked, let alone in that condition. 'She's made a very helpful statement anyway,' he added. 'Now we know that Smith didn't leave until this morning. And the fingerprints that were on the telephone in Jasmine's office matched the prints in his flat, so presumably he made the 999 call before he went off.'

'Were any of his prints in her sitting-room?'

'Yes,' said Tait. Quantrill paused in mid-chew. 'In the kitchen as well,' Tait went on. 'After all, he was a friend of Jasmine's, so he was probably in and out of her house a good deal. But the murderer must have worn gloves to do the job, or else he gave the cabinet and the bottles he used a quick wipe. Apparently their surfaces are too blurred to provide any usable prints.'

· 'Sounds as though we can rule Smith out, then,' said Quantrill. 'As the murderer, anyway, otherwise he'd have taken off last night. I've been wondering what made him make the 999 call this morning anonymously, and then bolt, but I think I can see a possible reason. He may grow his own marijuana, but he can't produce cannabis resin in this climate. He needs money to buy that. So let's assume that he got quietly stoned on cannabis last night, and was sleeping it off this morning when Alison roused him. He hurried up to the house, saw the body, and also saw that the cabinet had been broken open and that some of the valuables were scattered on the floor. The temptation to steal them and sell them was too much for him, so he picked them up—that's when he got the blood on his clothes. After that, he'd have to bolt. And, naturally, he wouldn't want to give his name to police.'

'Why bother to telephone at all?' said Tait sceptically.

'For Alison's sake?' Quantrill suggested. He washed down the last crumbs of his roll with a swig of dark brown tea. 'All right,' he said irritably, 'what's your theory? There had to be some good reason for the man to take off.'

'Yes. From what I saw at the party, Smith's not an obvious murder suspect. Like most druggies, he's self-absorbed. Drugs do alter the personality, of course, but the effect of cannabis is to make its users inward-looking and passive and imaginative. It's the hard stuff, hallucinogens like LSD, that can trigger off latent psychoses.'

Chief Inspector Quantrill twitched his eyebrows and embarked on the consumption of a Lyons individual raspberry and red current pie: 'So?'

'So I can see two possibilities. One is that Smith had moved on from cannabis to another drug, like LSD, that he needed a lot more money to keep buying it, and that he was capable, under the influence, of murdering Jasmine Woods when she tried to stop him stealing her collection. I agree that we've found no evidence so far of any other drugs, but Jasmine told me that Smith had Yarchester friends who were on the drug scene, and he could have bought acid from them.'

'And what about his clothes? We agreed that the blood on the jeans we found this morning didn't indicate that Smith was the murderer.'

'True. But if any of his clothes were saturated with blood, he'd have tried to get rid of them this morning before he left. He might have dug them into the compost heap. The other possibility, of course, is that the murderer wasn't Smith himself, but one of his junkie friends. No doubt he babbled about Jasmine's collection, and gave them ideas. And a junkie in need of a fix doesn't care what he does to get hold of money to buy dope.'

'So you're suggesting,' said Quantrill heavily, 'that after Smith—or one of his friends—did the murder, he calmly stayed here in his flat overnight?'

'It's possible. He might have been too stoned to believe what had happened, until Alison told him.'

'But not too stoned to wipe the fingerprints from the bottles and the cabinet?'

'That was what he would have rushed up to the house to

76

do this morning, before he left. As you suggested, that would probably be when he got the blood on the clothes that we found.'

'I see ... And before he took off, he telephoned for the police?'

'Why not? It would be a good way of covering his guilt, because he'd think we would assume—as you assumed just now, sir—that he wouldn't dare to telephone unless he was innocent of the murder.'

It was one of the occasions when Chief Inspector Quantrill thought his sergeant too clever by half.

'All right, then,' he conceded irritably. 'We know we need Smith—what are you doing about catching him?'

Tait was clearly glad he had been asked that question. His answer was prompt. 'My guess is that he would have headed for Yarchester to join his friends. He probably went to ground before we had time to put out the alert for his motor bike. So I had a photofit picture made up, and I've sent it to the Yarchester division in the hope that they can ferret him out. The drug squad boys know the likely areas of the city. I've also asked for a watch to be put on the railway station, the bus station and the airport, in case he decides to move on.'

Quantrill concurred; impossible not to approve of his sergeant's efficiency. 'But the fact is,' he pointed out, 'that Smith was still here this morning, and the murder was committed yesterday, so it's yesterday we need to concentrate on. Paul Pardoe, the brother-in-law, admits to having been near here, so I'm getting his story checked. Did you find a will at Yeoman's, by the way?'

'Yes. Jasmine was a practical woman and kept her affairs in order. She made several bequests to charity, and left £10,000 to her aunt, Mrs Agnes Gifford, in gratitude for her kindness to herself and Heather when they were children. If the aunt predeceased her, that money was to go to her sister, Heather Pardoe. In any event, the bulk of the estate was to go to her sister.'

'So the Pardoes will do pretty well out of her death. Her house alone will fetch sixty or seventy thousand. Paul wasn't sure that they'd get anything from Jasmine's estate, but he had hopes, obviously ... And ten thousand to Mrs Gifford, eh? That certainly gives Rodney Gifford a motive for making sure that Jasmine Woods didn't outlive his mother.'

'If he knew about it,' said Tait. 'It's sensible for a woman of Jasmine's age to make a will, if she has a lot to leave, but I doubt if she'd talk about it.'

'You may be right. Anyway,' said Quantrill regretfully, 'I've had to rule Rodney Gifford out. Pity... Well, what about yesterday? Were your men able to get any useful information from the neighbours about Jasmine Woods's movements?'

'Very little, except that she was alive and well about 1.30, when her drinks party finished. But neighbours is a relative term, after all—there's no one living within a quarter of a mile of the house on either side.'

'There's a lot of time unaccounted for, then,' said Quantrill. 'When I saw Heather Pardoe this afternoon, she told me that she tried to telephone her sister at about 8.30 yesterday evening, and got no reply. Until the time of death is established, we don't know whether Jasmine was out at 8.30, or whether she was already dead. So let's go back to the drinks party, and start interviewing the people who were there. Who were they?'

'As I guessed,' said Tait, 'Jonathan and Roz Elliott. They live in the Old Rectory, on the outskirts of the village. Jonathan acted as Jasmine's verbal sparring partner, and I suspect that there was frustrated lust in it on his side. All right if I come with you, sir? It should be an interesting interview.'

And even if it weren't, Quantrill thought, Martin Tait could be relied upon to liven it up.

East Anglia has a great many medieval churches, and too few twentieth-century parsons to go round. As a consequence the ecclesiastical parish of Thirling, like many others in rural areas, no longer had a resident incumbent. Instead, it had been grouped with six neighbouring parishes and put in the care of two parsons of the new generation: busy, enthusiastic young men who whizzed round their modest empire on motor scooters, wore jeans and sweaters, liked to be known as Tim and Barry and had the temerity to address God, in church, as 'you.'

The inhabitants of Thirling—and especially those who never went near the church except for weddings and christenings and funerals, and so were unable to recognize Tim and Barry when they saw them—were affronted. They liked a parson to *be* a parson, they said to each other, convinced that parsons had no business to be as other men.

It was not that anyone had ever had much time for the last rector of Thirling, old Mr Jennings, when he was alive. He wasn't reckoned by the older inhabitants to be a patch on his revered predecessor, Canon Phillips; but at least the stooped, dog-collared figure had been immediately identifiable. Mr Jennings always knew the names of his parishioners, whether they went to church or not, and greeted everyone he met as he perambulated in the village.

Unlike Canon Phillips he had no private income, but he had allowed Thirling to continue to take it for granted that it was his large, back-breaking garden that would be used for the village fête, and his wife's threadbare drawing-room for meetings of the mothers' union. The rectory where they lived had been built in the 1860s, in the architectural style subsequently nicknamed 'ecclesiastical commissioners' Gothic.' The commissioners of the day had reasoned that a parson, being accustomed to officiate in a medieval church, would want to live in a house which incorporated as many medieval features as possible. At Thirling these included steeply pitched roofs, a battlemented porch, lancet windows, flagstone floors, howling draughts, and acute discomfort.

The new parsons, Barry and Tim, would have none of it. When they were appointed to the Thirling group of parishes, they had each taken one look at the empty barn of a rectory and had said, in their perennially youthful idiom, 'No way.' They had insisted on living in small modern houses in other villages in the group, and the rectory was put up for sale by auction.

The villagers had very much hoped that the Old Rectory would be bought by someone who would live in it in the style to which the house had been accustomed in Canon Phillip's time—an organizing upper-middle class couple who could be grumbled about behind their backs but relied upon to devote their time and energy to the smooth running of local affairs. Instead, it was bought by Jonathan Elliott, television personality and brilliant satirical novelist, and his wife, Roz, a sociology lecturer at the University of Suffolk in Yarchester, whose combined income—with the addition of some capital inherited by Roz from her grandmother—enabled them not only to pay an inflated price for the house but to renovate it completely. Now damp-proofed and draught-excluded, double-glazed, centrally heated and extensively plumbed, the ecclesiastical commissioners' Gothic fantasy had become agreeably comfortable.

The Elliotts had three children, each of whose births had been planned to coincide with a long vacation and so to interrupt Roz's work schedule as little as possible. The house was still too large, even for a family of five and even though Roz and Jonathan each had a study. To fill it, the Elliotts had living with them a succession of Roz's girl students, who found the Old Rectory a temporary haven from whatever emotional, financial, sexual or academic problems threatened to overwhelm them.

It was not a matter of charity, Roz Elliott asserted, but an expression of feminist solidarity. She found it difficult to admit to anyone except her closest friends that it was the only way in which she could possibly come to terms with the embarrassing fact that she was a capitalist. To her husband, when he complained about the invasion of his privacy, she pointed out the unsought side-effects: the students naturally wanted to express their thanks, and it would be unsupportive not to allow them to do so in a practical way. The Elliotts were able to get their house cleaned—after a fashion—and their children minded in their frequent absences, without feeling that they were exploiting anyone.

The villagers' disappointment that the owners of the Old Rectory were not in the least concerned with local affairs was lessened when they realized that Jonathan Elliott appeared regularly on television. His Books and Writers programme had never before appealed to Thirling viewers, but now they all turned to it; not because they were interested in what he or any of his guests on the programme had to say, but because it gave them a vicarious sense of importance to know that during the course of the following week they would meet him in the village or serve him in the shop or the pub or the post office. There were hopes that he might even be prevailed upon to make a celebrity appearance at the next fête, to be held on the village green. A deputation had been sent, a decent interval after his arrival in the village three years previously, to ask him to allow the fête to be held in his garden, but the request was never put. The members of the deputation had retreated down the drive before they got as far as the house, appalled to find that the once-smooth lawns were now a grazing ground for livestock.

'Mind the geese,' said Chief Inspector Quantrill as Tait's car scattered them.

'They shouldn't be allowed to stray,' said Sergeant Tait, who had recently had a disconcerting confrontation with a goose when he called to make enquiries at a farm.

'It's a private drive. And one way of getting the grass cut, I suppose.'

The two detectives approached the old rectory in Tait's up-and-coming Citroën, which he parked with a flourish on the gravelled circle originally designed as a carriage sweep. Tait looked cautiously about him before getting out of the car, and was relieved to see that the geese were confining their attention to a large area of rough, brilliantly green spring grass that sloped down from the carriage sweep to an over-grown pond. Beyond the pond was a hedge, above which rose the flint tower of Thirling church.

Quantrill eased himself out of the small car and looked incredulously at the Old Rectory. 'Why on earth would anyone want to buy an ugly pile like this?'

'Space,' explained Tait. 'It's an architectural absurdity, I agree, but it has space and character. I like big old houses, too; I couldn't bear to live in a featureless little suburban box.' He remembered too late that this was a cruelly accurate description of the Chief Inspector's own house.

'Better find out whether you can afford to heat your big old house before you buy it,' snapped Quantrill. 'But, then, of course,' he added with heavy sarcasm, 'when you're Chief Inspector . . .'

That was exactly the line Tait was thinking along. Not that he'd ever consider going in for a mid-nineteenth-century Gothic house, or for geese in the garden. Something rather more manageable, he decided: a compact house, Georgian or at the latest early Victorian, built at a time when architects still understood that style was a matter of line and proportion rather than of spurious ornamentation. He certainly would not want a massive gothic front door, such as they were now walking towards, surmounted by a ridiculous battlemented mezzanine tower—

But Martin Tait was not a detective for nothing. Quantrill was too disgruntled to notice the sudden movement on the top of the tower, behind the crenellation, but Tait saw it. He gave the Chief Inspector a vigorous push, just as a bucket of water was emptied over the battlements to fall with a splash on the gravel between them.

'Next time,' piped a threatening voice from above their heads, 'it'll be boiling oil.'

'What the hell—?' spluttered Quantrill, retaining his balance with difficulty.

'It's a kid,' said Tait. He called back sternly: 'Watch it, Buster!'

A dark curly head rose above the battlements, which proved to be no more than knee high to a twelve-year-old. 'I didn't pour the water *over* you,' the boy said. 'I could've, if I'd wanted to, but I didn't. I'm repelling unwanted suitors,' he added, cheerfully unaware that there was anything anachronistic about carrying on such a medieval activity while wearing a Star Wars T-shirt. 'Which of the students have you come to see, Claire or Mandy?'

'Neither,' boomed Quantrill. 'Is your name Elliott?'

'Yes—I'm Piers.'

'Right, Piers. I'm Chief Inspector Quantrill, and I've come to see your father if he's at home.'

The boy's ebullience subsided. He lowered his voice: 'Oh, Lord—do you have to?' He scrambled over the battlements and down a knotted rope that hung at one side of the tower, almost falling down the last few feet in his hurry. His agitation was so genuine that Quantrill relented and spoke more kindly.

'It's all right,' the Chief Inspector assured him, 'we shan't mention the water.' He flicked his damp sleeve. 'Just a few splashes, no harm done.'

Piers shook his head. 'It's not that. Jonathan's in a foul

temper, and when he's in that kind of mood it's always best to leave him alone. If you disturb him, he'll be even worse when you've gone. Couldn't you come back and see him tomorrow?'

'Sorry,' said Quantrill. 'Official business.'

'What's upset your father?' Tait enquired in a matey voice. 'I mean, is there any particular subject we ought to avoid mentioning to him?'

'Yes,' said the boy. 'Jasmine Woods.'

Quantrill and Tait both blinked rapidly and avoided each other's eyes. 'Any particular reason?' asked Tait.

'Well, she's dead,' said the boy. 'I know that, Claire and Mandy were talking about it when I got home from school. She died today. Pity, she was nice—quite interesting to talk to. But Jonathan isn't wild because she's dead, he's been wild ever since yesterday lunchtime. He and Roz—that's my mother—had a row about Jasmine yesterday afternoon. I know, I heard them.'

'Yes, well,' said Quantrill hastily. He had scruples about obtaining ingenuous information from children concerning their parents. 'I'm afraid we do have to see your father. Could you take us to him, please?'

The boy shook his head. He twisted at the wrought-iron door handle with both hands and pushed the massively hinged door ajar. 'Down the hall,' he pointed, staying firmly where he was, 'first passage on the left, second door on the right. And rather you than me.'

15

'Piers! Piers, don't!'

The policemen turned in the doorway. Two more children were running up from the garden, one a much smaller and grubbier version of Piers, the other a girl about ten.

Unlike the boys, she was neat in appearance; almost prim. Her straight light-brown shoulder-length hair was held back by a band of ribbon, and she wore a plain blue denim skirt, a clean white T-shirt and knee-length socks that were horizontally striped in blue and white. She reminded Quantrill of someone. He dredged his memory and came up with one of the illustrations in Alison's childhood copy of *Alice's Adventures in Wonderland*.

'Yes, Alice. Alison . . . For a fiercely protective moment he thought of his daughter, and of the emotional shock she had sustained. He felt for her all the more keenly because the small girl in front of him had all of Alison's childhood neatness, and a look of distress about her, too.

'You *can't* disturb Daddy!' she was protesting to her elder brother.

He shrugged. 'I can't help it, Vanessa—it's not me that's doing the disturbing. It's not my fault they want to see Jonathan. They're policemen.'

'Well, tell them he's not seeing anyone.'

'They won't *be* told.'

'Did you explain why?'

'Yes.' Piers suddenly went bright red. 'Well . . . sort of . . . '

'You didn't let on about—?'

'Well . . . '

His sister, younger and half a head shorter, glared at him with contempt. Quantrill had at first been surprised that a woman as uncompromisingly liberated as Roz Elliott had managed to produce such a conventional daughter, but evidently Vanessa had inherited her mother's strength of character. 'Idiot!' she told her elder brother. She glanced at the smaller boy, who had been following the conversation apprehensively, all dark curls and big eyes and open mouth. 'Push off, Toby,' she ordered.

Toby went. Vanessa turned to the policemen and gave them a grave, social smile. 'I'm so sorry,' she said sweetly, as though she assumed that they had been deaf to her exchange with Piers, 'but Daddy's very busy and this isn't a good time to interrupt him. He's creative, you see, and creative work is very difficult. It needs complete concentration. Perhaps I could give him a message for you?'

Quantrill refused with equal politeness, wondering what

the girl was trying to conceal. The row between her parents over Jasmine Woods? But why should she think that significant? Her brother didn't; didn't even seem to know that the woman had been murdered. But, then, Vanessa was clearly more perceptive than Piers. 'Is your mother in?' Quantrill added kindly.

'No—she's gone to the university, to a union meeting. I expect she'll be staying in Yarchester overnight, because she's going on to Birmingham tomorrow to talk to a women's group. We've got two students living here, they're out in the garden if you'd like to see them instead—'

'No, thank you,' Tait intervened firmly. He was anxious to start talking to the man who had quarrelled with his wife about Jasmine Woods just a few hours before the murder. It wasn't difficult, he thought, to guess what had occasioned the quarrel.

Vanessa Elliott sighed. 'All right,' she said reluctantly, 'you can see him. But what you have to understand about Daddy is that he works under considerable stress. He's on television, you see. He always looks relaxed on his programme, but he's really very tense. He's preparing now for tomorrow's programme, and that means that the tension is building up. He's—well, a bit difficult. That's what Piers should have explained to you. You have to make allowances for Daddy because of the stress of his work.'

'Right,' confirmed Piers, still pink with mortification but anxious to demonstrate family loyalty.

'I'll bear it in mind,' said Quantrill. 'First passage on the left, second door on the right, I believe?'

'I'll come with you,' said Vanessa. 'If you're on your own,' she explained primly, 'he might swear.'

But Jonathan Elliott said nothing at all. He sat over a portable typewriter, one elbow on either side of it, his shoulders hunched, his face half hidden by his long thin hands. He made no movement as his daughter went in, apologized for disturbing him and said that two policemen had come to see him; but his fingers tensed.

Vanessa gave him a half-protective, half-exasperated look. She smiled and shrugged at the visitors and went out, closing the door softly behind her.

'This is Chief Inspector Quantrill, I'm Sergeant Tait,

County CID. You may perhaps remember me, Mr Elliott, we met at a party about six weeks ago.'

Elliott lifted his face from his hands, and the youthful darkness of the curls on top of his head was immediately qualified by his greying sideburns. His face was set, strained, grey with fatigue and with odd patches of stubble left after a careless shave. In contrast, his long pointed nose was sharp and white. His heavy eyelids flicked up for a moment while he looked at Tait, and then lowered again.

'If you say so.' His voice was harsh, his north-country intonation more pronounced. 'What do you want? I'm going up to London to do a programme tomorrow, and I haven't time to concern myself with anything else.'

'Criminal investigations, Mr Elliott,' pointed out Quantrill, 'take precedence over television programmes. We're enquiring into the murder of Jasmine Woods.'

'So I gather. The local woodentop was here earlier.'

The Chief Inspector gave him a huffed look. 'One of my officers was making preliminary enquiries. He saw your wife, I understand?'

'Yes.' It was, apparently, all Elliott wanted to snap out on the subject. He glanced angrily at the typescript he was working on, ripped it from the machine and began to screw it up; but then he changed his mind. He smoothed out the sheet of paper on his desk and at the same time expanded his answer, phrasing it with rather more civility.

'I didn't see your officer myself—he caught Roz just as she was going off to Yarchester. She was able to give him all the information he needed. We went to Jasmine's for drinks at midday yesterday, and left just before half-past one. Jasmine was alive and well at that time. Roz and I spent the rest of the day at home, and we saw and heard nothing unusual. There's nothing else I can tell you.'

'And that was the last time you saw Jasmine Woods?'

'Yes.' Jonathan Elliott got up from his desk and walked to the double-glazed gothic patio-door of his study. Outside, the evening sun, low under a rain-dark sky, picked out the yellow of the daffodils that sprouted haphazardly from tussocky grass. Beyond what had been a back lawn, half a dozen different trees were beginning to put out leaves in assorted shades of green.

He turned to the policeman again. He was over six feet tall, about the same height as Quantrill, and he made a point of addressing himself to the air above Tait, the shorter man's head.

'Look, I'm really cut up about Jasmine's death,' he said abruptly. 'I want to make that clear.' He walked back to his desk and picked up the creased sheet of typescript, smoothing it with nervous fingers. 'What you have to realize is that I work under pressure—first to a deadline, and then in conditions of stress: under lights, in front of cameras and with guests who are totally unpredictable. No, not just unpredictable—they're bloody terrifying. Sometimes they're dry, sometimes they won't stop talking, sometimes they're drunk. You've no idea of the strain I'm under, trying to look relaxed while my guts are churning with anxiety.' He pushed the curls off his forehead, suddenly embarrassed. 'Well, that's not your concern, is it? But, whether or not you've a criminal investigation on hand, my work has to go on. I can't stop because Jasmine's been murdered—but I want you to know that I do mind about her. She was a good friend.'

He sank into his chair, snatched a blank sheet of paper and rammed it into his typewriter. 'So,' he continued, his mouth tight, 'I'm working today and tomorrow under even greater difficulties than usual. Do me a favour, will you? Get the hell out of here and do your investigating somewhere else, so that I can get on with my work.'

Quantrill and Tait glanced at each other. The Chief Inspector nodded; his sergeant could carry on with the interview. It was Tait who had met Jonathan Elliott at Jasmine Woods's party, and suspected him of having designs on her; it was Tait who was getting hot under the collar because he'd been told to get the hell out of there. If Quantrill had taken umbrage every time he'd been told that, in the course of his police career, he'd be as much a nervous wreck as Elliott. He sat down, uninvited, to watch and listen.

Tait made a cool start. He propped himself against a bookcase, crossed one ankle over the other and folded his arms. 'Ah,' he said, superficially tolerant, 'but we still have some investigating to do here. Primarily into your relationship with Jasmine Woods.'

Elliott flicked him a sharp look. 'My relationship with Jasmine? I told you—friendship.'

'Come off it. I saw the way you looked at her, at that party we both went to. It might have been nothing but friendship on her side, but it was more than that with you. You fancied her.'

'And so did you, brother!' Jonathan Elliott was on his feet, his face darkening, his nose jutting with anger. 'Oh, yes, I remember you at the party, though I didn't realize at the time you were a copper. I was amused—another hopeful new boy joining Jasmine's entourage. How far did you get with her?'

Tait straightened, suddenly conscious of his comparative lack of height. 'I didn't bother to pursue her,' he said stiffly. 'I had other interests—I was there with a girl-friend.'

'Oh, yes—I noticed her vaguely. She was the one Jasmine took on as her secretary, wasn't she? A rather dim little piece, I thought.'

Chief Inspector Quantrill's eyes bulged. 'The young lady you're talking about is my daughter!' he intervened. 'Are you trying to change the subject, Mr Elliott?'

Tait moved towards the desk, fixing Elliott with an ice-blue stare. 'And how far did *you* get with Jasmine Woods? Or was that your trouble—that you've wanted her for two or three years and have never been able to get anywhere at all? It must have been very frustrating, living so close to an attractive woman who wasn't interested in you.'

Elliott sat down abruptly, fiddling with the paper in his typewriter. 'Don't fictionalize,' he snapped. 'All right, I admired Jasmine. What man wouldn't? But like you, I didn't pursue her. I had no need to—I'm very happily married.'

'To a wife who believes in women's lib?'

'Oh, yes! Just because—quite rightly, in my opinion— Roz rejects the traditionally subservient wifely role, it doesn't mean that our marriage is unsatisfactory. Far from it. We're a partnership. We share our domestic pleasures and we divide our domestic responsibilities, so that both of us get involved and neither of us gets exploited. And that applies to sex, too—exploitation is out. It makes for an ideal form of marriage. I can thoroughly recommend it.'

There was a knock on the door. Elliott shouted an irritable 'Come in!' The door opened and an alarmingly advanced pregnancy appeared, topped by a young, small, nervous face. 'S-sorry to bother you, Jonathan,' said the girl timidly, twisting her ringless hands, 'but Vanessa said you had visitors and I wondered if you'd like c-coffee. Or anything.'

Elliott waved her impatiently away. The girl, an obvious subscriber to the tradition of feminine subservience, went. Tait raised his eyebrows.

'One of my wife's students,' explained Elliott. 'She lives here.' Tait's eyebrows stayed up, provocatively. 'I mean,' Elliott continued, reddening, 'she came to live here after— Hell, if I did it at all, it certainly wouldn't be on my own doorstep!'

Tait indicated silent, offensive disbelief. Elliott began to smoulder.

'Tell me about yesterday,' Quantrill suggested hastily. 'You and your wife went to Jasmine Woods's house about midday, you said. Was anyone else there?'

Elliot's reply was sulky. 'Yes, Gilbert Smith. He's a friend who does her garden. He was in the kitchen, drinking coffee when we arrived, but he drifted off after about ten minutes.'

'Was he high?'

Elliott looked at the Chief Inspector with wary surprise. 'You know about him?'

'We know he smokes cannabis. Does he take any other drugs?'

'Not as far as I know.'

'Was he high when you saw him yesterday?'

'I'm no expert. He's usually vague, anyway.'

'Did he say anything about what he intended to do for the rest of the day?'

'No. He just finished his coffee, said, "See you," to Jasmine and wandered away.'

'Hmm. Was anyone else there, apart from you and your wife?'

'No.'

'And did Jasmine Woods say anything about what *she* intended to do for the rest of the day? Was she expecting any callers? Did she say she was going out?'

'No.' Jonathan Elliott began to drum his fingers impatiently on the cover of his typewriter.

'You left Yeoman's about half-past one, you said. Did you and your wife leave together?'

The drumming paused. 'No—Roz left about ten minutes before I did,' said Elliott slowly.

'In order to get your lunch ready?' mocked Tait. 'But I thought yours was a liberated marriage?'

'*Not* to get my lunch. It was a sunny day and she decided that she'd like to walk back. I stayed because there was something I wanted to discuss with Jasmine—a book she'd read that I intend to mention in my programme this week.'

'I thought you disapproved of her literary opinions,' said Tait.

'Of her output, not of her opinions.'

'And did the fact that you stayed behind to talk to Jasmine Woods cause any difficulties between you and your wife when you got home?' Quantrill asked.

'No, why should it?'

'It's not the kind of thing my wife would approve of.'

Elliott gave him a thin smile. 'You must have a very conventional marriage, Chief Inspector.'

Quantrill declined to be provoked. 'Did you and your wife quarrel over Jasmine Woods yesterday afternoon?'

'Good God no. We talked about her, yes, but that's all.'

'What did you do, after you got home?' asked Tait. 'What did you do for the remainder of the day?'

'Oh—I had some bread and cheese and got on with my work. I was here working until the early hours of this morning. Look, you're not trying to suggest that I had anything to do with Jasmine's death, are you? Because I can tell you right away that that's preposterous!'

'We're interested in the fact that as far as we know at the moment, you were the last person to see Jasmine Woods alive.'

'Sorry, but you've got your facts wrong. Just as I was leaving Yeoman's yesterday, another car drove up.'

'Why the hell didn't you say so earlier?' Tait snapped. 'Can you describe it?'

'A dark blue Volvo Estate with an S registration. A local car—I've seen it around Thirling.'

'Do you know who it belongs to?' the sergeant demanded. 'Who was the driver?'

Jonathan Elliott's long nose seemed to twitch with satisfaction. He bent over his typewriter, tapping it at practised speed with one finger of each hand. 'How should I know? You're the detective.'

'I'll do him for wasting police time,' snarled Tait, 'if for nothing else. He must know damn well who that car belongs to.'

'He also knows we can have it traced through the computer,' said Quantrill. 'You gave the man a fair amount of aggro, so I'm not surprised he didn't feel co-operative.'

The two policemen were sitting in Tait's car just outside the gates of the Old Rectory, waiting for information abut the Volvo Estate. 'Elliott's a possible, quite definitely,' Tait asserted. 'What about that row he had with his wife over Jasmine?'

'We've got no proof of that. Oh, I know his son said that he heard a row going on, but children always magnify things. Alison used to get quite upset, when she was small, if she heard me having an argument with her mother. She always assumed that we were quarrelling, but most of the time we weren't—it was simply our way of coming to domestic decisions. So I wouldn't give much weight to what the boy said.'

'But his sister was definitely trying to cover something up.'

'Girls are like that,' stated Quantrill with authority. 'They're secretive by nature.'

Tait felt ill-equipped to dispute the matter. He was irritated. Everyone seemed to be trying to put him down. When his radio bleeped he answered it sharply.

There were two pieces of information for them. First, a preliminary post-mortem report confirmed Tait's hypothesis that Jasmine Woods had died the previous day. The pathologist estimated the time of death to be between eight and nine in the evening. Secondly, Gilbert Smith had gone where Tait had guessed. His motor cycle had been found abandoned on waste ground in Yarchester.

Chief Inspector Quantrill looked at his sergeant with wry

approval. 'There had to be some good reason why they picked you for accelerated promotion,' he admitted.

Tait grinned, restored to humour. 'Makes yer spit, don't it?' he said immodestly.

The radio bleeped again. A dark blue 'S' Volvo Estate car was registered in the name of George Eustace Hussey, of the Antique Shop, The Street, Thirling.

16

Dressed, but still in her bedroom because she wanted to be alone, Alison sat staring at a bowl of lukewarm mushroom soup. She had not wanted any supper—certainly not the liver and bacon that her mother had proposed—but had agreed to soup for the sake of peace. Now the smell of it nauseated her; and the greyness, the black-flecked greyness, reminded her of a greyness she had seen earlier that day, a puddle of it that had oozed through the white and red splinters of Jasmine's skull—

She managed to reach the bathroom without either vomiting or fainting, and flung dizzily to the washbasin. The hollow-eyed face that stared back at her from the mirror, swinging in and out of focus, seemed completely strange. She had sometimes, during the emotional upheaval of her love affair in London, looked at a mirror with amazement that so deep an unhappiness could leave so little trace on her features; now she knew that her hurt over Gavin Jackson had been comparatively superficial. Her discovery of Jasmine Woods's mutilated body was traumatic. It had changed her, and the change was reflected in her face.

In the two months since she had left London, she had almost forgotten Gavin. There had, after all, been nothing particularly wonderful about him: he was good looking and amusing and occasionally kind, but more often casual and inconsiderate. She had told Jasmine about him, soon after she began work at Yeoman's and when Jasmine said, 'He does sound a bit of a pig—I recognize the breed, I've met one or two like him. You know, I suspect that it's your pride that has been dented, as much as your heart,' she had been obliged in honesty to agree.

'You're an attractive girl,' Jasmine had added, 'and there's no doubt that someone else will be after you quickly enough. You probably feel at the moment that you can never fall in love again, but you will, of course. Only don't for heaven's sake make the same mistake; don't undervalue yourself by going for another Gavin. There are alternatives, you know.' And she had smiled encouragingly: 'That's what's so interesting about life—it really does have infinite possibilities for change.'

But not anymore, for Jasmine.

It was incredible. Impossible to believe that Jasmine was dead, when her face was so familiar, her voice so clear in Alison's head. That was one of the horrors: the fact that she had spent an hour in the office at Yeoman's that morning busily audio-typing, transcribing the tapes that Jasmine had recorded during the weekend, while her friend's body lay in the next room, bludgeoned and violated.

And what exacerbated Alison's pain was the memory of the chattiness of the tapes. Jasmine Woods—probably because she lived alone—thought aloud. The tapes were a personal communication between herself and her secretary, a friendly acknowledgement of their dual involvement in the production of the next romantic thriller; they provided an occasional giggle in the middle of the serious business of keeping the Jasmine Woods industry going.

'Right, then,' that morning's tape had begun briskly, 'Chapter Six in the Paris-in-the-late-1930s saga. I've been going through the last chapter you typed, and I'm not happy about the cliffhanger—on reflection, our heroine's new predicament is even more unlikely than usual. I mean, she'd have known perfectly well that she was walking into a trap—she couldn't be *that* stupid... or could she? Hmm. Trouble is, in this genre, if our heroines used their heads, they'd never get involved in the first place, and we'd have no plots at all. Anyway, I've altered the ending of the last chapter slightly, so don't be surprised by the apparent inconsistencies. Here we go with Chapter Six: *It was a cold and draughty prison, noisy with the wind that moaned through slatted openings in the thick walls. The sun had already set, and the dusk in the chamber was further darkened by a monstrous, unidentifiable bulk that loomed over the wooden floor where Hannah had fallen. She put out*—Help, did I say Hannah? Sorry, that was the girl in the last book! Anyway, you know who I mean: Laurel. *She put out a tentative hand to touch its side. It was cold as iron. It was iron.* "Was" underlined, paragraph.

'*Her fingers slid down a great outward curve and then reached a thick rim. She stood up cautiously and tried to measure its extent, first with her hands and then with her outstretched arms. It was huge, of incalculable size. And yet, incredibly, as she pushed at it, it seemed to move a fraction. Then as her eyes became accustomed to the gathering gloom, she saw the shape of a great bell* semicolon. *A massive mouth, x tons*—see if you can look this one up for me, Ali dear, I've no idea what a church bell weighs. I agree that Laurel didn't know either, but I like to get the details more or less right. Credibility wherever possible, that's my motto. And I'd like to be alliterative if I can, two tons or ten tons or whatever. Where was I? *X tons of suspended metal that would soon, as it did every evening, begin to swing in its cradle and bawl out across the rooftops of Paris. She realized with mounting terror that she had been locked in the bell tower of the cathedral of Notre Dame.*

'And Lord knows how I'm going to get her out without a faithful Quasimodo lurking near, but no doubt our hero— hell, there's someone at the back door. It's only ten to twelve. Roz and Jonathan are coming for drinks but I didn't expect them as early as this. Oh, well, don't go away, Ali, I'll get back to you after they've gone.'

Alison could hear it again, word for word, with every nuance clear: the wry amusement of the asides, the serious competence of the narrative, the easy affection of the 'Ali dear.' And it was at that point that she had switched off the recorder to put a fresh sheet of paper in the typewriter, checked her watch and decided that it was time Jasmine appeared with coffee.

The Chief Inspector's Daughter

She had waited a few minutes longer, pondering the best source of information about the approximate weight of one of the Notre Dame bells—the Dean's office at Yarchester Cathedral? the *Encyclopaedia Britannica* at the county library? the French tourist office in London?—and had then realized how quiet Yeoman's was. Too quiet. She hurried to the hall, called Jasmine's name, then opened the sitting-room door. At first it was gloomy because the curtains were still drawn, and that in itself surprised and alarmed her. She had pulled them back, flooding with April morning sunshine of the kind that is too brilliant to last the day; she had turned from the window and then she saw...

What she had seen was etched on her mind's eye, engraved as though with acid. Every detail was so appallingly vivid that she could cope with it only by trying to shut it out of her consciousness. The policewoman, Beth Knowles, had asked her for details; had suggested that she might remember more when she got over the shock. But that was naïve. Alison could remember it all, now. She doubted that she would ever forget it. Her problem was to keep it away, to keep a shutter pulled down over it.

But it kept coming back. If she left her mind unguarded even for a moment, the shutter would fly up; once again she would turn from the window to look at the room, lit up like a stage set. Something was wrong, she had known that at once, even though from where she stood she could not see the alcove that contained the wrenched-open display cabinet, or the sofa behind which—

Something had been wrong with the room. Jasmine had invited her to stay for supper on several occasions, and they had usually had the meal in the sitting-room—an omelette or a salad, with a glass of wine, eaten from trays on their knees while they listened to records or talked about every subject that came into their heads. And so Alison knew the room quite well.

Because she was a working woman, a best-selling author preoccupied with writing and proofreading and business correspondence and accounts and fan mail, Jasmine Woods had no time to spend on rearranging her sitting-room; things were always kept in the same place. And because Alison always sat in the same armchair, close to the window from which she had turned that morning, the roomscape was almost as familiar to her as that of her own bedroom.

And there had been something wrong with Alison's bedroom. She had known it the first morning after she returned from London, sitting up in bed and looking with sad adult eyes at the relics of her childhood and adolescence that decorated the room. Each of her possessions lived in its particular place, and when she left home she had instructed her mother that nothing must be changed. But Molly had accidentally broken something while she was dusting the room ready for her daughter's return, and had not thought it worth a confession.

It was not that Alison cared greatly, when she noticed her loss, because she had already decided to send most of the things to a children's home and to redecorate her room; but she did not fail to notice. Ridiculous that among so many fubsy animals in wool and felt and fur and wood and glass he should spot the absence of one small pink china rabbit...

Something, she knew—apart from the treasures in the cabinet—was missing from its accustomed place in Jasmine Woods's sitting-room. If she thought about it, she knew that she would remember what it was. But thinking about it— about the room, about Jasmine—was precisely what she did not want to do.

Perhaps the missing object was significant; no doubt WPC Knowles would have been glad to have some information, however marginal, to pass on to the Chief Inspector. Perhaps it would help her father to find Jasmine's killer.

But what good would that do Jasmine? Alison was not interested at that moment in either justice or retribution. Nothing could bring Jasmine back or undo what had been inflicted upon her... the horror of what had been done to her... or take away the memory of that sight, the head, the limbs, the blood—

Molly, listening anxiously at the foot of the stairs, heard her daughter retching in the bathroom. She waited until she heard Alison return to her bedroom, then went upstairs with the offer of a cup of tea.

'No, Mum! For goodness sake stop trying to force food and drink down me! I'm not convalescent, I just want to be left alone.'

Molly tried not to look hurt. 'Would you like to go back to bed, then? Another sleep would do you good.'

'No! If I sleep, I'll dream, and that's the last thing I want to do. I might go for a walk—'

'But it's getting dark. And anyway, I don't think that would be wise, dear. A reporter from the local paper called about an hour ago, wanting to talk to you. I said you were asleep, to put him off. Your father wouldn't like you to talk to anyone outside the police about what's happened.'

'Do you think I *want* to talk to anyone about it?'

'Well, you'll have to talk to your father. He thinks you might be able to remember something that will help him. He rang a little while ago to ask how you were, and said he'd come to see you as soon as he could.'

'Oh, no . . . ' Alison could imagine how it would be: her father, kind, patient, intolerably persistent, forcing her to turn again from that window at Yeoman's and look minutely at every detail of the murder scene . . . forcing her not only to look, but to describe . . . 'No, I can't do it! I won't, he can't expect it of me! She wasn't just my employer, she was my friend—'

'But you'll *have* to talk to him,' said Molly earnestly. 'It's your father's job to find out as much as he can.' She frowned, her eyes soft with anxious sympathy. 'I suppose Martin Tait could do it instead, if you'd prefer that. Would you rather talk to Martin, dear?'

Alison flung herself face down on the bed, thumping her pillow with anguished frustration that her mother understood so little of what she was going through. 'No! Oh, God, can't you get it into your head that I don't want to think about it or to talk about it to anyone? Haven't you any imagination?'

'But, Alison, it's a police matter. It's official, you must realize that.'

'I don't care. I don't give a damn about the police. What can they do to bring Jasmine back?'

'Ssh, dear, ssh. You rest here quietly, and later on I'll bring—'

Alison rolled over and sat up. Her eyes were feverishly bright, her fists clenched. 'Just leave me alone,' she said in a low, angry voice. 'Do you hear? That's all I want, from any of you. For God's sake leave me alone.'

17

'This antique dealer we're going to see, George Hussey—isn't he one of the men you met at Jasmine Woods's party?' Quantrill asked.

'Yes, and one that I didn't take to: overdressed and smarmy and patronizing. The type who makes such a point of being a ladies' man that you automatically suspect that he dislikes women.'

'Oh, yes? What was his attitude to Jasmine Woods?'

'Effusive. Apparently she'd been a customer of his from way back, and he'd sold her most of her netsuke—before they started shooting up in value. He'd known exactly how much her collection was worth. He was open enough about it; told me that she'd enriched herself at his expense but that he valued her custom and friendship too much to bear a grudge . . . or words to that effect.'

'Har,' said Chief Inspector Quantrill.

The country road circled a walled churchyard, and was immediately transformed into the village street. Lest there should be any doubt as to its identity, a plaque erected by the district council bore the name The Street. This was doubly superfluous, since there were no other streets at all in the village. The remainder of Thirling consisted of outlying farms and former farms, like Yeoman's.

But although it was a small village, Thirling took itself seriously. The Street was no cottagey, flower-bowered picturesque straggle, but a double line of buildings in an interesting mixture of ages and sizes and styles and functions; a proper, business-like place, with a garage, a pub, a butcher's shop and a general shop-cum-post office interspersed among the houses. Most of the buildings fronted directly on to the pavement and were faced, if not entirely constructed, with brick or stone. One of the larger houses, Regency, in grey brick with a central bow window surmounted by a delicate ironwork veranda, was lettered discreetly 'Antiques.'

Tait parked at the side of the road a few yards beyond the shop, and the policemen walked back to it. Dusk was gathering, and the lights were on in the display room. The antiques, seen through the window, appeared to be distinctly up-market: a few carefully chosen and presented pieces of furniture, chiefly in mahogany or rosewood. There were some smaller inlaid wooden items—portable writing desks, jewel boxes, tea caddies—and against the Wedgwood-green walls stood two display cabinets containing porcelain and silver.

No one was in the lighted room, but as the men approached the door a car nosed out of the arched gateway at the side of the house. It was a big BMW with a Belgian registration, driven by a man with a cigar in his mouth. He gave a perfunctory glance left and right, snapped his headlights full on and zoomed up the street as though he had never heard of speed limits.

'Get him?' said Quantrill; it was not speed he was concerned about.

'Got him,' said Tait, scribbling in his pocket book. He hurried back to his car to radio a message to county headquarters, and then rejoined the Chief Inspector. There was a discreet 'Closed' notice on the main door leading to the display room, and so they walked through the gateway to the side door. A slim young man with a bush of curly hair and tinted metal-framed glasses stood in the doorway, pulling a short leather jacket over his thin black sweater.

'We *have* just closed,' he said, in tones that suggested that it might be no trouble at all to re-open. He looked the policemen over with interest.

'We're not customers,' said Quantrill.

'Pity. Personal for Mr Hussey, then?' He smiled at Tait, opened the door a little wider and called, 'George—couple of fellas to see you.'

'Coming,' said a plummy voice from inside the house. George Hussey's well-tailored paunch sailed towards them down the passage with a following breeze of aftershave. 'Good-night, then, Christopher. Thank you for staying on while I was busy.'

'No trouble. Any time, George, you know that. 'Bye.'
The young man, Christopher, smiled again at Tait. 'You must
come earlier another day, and I'll give you a conducted tour.'

'It wouldn't be worth your while,' said Tait equably.

Christopher laughed, swung himself into a small open
car that stood in the cobbled courtyard, and waved at the
three men as he began to roll past them.

'See you tomorrow,' Hussey called.

'Looking forward to it.' Christopher's car disppeared
through the arch into the street.

'My assistant,' Hussey explained. 'He did tell you that
we're closed?'

'We're not customers,' Quantrill repeated with brisk
distaste. He had been a policeman in the days when homo-
sexual relationships, even between consenting adults in private, were illegal. He had no wish for the reintroduction of
that particular law—in his experience it had been a blackmailers'
charter—but he was too old a copper to shed his prejudices
easily and he was confident that he knew a couple of queers
when he saw them. He introduced himself and his sergeant.
'May we come in?'

Hussey backed away from the policemen, his small mouth
opening with evident alarm. His dark-rimmed glasses slipped
down the bridge of his nose, but he adjusted them quickly.
'Well . . . yes, come in, but I can assure you—'

He retreated reluctantly down the passage, which led to
a semi-circular inner hall. A delicate staircase with no visible
means of support curved up against one wall. From a niche at
the foot of the stairs a plaster bust lettered *Homer* stared
blindly towards a bust in another niche, an equally sightless
Cicero. The hall was furnished with an early nineteenth-
century Grecian sofa; Hussey motioned halfheartedly towards
it, but Quantrill preferred to stand.

'We're interested in netsuke, Mr. Hussey. Netsuke and
Chinese jade.'

The antique dealer smoothed back his already smooth
hair. He was standing directly under a wall light which gave
his dark hair an oddly matt appearance; dyed, Quantrill
decided with pitying contempt.

'Netsuke . . .' repeated Hussey uncertainly. 'Well, I think
I have a few I can show you, but they're rather poor speci-

mens, I'm afraid. One doesn't often come upon good netsuke now, more's the pity. And I haven't any jade at all.'

'Has anyone tried to sell you any netsuke or jade today?' Quantrill asked.

'Today? No . . . why should they?'

'Haven't you heard about Jasmine Woods?' said Tait.

Hussey's head jerked round. 'Jasmine? Of course, the village has buzzed with the news. I believe that one of your policemen was making enquiries earlier today, but it was Christopher who saw him. I was out. Yes, poor Jasmine—a terrible tragedy.' He stared at Tait through his thick lenses. 'Aren't you a friend of hers? Didn't I see you at her last party?'

'Yes. We talked, if you remember, about her netsuke—most of which you said she had bought from you at ridiculously low prices.'

The man's hands flew to his bow tie. He adjusted it, smiling unconvincingly. 'I believe I did joke about the value of her collection. One likes to know that one's advice has benefited one's friends.'

Quantrill found the use of 'one' irritating and pretentious. 'Her jade and netsuke were stolen,' he said abruptly. 'We're anxious to find the thief.'

'Naturally,' Hussey agreed. 'Of course, if anyone were to bring any of the pieces to me, I should recognize them immediately.' He took several short steps towards the policemen, evidently hoping to shepherd them back down the passage. 'Rest assured that if I see or hear anything at all suspicious, Superintendent, I shall notify you at once. One does one's best to cooperate with the police.'

Quantrill elected to sit down, finding the Grecian sofa as unyielding as it looked. 'Just Chief Inspector, thank you. Tell me, Mr Hussey, what was your Belgian customer buying?'

'Er. . . Belgian?'

'The man who went off in the jet-propelled BMW five minutes ago,' said Tait. 'Weren't you busy with him while your assistant stayed to mind the shop?'

'Oh—*that* Belgian. One has so many foreign customers. Mr Wouters visits me quite often, and I like to offer him a drink and a cigar in my sitting-room while we do business. He specializes in silver, and I had found a rather handsome pair of Georgian candelabra for him.'

'Did you sell him any netsuke?' Quantrill asked. 'Or jade?'

'No! I told you, I haven't jade at all, or any netsuke that would interest him. Good heavens, do you want to search the premises?'

It was a waspish retort rather than an invitation, but Quantrill accepted it promptly. Not that he imagined there would be anything to find, but it was too good an offer to refuse. He sent Tait out to the car to call up a couple of men.

'I couldn't help wondering why your Belgian friend was in such a hurry,' he told Hussey.

'He had a boat to catch, I imagine.'

'Probably. But just to be on the safe side I've sent word through to Customs to be on the lookout for him. We don't want any of Jasmine Woods's collection to slip out of the country without our knowledge.'

Hussey's head lifted, stretching its supporting fold of flesh. 'Are you suggesting that I sold any of her collection to Mr Wouters? That I had it to sell?'

'Not necessarily,' said Quantrill. 'I expect he goes to other antique shops while he's over here. But the Customs men will talk to him. Sergeant Tait and I are more interested in Jasmine Woods.'

'When did you last see her, Mr Hussey?' asked Tait, who had returned and was now standing with one elbow propped on the ledge next to Cicero.

Hussey went to the niche and moved the white bust to one side with ostentatious care. 'As a matter of fact, yesterday afternoon. We've known each other for years, as I think I told you. Poor girl . . . Yes, a customer on Saturday sold me a delightful Victorian silver *porte-bouquet,* and I thought Jasmine might like it. I knew that Mr Wouters would be coming today and that he would be interested, so I wanted to give her first refusal. Such a charming girl—Thirling will be a desert without her.'

'You know her very well, then.'

'Ah, no. Only moderately well. We saw each other, informally, quite often, but we didn't exchange confidences. We respected each other's privacy.'

'About how long were you with her yesterday?' Quantrill asked.

'Let me see—I went there about 1.30; Jasmine and I both live alone, and we keep irregular hours. I must admit that I hoped she'd suggest luncheon, and she did; a very palatable *omelette aux fines herbes*. After that we drank coffee and talked cookery and antiques for a while, and I left in mid-afternoon. I came back just before four o'clock.'

'Was anyone else at Yeoman's while you were there?'

'No one—though Jonathan Elliott was leaving just as I arrived.'

'Did she say anything about seeing anyone else yesterday, or about going out?'

'She did mention that her sister had invited her to supper in Yarchester, but she wasn't sure whether she would go. She said that she hated to ruin her brother-in-law's Sunday—they didn't get on, you know. Besides, she wanted to work. When she had a book on the go, Jasmine usually worked every day, but yesterday had turned out to be rather more social than she'd expected. Apparently Smith—a tiresomely scruffy boy, I've always thought, but Jasmine was very kind-hearted and tolerant—invited himself in for coffee; and then the Elliotts went there for drinks; and then of course my own visit was unexpected. She didn't say for sure, but when I left, my impression was that she intended to spend the evening working on her book.'

'And what did you do, after you returned here?' Tait asked. 'How did you spend yesterday evening?'

Hussey bridled a little. 'If it's of any interest to you, I took a nap. Then I cooked myself a steak, somewhere about seven o'clock, and watched television for the rest of the evening.'

'Alone?'

'Of course alone. I live alone, I told you.'

'I thought you might have had company for the evening. Your young friend Christopher for example?'

Hussey's plump jaw tightened. He was angry, but he covered his anger with disdain. 'My private life is my own concern, Sergeant,' he said, 'but as it happens you have drawn quite the wrong conclusion. As I told you, I spent yesterday evening alone watching television: a Pinter play on BBC2. And don't start wondering whether I simply looked that up in *Radio Times*, because I can tell you exactly what the set looked like and what the cast was wearing—'

'Don't bother,' said Quantrill. 'Not for the moment, anyway. We'll probably come back to you.'

'We shan't find any of Jasmine Woods's jade or netsuke in his possession,' said Quantrill. 'If he did handle them, with or without knowing anything about her death, he'll either have hidden them somewhere else or got rid of them as quickly as possible. He was shifty about something, that's for sure.'

'No one likes admitting that he was alone with a murder victim shortly before the event,' said Tait. 'And there are all kinds of other reasons why he might have a guilty conscience. Perhaps he's been fiddling his income tax, or his VAT returns.' He stopped his car a short distance down the street from the antique shop, and switched off the engine while they discussed their next move.

'Anyway,' said Quantrill, heavy with disapproval, 'it's going to be worthwhile keeping an eye on Mr Hussey and his friend Christopher.'

'That sounds remarkably like prejudice,' said Tait, fingering the steering wheel of his Citroën with absent-minded pride.

'I don't deny it. You didn't like the man either.'

'I didn't like him socially. I couldn't stand his patronizing attitude. But I don't get uptight about anyone's propensities, as long as they're not illegal. As he said, people's private lives are their own concern. I provoked him quite deliberately, just to get his reaction, and you heard what he said: he was far more concerned with spitting in my eye than providing an alibi for himself. No, I'm inclined to believe him. I doubt if he's anything other than a lonely, fussy old bachelor. I'm sure he's far too fastidious to be an accessory to a crime like that.'

Quantrill drummed his fingers on the dashboard as he watched two uniformed constables who had appeared under a lamp on the other side of the street. Small as the village was, they were still trying to complete their house-to-house enquiries by calling on the people who had been out during the day. That was what most detective work consisted of, a time-consuming slog of questioning and checking facts. Judgement came into it, of course, but judgement without facts to back it—as he had cause to know, with Rodney Gifford—was irrelevant.

'Hussey's an unlikely accessory, I grant you,' he stated. 'But if murders weren't done by, or in connivance with unlikely people, they wouldn't be so difficult to detect. After all, we don't know what the circumstances of the murder were. I reckon that, given enough passion or greed or fear, almost anyone is capable of almost anything.'

'And I was the one your daughter once reproved for thinking the worse of people!'

'Let's say that we've both got nasty suspicious minds.'

Quantrill tore the wrapper from a packet of mild cigars, and took one out. Tait, a non-smoker, glared his disapproval and opened the car window to its fullest extent. The Chief Inspector coughed as the sharp evening air reached his lungs, paused with the cigar in one hand and his lighter in the other, and sniffed appreciatively.

'Aha! Cliffie the chippy—just what we need.'

A tall old van, well known in and around Breckham Market, had trundled up behind them. In one side of the van body was a large sliding window; from the roof protruded a flue that puthered aromatic smoke. The van parked a little further up the street. Immediately, the interior was lighted up and the driver's mate, a pale man in a soiled white apron, began to shovel raw potato chips from a plastic bucket into a vat of hot cooking-oil. Half the population of Thirling promptly emerged from their houses to collect fish and chips for supper.

Quantrill put away both cigar and lighter and gladly produced a pound note. 'Have this on me,' he said.

'Damn it, this isn't a police van,' protested Tait indignantly. 'Fish and chips will stink my car out.'

'I'll have plaice,' said Quantrill, 'if Cliffie's got any, otherwise cod. Not too many chips. Plenty of salt, but go easy with the vinegar.'

Tait muttered insubordination.

'Stop making a fuss,' said Quantrill, 'and go and join the queue. I'll do the same for you when you're Chief Constable.'

'This looks like a dead end, at the moment, Martin. I've just been talking to the incident-room, and no-one they've interviewed saw any person or vehicle going to or coming from Yeoman's after the time when Hussey says he left. So presumably, as he suggested, Jasmine Woods decided to spend the rest of the day at home. And presumably the next visitor was her killer.'

Tait, having decided that the only way he could bear the smell in his car would be to succumb to the Chief Inspector's offer, blew on a hot chip.

'No word from Yarchester about Smith, I suppose?'

Quantrill crunched a piece of fishy batter. 'No. They're all sitting on their behinds having refreshments instead of going out looking for him.'

'I'm interested in the fact that Smith called on Jasmine yesterday morning, and was interrupted by the Elliotts,' said Tait. 'Oh, I know that he lived in the garden, so he must have been in and out of her house a good deal; but he'd been there a couple of years, and if he had any part of her murder, something must have happened yesterday to trigger it off. We know that he spent money on drugs, and he might have got to the stage where he needed more money than he earned. Perhaps he went to see Jasmine yesterday morning to try to get a loan. But I know that she disapproved of hard drugs, and I think she'd refuse. And then the Elliotts arrived, and after them Hussey. By the evening, Smith would have been getting desperate.'

'It's a possibility,' agreed Quantrill. 'We badly need Smith, but until Yarchester finds himself, or forensic comes up with some evidence that definitely ties him in with the murder, we can't be sure that he did it. So we have to go on looking elsewhere and I was thinking, while you were getting the fish and chips—by the way, was there any change from my pound?'

'You've been overtaken by inflation. I had to put in another 10p.'

Quantrill grumbled about the cost of Cliffie's new-fangled white wrapping paper and cardboard trays. 'When I was a kid we ate fish and chips out of newspaper. Very educational, especially when it was the *News of the World*. Anyway, it occurs to me that we might have been concentrating too hard on the people we met at that party. On the face of it, several of them had motives that might have led them to kill her.

And Gilbert Smith and her brother-in-law Paul Pardoe and Hussey all had the opportunity.'

'So did Jonathan Elliott,' said Tait. 'That study of his has a patio-door—he could have slipped out of there after dark and walked down to Yeoman's without anyone else in the family knowing that he'd gone.'

'All right, they all had the opportunity. But if we hadn't known Jasmine Woods, and met those men at her party, I think we'd have paid more attention to the way the murder was done.'

'With hatred, you mean. Yes, it wasn't simply murder in furtherance of theft, we all saw that right away. Whoever killed Jasmine might have wanted her jade and netsuke; alternatively he might have taken them just to make us think that was why he did it. But we could see for ourselves that there was a much stronger motive for the murder than that. And—excluding Smith, because druggies might do anything—the men we've interviewed haven't really been sufficiently strongly motivated to do that kind of murder.'

'With the exception of Rodney Gifford,' Quantrill amended, chip in hand. 'He was strongly motivated, all right. With half a bottle of her wine inside him, he was licking his lips over the prospect of making her suffer. The only snag is that he lives seventeen miles away, there's no public transport out here on Sunday evenings, he doesn't own a vehicle and he's got his dear old mother as an alibi...'

Quantrill brooded for a moment. Tait ignored the interruption.

'Jasmine told me, at her party, that most of the guests were relations and neighbours rather than personal friends. In other words, we haven't yet met any of the people she was really involved with. We know nothing about her private life. While I was at Yeoman's this afternoon there was a telephone call from her publisher, asking for news. I spoke to him myself. He was shocked by the murder. He'd known her for years and regarded her as a friend, but he didn't seem to know much more about her than George Hussey did. He knew that she had friends in London, but he couldn't tell me who they were. And I don't think there was any doubt that Jasmine had an active private life—she told me once that she thought we were all entitled to our private pleasures. So presumably there's a lover about somewhere, and possibly an ex-lover, or two. There's certainly an ex-husband, name of Potter—'

The Chief Inspector stopped brooding and screwed the wrapping paper round the remains of his fish and chips. 'You're right, Martin. It's the men who have loved her who are most likely to hate her—and particularly the ex-husband, now that she's rich and famous. Right, see if you can track him down. I'll go back home and have a word with Alison. I must see her anyway, to get some details filled in, but I'll also ask her about Jasmine's current men-friends. Alison's bound to know something about them. It wasn't just an employer-employee relationship. I bet she knows a lot more about Jasmine Woods than anyone else round here. By God, she can probably put her finger straight on the man we want!'

Sergeant Tait snatched up their supper wrappings, leaped out of his car and stuffed them in the rubbish bin outside the village shop. He sprinted back to the driving seat and switched on the ignition. 'Straight to your home, sir?'

But Quantrill had gone broody again. 'No, hold hard,' he said slowly, 'I can see Alison later. I was thinking about Rodney Gifford. His mother told me that they were both watching television last night—BBC2, she said. That was what George Hussey said he was watching, wasn't it?'

'Yes. A play by Pinter.'

'Who's he?'

'A modern English playwright.' Tait had never been interested in the theatre, and his job absorbed most of his time and energy, but he tried to keep up with the Arts pages of the *Sunday Times*. A quick glance through the reviews was, he found, a surprisingly effective substitute for going to plays and films and reading books.

'Does he write romantic plays?' asked Quantrill. 'The sort of thing Rodney Gifford's mother might enjoy? She's a dear old soul, pushing eighty; used to love going to the pictures to see Clark Gable.'

Tait smiled knowledgeably. 'I doubt she'd enjoy Pinter, then.'

'That's what I was wondering. I think the chances are that she'd sleep all the way through it . . . Get moving, Martin. Alison's information will keep. I'm going back to talk to Gifford.'

'But he lives in Yarchester, and you said he hasn't any transport.'

'I know. But that doesn't mean that he can't drive, does it?'

18

'Oh—it's Mr—er Roddy's friend, isn't it? How nice of you to call back.'

Mrs Gifford stood in the doorway of the semi-detached house in Rowan Road, peering uncertainly up at Chief Inspector Quantrill in the dim light from the hall. She looked very weary; smaller and frailer then she had seemed that morning. She had exchanged her bunion-shaped shoes for a pair of carpet slippers, and her neat cardigan for a heavier hand-knitted jacket that she clutched to her throat as though she were cold. 'It's rather late, though,' she went on. 'Roddy's in his room, working, and he doesn't like to be disturbed. And I shall be going to bed just after ten.'

'I'm very sorry to bother you, Mrs Gifford, but I'm afraid that I need to have another word with your son.'

'He's very upset, you know,' she said. 'I don't think he wants to see anyone. We're both upset. His poor dear cousin Jasmine is dead—a wicked murder—' She pulled an inadequate wad of handkerchief from her sleeve and searched for a dry corner to dab her eyes with. 'But then, I expect you've heard about the tragedy—you were a friend of Jasmine's, weren't you?'

Quantrill offered his sympathy. 'But I must tell you,' he said, 'that I'm a police officer, and I need your son's help. May I come in?'

He stepped firmly into the hall. Mrs Gifford stood pale

and alarmed. She held her arms crossed on her thin chest, with both hands hugging the collar of her jacket close to her corded neck.

'Who is it?' called Gifford's deep, fierce voice from upstairs. 'Who the hell is it?'

'Rodney!' his mother piped with tearful reproof. She tried to reassure herself. 'He doesn't usually swear, he's a good boy. I'm sure he'll help you in any way he can,' she told Quantrill. She raised her voice again. 'Someone to see you, Rodney.'

Gifford came thundering down the stairs. As soon as he saw the Chief Inspector he stopped dead, one hand grabbing at the banister, one shabbily carpet-slippered foot poised in mid-descent. He glanced back the way he had come, and for a moment Quantrill thought that he was going to bolt for his room.

'Just a couple of queries,' Quantrill assured him. 'You could help me too, Mrs Gifford, if you will.'

Gifford came reluctantly to ground level, complaining about the inconvenience of the call. Quantrill held open the sitting-room door for both mother and son, and followed them in. A big old-fashioned monochrome television set was switched on, though the sound was turned down.

Mrs Gifford sat down nervously in an unyielding armchair. Her son stood in a protective Victorian position behind her, one hand on her shoulder, head up, ears protruding scarlet through his hair. 'What did you want to ask Mother?' he demanded.

Quantrill sat opposite the old lady. He gave her a reassuring smile. 'I'd just like to know whether you have a car, Mrs Gifford.'

'We haven't,' growled Rodney. 'You know that, I told you this afternoon.'

His mother glanced up at him. 'Well, we did have a car, Rodney, don't forget that. When your poor dear father was alive.' She proceeded to tell the Chief Inspector more than he wished to know about the family car, and her decision to sell it after her husband had died, at the time when Rodney was being successful in London. 'And after he came home to keep me company, we decided that a car was an unnecessary expense. Not that we couldn't afford one, of course, Rodney's father left me fairly comfortable, and then there's my pension...'

Quantrill met Gifford's uneasy eyes. 'You can drive, then?'

'Of course he can,' said his mother proudly. 'His father taught him to drive—he's had a licence ever since he was eighteen, haven't you dear?'

'I see. The other thing I wanted to ask you about, Mrs Gifford,' said Quantrill, 'is yesterday evening. I wonder if you'd mind telling me exactly what you did?'

'I told you about that, too,' her son intervened fiercely. 'Last night my mother and I sat here watching television.'

'Yes, of course we did,' she agreed. 'We always do on Sunday evenings.'

'Did you enjoy the programme?'

'Oh, yes. Not that you get the same atmosphere as a cinema, but I quite enjoy television.' Her eyes were drawn towards the silent screen where a spaghetti-Western film was in progress: Clint Eastwood, thin, unshaven, expressionless, with Stetson on head and cigar in mouth was—apparently without removing either—about to give a girl in vaguely Victorian fancy-dress exactly what she was asking for.

'Did you watch a film last night?' Quantrill asked.

Mrs Gifford dragged her eyes from the screen with shocked reluctance. Her son strode over to the television set and switched it off, muttering his distaste for such offensive rubbish. 'I've told you, Mother, you should stick to BBC2. That's what we were watching last night, a play by Pinter.'

'Good, was it?' Quantrill asked her, smiling encouragingly. 'My wife always enjoys watching plays.'

'Well...' Mrs Gifford's rheumaticky fingers picked shyly at the hand-embroidered linen cover on the arm of her chair. 'It's really the hymns I enjoy most on Sunday evenings. After that, I often take a nap.'

'And why not?' said Quantrill. 'I fall asleep in front of the set myself, if I've had a busy day. Were you asleep for long, last night?'

'Let me see... we had tea in here, we always do that on Sundays, and then Rodney washed up while I watched the hymn-singing. And then he brought me another cup of tea;

that's what he does every Sunday evening. Such a good son to me.'

'And then you saw the start of the play?' Quantrill prompted.

'Oh, no, it's "The World about Us" first; animals, you know, and sometimes birds.'

'Which was it last night?'

'I'm not sure—I think I must have dozed off.'

'But you woke for the start of the play?'

'Now you come to mention it, I don't think I did . . . I can't remember the play at all. Surely I didn't sleep all the way through it, Rodney?'

'You just dozed on and off, Mother. We discussed the plot at one point, don't you remember?'

She shook her head. 'Isn't it silly of me? All I can remember is you waking me up with my Horlicks and biscuits and telling me that it was nearly eleven o'clock!'

'Oh—you fell into such a sound sleep towards the end of the play that it seemed a shame to wake you. No wonder you're tired this evening, after such a late night.' He turned angrily to Quantrill. 'Have you quite finished?'

Quantrill addressed the old lady. 'Thank you, you've been very helpful. I'd just like to have a word with Rodney—out in the hall, perhaps?'

'No, no.' Mrs Gifford got stiffly to her feet. 'You couldn't stay for tea this afternoon, so you must have some Horlicks now. I'll go and make it. After all, you were one of poor dear Jasmine's friends . . .'

She went out to the kitchen. Quantrill stood facing her son.

'Right, Mr Gifford.' He pulled out his notebook. 'I took the precaution of checking last night's television programme before I came here: "The World About Us" started at 7:15 last night. It was about an expedition in the Himalayas, incidentally, so I don't think your mother can have taken much interest in it, do you? And if you didn't wake her until eleven, she must have been asleep for all of three hours, possibly nearer four.'

Gifford's tongue flicked across his wide mouth. 'And what concern is that of yours?'

'The pathologist who did the autopsy on your cousin

112

Jasmine puts the time of her death between eight and nine last night. What were you doing at that time, Mr Gifford?'

'For God's sake, I've told you! Sitting here with my mother, watching television!'

'I see. Someone else I've interviewed this evening said that he was doing just the same thing—watching the play on BBC2, I mean. I asked him,' said Quantrill, bluffing—or lying—as detectives often find it expedient to do, 'to give me full details about the sets and what the actors were wearing. So if you'd like to do the same, Mr Gifford, and if your recollections tally with his, I shan't have to trouble you any further.'

There was a long pause. From the kitchen, Mrs Gifford's voice could be heard in a quavering rendering of a hymn for Palm Sunday, which she must have heard on television the previous evening. Her son's face looked a dirty grey under his gingerish hair.

'I've got nothing to say,' he muttered. 'Except that I don't know anything about Jasmine's death.'

'Did you go to her house last night?'

'No.'

'So where were you?'

'I've got nothing to say.'

'Then I'll have to ask you to come with me to the station.'

'You can't arrest me! You've got nothing against me!'

'I'm not arresting you, Mr Gifford—simply asking for your co-operation. If you're not prepared to talk to me here, it'll have to be the station.'

He licked his lips again. 'I can't leave mother alone, she'd be worried sick.'

'I thought of that. I brought one of the Yarchester policewomen with me—she's waiting outside in my car. I daresay she'll enjoy a nice chat and mug of Horlicks with your mother while you're helping me with my enquiries.'

'Sure of yourself, weren't you?' sneered Gifford bitterly.

For a moment, Quantrill saw him again as he had seen him at Jasmine Woods's party. He recalled the wolfish way Gifford had looked at his cousin, his gesture with the wine bottle. He recalled the relish with which Gifford had said, *A bit of suffering would do cousin Jasmine a world of good*. Yes, he was sure that he had found the murderer.

He might, with reason, have felt at that moment a surge of anger. After all, he had known and liked the victim; and then, there was his daughter's connection with her. Jasmine Woods was beyond either help or suffering now, poor woman, but Alison might well be emotionally scarred for the rest of her life by what she had seen when she found the body. On her behalf, if not the victim's, he might have been moved to anger against Rodney Gifford.

Alternatively, he might have had a sense of triumph. Suspicion and dislike had not been enough to bring in Gifford, but persistent questioning had paid off; with luck, he was going to be able to wrap this case up inside a day, and that would be a personal record.

But Quantrill felt neither anger nor triumph. He felt tired; dispirited by the years he had spent in trying to clear up the dirt, the follies and greeds and overflowing emotions, the sickness of humanity. What saddened him most was that, ultimately, it was not only the victims of murder who suffered but the innocents on the periphery of every case: the ones who were left to manage as best they could, the wives, the husbands, the children, the parents, not only of the victim but of the criminal. Old Mrs Gifford, for example, unsuspectingly singing hymns as she made them all a bed-time drink...

'Get your coat on, Roddy,' he said wearily. 'Your mother won't want you to catch cold.'

At fourteen minutes past ten, as Quantrill was driving through the dark towards Breckham Market, with Rodney Gifford dumb and tense on the back seat beside a uniformed constable, he was called up on the radio.

'Chief Inspector Quantrill? Your wife is trying to get in touch with you, sir. Could you ring home as soon as possible?'

He answered impatiently, 'I'm bringing someone in for questioning. Tell my wife I'll call her as soon as I get back to Breckham—about twenty minutes.'

'Mrs Quantrill said it was urgent, sir. She sounded very distressed. Something to do with your daughter.'

He jammed on the brakes outside a telephone call box in the next village he passed through. The directories had been rumpled and torn, the floor was littered with cigarette ends

114

and worse, and the receiver was sticky; but at least the telephone worked.

'Molly—it's me. Is Alison all right?'

His wife's voice was so thick with tears that he could barely understand her. He had to ask her to repeat her words.

'I don't know. I don't know how or where she is. Oh, Douggie—she's gone. She's run away.'

19

'There's no point in panicking. Let's take this calmly,' said Quantrill, pacing up and down like an expectant father in a Laurel and Hardy film.

'I'm not panicking,' protested Molly tearfully. She stood in the doorway of the sitting room, biting her lower lip. She might have been said to be wringing her hands, except that the action was clearly involuntary; her hands wrung themselves, kneading and plucking at each other without her knowledge or intent. 'I'm sorry I had to bother you when you're working, I know you hate me to do that, but I was at my wits' end.'

He sat down, trying to ease the tension. 'Yes, of course—you did the right thing. There's no problem, Martin Tait's keeping my suspect warm for me. Now, let's consider this bit by bit. When did you last see or hear Alison?'

'About a quarter past seven. She wanted me to leave her alone, so I did. I've been so worried about her all day, and I kept popping in and out to see how she was. But from a quarter past seven I did as she asked, and sat in here watching television. Then I went upstairs just before ten to see if she wanted anything, and she was gone.'

'What about Peter? Did he hear her when he went up to bed? Have you asked him?'

'Yes, but he said not. I told him to be quiet—you know how noisy he usually is, running taps and banging doors—so as not to disturb her. He said he couldn't hear her transistor, so he thought she must be asleep.'

Quantrill went out of the room and up the stairs to Alison's bedroom, his wife following. The girl had made her bed, and had left the room tidy. If it were not for the absence of the teenage animal collection that she had left behind when she went to London, and the redecorating she had recently done, it would have looked as though she had never returned home.

'What did she take with her?' he asked.

'Not very much. At first I didn't realize that she'd taken anything. She'd said during the evening that she thought she might go for a walk, you see, and I assumed that was what had happened.'

'At this time of night?'

'Oh, but she was in a very odd mood, Douggie. Very distressed and restless and angry; and her stomach was upset, too.'

'I'm not surprised,' said Quantrill. 'Good grief, it was a hell of an ordeal the poor girl went through, seeing—well, never mind. Go on.'

'Well, I looked in the bathroom, just to make sure she wasn't there, and then I saw that her toothbrush had gone. So I went through her room and it looks as though she's taken her small suitcase and a few clothes. Just enough for a day or two.'

'Hmm. And you say you rang round some of her Breckham friends?'

'She didn't have many. I mean, she hadn't bothered to get in touch with many of them since she'd been back—she was too taken up with her new job. I checked that her bicycle was still in the garage, and then I rang the railway station. Jack Collins is the booking clerk tonight, and he knows her of course, but he said he hadn't seen her either. After that, I had to ring you. I mean, you do hear of such things . . .'

Quantrill patted his wife's shoulder absently. 'You did right, Molly. Now, you're sure she didn't leave a note anywhere?'

'Peter helped me look. We couldn't find a thing.' She hesitated, blushing a little. 'I couldn't find any letters she'd received, either; I searched, while I was waiting for you. I mean, I thought perhaps she had another boy-friend somewhere and that she might have gone to him, but there were only a couple of letters she'd had from Jennifer.'

'That's where she's most likely to go, now that Jennifer's moved out of the nurses' home into a flat,' said Quantrill, with more confidence than he felt; his daughters had never been very close to each other. 'Look, what we have to remember is that Alison's nineteen. She's an adult. We had no idea what she got up to while she was in London, and after eighteen months there she should be capable of looking after herself. But I do need to talk to her—and after the shock she had this morning she'd be better at home than travelling. She was in an odd mood, you say?'

Molly nodded wretchedly. She sat on the edge of the empty bed, still twisting her hands together. 'It was partly my fault, I suppose. I wanted to help her, and that made her impatient and cross—she's a lot like you in that way, you know; I try to do my best for all of you—' She choked into silence, wiping tears from beneath her soft brown eyes with her fingers.

Her husband sat down beside her, suppressing a sigh. 'Anyway,' Molly went on, her voice high and uncertain, 'when she said she might go for a walk I told her that you wouldn't want her to. There was a reporter hanging about earlier, trying to ask about the murder, but I sent him off. I told her that you'd want to talk to her yourself as soon as you could, and that was what really upset her. She said she wouldn't talk to anyone. She was so angry, I've never seen her like it—she shouted and swore and told me to leave her alone. *For God's sake leave me alone,* she said, and that's the last thing she said to me—'

Molly pressed both hands against her face and sobbed. Quantrill put his arm affectionately round her shoulders, a simple gesture that he had not made for a long time. 'Come on, Molly, don't upset yourself, it's understandable that she doesn't want to talk about the murder. She didn't mean to be angry with you, she was just overwrought. That's how it is with me sometimes when I'm worried about the job, I take things out on you—but you know I don't really mean it.'

He patted her shoulder briskly. 'Now, look, let's be sensible. Alison has simply gone off to stay with Jennifer, or with a friend somewhere, and as soon as she gets there she'll ring us. There's nothing at all to worry about. But I'd like you to find me a photograph of her, and write down a description of what you think she was wearing, so that I can get the boys to find out whether she's been seen in Breckham tonight. It'll be a useful exercise for them. All right?'

Quantrill kissed her temple, and stood up. His wife gave a childish, surprisingly endearing sniff and a hiccup. Then she shook her head, refusing to be fobbed off.

'No, it's not all right, Douggie. I know why you want to talk to Alison—it's because you think she may know something that will put you on to the murderer. And meanwhile he's on the loose—'

'You're wrong there. I've just taken him in for questioning.'

Her frown lightened. 'Have you arrested him?'

'Ah, well—not yet, we do have to be absolutely sure—'

'You mean, the man who did it may still be on the loose while you're questioning someone else?' She began to panic. 'But, Douggie, don't you see? Alison may be in danger. The murderer could have been watching for her, waiting for a chance to—to—'

'I never heard such squit in all my life, woman!' protested her husband. 'You've been watching too much television, that's your trouble. Of course Alison's not in any danger! If you've got nothing better to do than worry your head about that—'

Molly's tension slackened a little. 'You're not worried about her, then? Truly?'

'Of course I'm not!'

Chief Inspector Quantrill was lying again.

20

In an interview room at Breckham Market police station, watched impassively by a grey-haired constable who had seen it all before, Rodney Gifford was, literally, sweating. The air of the small room was sharp with his nervous emanation.

Chief Inspector Quantrill was tense, too. Usually he liked to make the soft approach at an interview, to offer tea and cigarettes, to be so kindly that his suspect failed to see that a verbal trap was being set for him. But this time, Quantrill had too much at stake to go softly. For Alison's sake, for his own and his wife's peace of mind, he wanted confirmation that it was Gifford who was the murderer; and he wanted it quickly.

He slammed the door behind him. 'Right, Mr Gifford,' he snapped.

The man, sitting at a table with his hands clenched in front of him, raised his large head. There was a line of sweat on his upper lip and he brushed it away with the knuckle of his forefinger, first from one side and then from the other, as though he were brushing up a moustache. He blinked his pale ginger eyelashes nervously, but said nothing.

'Where were you yesterday evening?' Quantrill demanded, leaning his hands on the table and glaring at Gifford from under his heavy eyebrows. 'And don't give me any of that stuff about watching television, because I know you weren't. Where were you?'

Gifford's tongue flicked across his lips. 'I'm not saying anything,' he said, 'except that I had nothing to do with my cousin Jasmine's death.' His voice cracked. 'What possible reason could *I* have for killing her? *I* shan't inherit anything from her. Why don't you badger her sister's husband, Paul Pardoe, about it? He's got far more to gain from her death than I have.'

'Come off it,' said Quantrill curtly, pulling out a chair and sitting down opposite him. 'Whoever killed Jasmine Woods made away with her collection of jade and netsuke; he's hoping to make a small fortune, whether or not he stands to inherit anything from her estate. You had a very strong financial motive, Mr Gifford—quite apart from the personal one.'

'I don't know what you mean,' said Gifford sourly.

'No? Don't forget, I saw and heard you at your cousin's party, being bitter about her success and your own lack of money. And other people heard you, too,' Quantrill asserted, without regard for fact. 'You had more than one motive for killing her, and you had plenty of opportunity while your mother was asleep. What did you give the poor old dear, incidentally—sleeping pills?'

Rodney Gifford reddened to the far-flung tips of his ears and muttered something fiercely unintelligible. Quantrill let that pass.

'So,' he continued, 'you put your mother safely to sleep yesterday evening, and then sneaked out of the house. What transport did you use, I wonder? Did you hire a car? Or steal one?'

Gifford glowered. 'I'm saying nothing—except that I wasn't anywhere near Thirling last night, and I didn't kill my cousin.'

'Prove it to me,' said Quantrill.

'I don't have to prove anything! If you think I killed Jasmine, *you'll* have to prove it—and you can't because you haven't any evidence.'

'It won't be difficult to get,' claimed Quantrill recklessly. 'We can easily check hired cars, and go over stolen and abandoned cars for fingerprints, or fibres from your clothes. And we can enquire round your friends and neighbours, to see if you borrowed a car yesterday evening. Would you like us to do that, Mr Gifford? Would your mother like it?'

The man stirred uneasily.

'And then,' Quantrill continued, putting on pressure, 'we'll search your house and garden. We probably wouldn't find anything as obvious as the stolen netsuke or blood-stained clothing, but its surprising how even tiny things can give a murderer away. For instance, Jasmine Woods's murderer almost certainly has some fragments of ivory from a smashed netsuke on the sole of one of his shoes. So we'll go through your house and clothes with a nit-comb, Mr Gifford—'

'You couldn't do that,' protested the man, 'not without a search warrant!'

'You're right. But remember, I heard what you said about your cousin at her party. That's enough for me to be able to get a warrant without any trouble at all.' It wasn't true. Getting a warrant wasn't easy, but hopefully Gifford did not know that: hopefully he would prefer to make a confession. 'It'll upset your mother of course,' went on Quantrill. 'Break her heart, poor old soul, I shouldn't wonder. But if you won't co-operate, we'll have no alternative.'

'No—wait!' Gifford licked his lips nervously. 'I want to protect my mother, that's the whole point . . . Look, I went into Yarchester yesterday evening. I—I went to the cinema.'

Quantrill raised a disbelieving eyebrow. 'I see . . . With someone? A woman friend? Someone you didn't want your mother to know about? But you'll have to tell me who it was, if you expect me to believe you.'

'I wasn't with anyone.' Gifford began to speak in a rush. 'I went alone. I didn't want to pretend to my mother that I went with anyone else because—well, I haven't many friends. I very rarely go out, and she would have been inquisitive if I'd suddenly said that I was going with someone to the cinema. And if I'd told her I was going alone, she would have wanted to come with me.'

'Hmm. And you're going to tell me that the film wasn't suitable for an old Clark Gable fan, I suppose? Porn, was it?'

Gifford twitched. He lowered his large head and wiped his upper lip again with his forefinger. 'It's not pornography,' he muttered. 'It's perfectly legitimate cinema, only it has an X certificate. I saw it reviewed in the *Observer*. It's rather—artistic; beautifully photographed. But it's just too explicit for my mother.'

'I can believe that. And I suppose, if I ask, you can give me enough detail about the film to convince me that you really did see it?'

Gifford looked up eagerly. 'Yes—yes, of course . . .'

'Yes, I bet you can. Once those films come to the city they're on for weeks. You probably saw it the previous Sunday, partly to enjoy it and partly to get the details in your head so that you could offer it as an alibi for last night. But your alibi won't work, Mr Gifford. An unsupported claim that you were alone in a Yarchester cinema last night isn't good enough. So unless you start telling the truth, I'll have to come and take your house apart round your poor old mother's ears—'

'But I *am* telling the truth!' Gifford's forefinger had become insufficient, and he wiped his sweating face with the back of his hand. 'You can search as much as you like, but you won't find anything. And my claim isn't unsupported, anyway. I—as a matter of fact, I've been to see that film several times. Every Sunday evening for the past four weeks. The girl at the box office recognizes me. She said to me last night, "Hallo, you again?" The bitch.'

Quantrill had felt increasingly sure that he had the right man, but now for the first time he wavered. 'She recognizes you—out of all those customers?'

Gifford held his head up, and his ears blazed through his hair. 'I do tend to be recognizable,' he said, half arrogant, half sour. 'Why don't you ask her?'

'You could have gone in, and slipped out again after the film started,' argued Quantrill with diminishing confidence.

'But I didn't. I left at the end of the film, just after ten. And as I passed the box office she said, "Cheerio, see you again next week."' His jaw tightened at the memory. 'God, if I could get her alone just for five minutes—'

His lips were drawn back from his sharp teeth; his eyes had a sadistic glitter. For a moment, sober as he was, Gifford looked as vicious as he had looked at Jasmine Woods's party.

Quantrill leaned forward. 'Yes, Roddy?' he said softly. 'If you could get her alone, what would you do?'

Gifford turned his head slowly to look at the Chief Inspector. He blinked, and began to relax: his eyes faded, his facial muscles slackened. Then he sighed, and made a wry confession.

'Nothing at all,' he said. 'That's my trouble. I can think of a lot of things I'd like to do to them, but never had the courage. I never do anything, except write and dream. That's been my trouble all my life.'

21

Chief Inspector Quantrill swore, and thumped the wall of his office with the side of his fist.

'I thought I had him, Martin—I really thought I had him. Almost as soon as I heard that Jasmine Woods had been murdered, I thought that Gifford was likely. And now he reckons he can prove that he spent the whole of yesterday evening in Yarchester, watching a sexy film . . . There ought to be a law against it.'

'You'll check his story, of course.'

'*You'll* do that,' retorted Quantrill. 'As long as you're a sergeant, checking's your job.' He looked at his watch, and that did nothing to improve his temper. The watch had been a Christmas surprise from his wife; an unusually expensive gift, because they had always been accustomed to exchange modest and predictable presents. Without either of his daughters at home to do his shopping for him, and knowing that Molly had a childish love of unwrapping things, he had last Christmas resorted to asking Patsy Hopkins to buy and gift-wrap a fancy bottle of bath oil and a pretty box of chocolates. To receive in return, instead of the expected socks and cigars, a watch that must have cost Molly at least a month's pay from her part-time job was an acute embarrassment.

He was even more embarrassed when Molly reminded him that it was only right he should have a good present, because he had that autumn bought her the sheepskin coat she had wanted for years . . .

He had thanked her profusely, of course. Difficult to explain that he'd bought the coat only to salve his conscience after falling in love with another woman. And now he felt obliged to wear the watch always, and it was a damned nuisance. Molly had ordered it from a mail-order catalogue, and had chosen one of the latest digital models; fine, except that Quantrill was one of those people for whom the measurement of time is visual. The figures on the watch meant nothing to him until he had converted them mentally on to a conventional face, just like that on his perfectly good old watch, which Peter—who really coveted the digital one—had now inherited prematurely.

He did a quick conversion—at least the figures on his new watch were on permanent display, and he didn't need to press a button to see the time—and found that 23.48 was just after a quarter to midnight.

'No point in trying to check Gifford's story now—you'd

better send someone to do that in the morning, but I haven't any hope that he was lying. So whoever did the murder is still loose—and Alison is still missing. Have you tried the bus depot?'

'Yes. There are only three buses out of Breckham Market after eight on weekday evenings, two to Yarchester and one to Saintsbury. I've got someone checking with the drivers at the other end; one report's negative, and I'm still waiting for the other two. I've tried the taxi firm, but their drivers didn't pick her up. I've also sent a man to visit the all-night cafés on the main London road, in case she went there to hitch a lift.'

Quantrill's eyebrows knotted with anxiety. He knew what so easily might happen to girls who hung about transport cafés late at night, trying to hitch lifts. Even if a sadistic murderer wasn't out searching for his daughter, she could find herself cabbed-up with some hulking lorry driver who was looking for a quick lay.

'I'll have to go home soon to see how Molly is. She was going to telephone my other daughter and one or two relations Alison might have gone to... but she'd have sent a message through for me if there had been any news.' He rubbed his hands over his face, feeling tired and baffled. A constable came in with the drink he had been sent to get from the machine in the bottom corridor, and Quantrill sat down heavily at his desk and reached for the beaker. The liquid was grey, which meant tea; coffee would have been brown, tomato soup orange. They all tasted much the same, warm, wet and powdery.

He took a dispirited swallow. 'It's not just that I'm anxious about Alison,' he said, 'though God knows I am, even though I keep telling myself not to exaggerate. But I felt so sure that she'd be able to tell us enough about Jasmine Woods's private life to lead us to the murderer—and now we're working blind again.'

'Not quite. There's the ex-husband, don't forget: Robert John Potter, who lived in Chelmsford at the time of the divorce. He could have moved away, of course, but the Essex police have found me three R.J. Potters living in the area. I'll go down there first thing, and see if I can find him. All right, sir?'

Quantrill nodded, glancing through a report that had

been left on his desk. A lucky constable had been sent on an extended pub crawl, following the route that Paul Pardoe alleged he had taken between Newmarket and Yarchester the previous evening. Each landlord had been able to confirm that Pardoe had called, and had sat alone with a drink and a Sunday newspaper, but no one could be positive about the timing of his visits. One of the pubs, the Rose and Thorn at Dodmansford, which he had visited somewhere between eight and nine o'clock, was only a fifteen-minute drive from Thirling.

The Chief Inspector passed the report to his sergeant. 'Pardoe had the opportunity, then,' he said. 'So did George Hussey, so did Gilbert Smith—all right, so did Jonathan Elliott. Let's hope that by tomorrow forensic will have found something definite for us to work on. That's the trouble with murder, it's mostly done by amateurs. Criminal records and informers are no use to us at all. No word from Yarchester about Smith, I suppose?'

'He seems to have covered his tracks pretty well, but the drug squad boys are still busy. I had another look at Jasmine's address book, by the way, but there are a hell of a lot of names in it, and no indication of priorities. And she was too discreet to keep private letters, unfortunately, so it'll take us a long time to work through the book, looking for lovers.'

Quantrill scratched his unshaven chin. 'It's Alison we need to help us,' he said. 'She's the one person who knows enough about Jasmine Woods to give us a lead.' He leaned back to swallow the last of the contents of his beaker, and then suddenly sat up, crushing the waxed cardboard in his large square hands.

'Hold hard—there was another girl I met at the party. She arrived just as I was leaving, so you wouldn't have seen her. Jasmine Woods's former secretary—she'd worked at Yeoman's for a couple of years, so she could probably tell us as much as Alison. More, perhaps. A pretty girl, Anne somebody. She'd just got engaged to a farmer, and she was showing him off. She said he lived somewhere in Norfolk, and that she was staying with him and his parents until the wedding. His name was—'

The Chief Inspector screwed up his face in an effort of memory, but his brains had furred over with weariness.

'—damned if I can remember. I can see the man well enough: prosperous young farmer, big and going bald early. Completely bowled over by the girl, though I wouldn't have said she was the country type. Anyway, I'll get them traced and go and have a word with her tomorrow, while you find the ex-husband. I don't know what you intend to do in the meantime, but I'm going to get some sleep.'

Chance, he knew, would be a fine thing; but then, Molly had had a distressing day and it would be unreasonable to hope that she would not be waiting for him. As soon as he opened the door she came hurrying, dressing-gowned in quilted nylon but not yet curlered.

'Did you get the right man?' she asked. 'Have you caught the murderer?'

'Well, no, it wasn't the man I thought. But the one we really want to interview is somewhere in Yarchester—his motor bike was found abandoned there this morning, so there's no need to worry about him as far as Alison's concerned.'

'But are you sure she didn't go to Yarchester? Have you found out where she went?'

'Not so far,' said her husband, trying to make it sound like good news, 'but Martin Tait's got the enquiries organized, and the station sergeant will let me know as soon as my information comes through. Did you manage to speak to Jennifer?'

Molly nodded, her face wretched. 'Jennifer was on duty, that's why I couldn't get through to her earlier. She hadn't seen or heard anything of Alison, but of course she'll ring back as soon as she does. *If* she does. The same goes for everybody else I've rung—everybody, even old Aunt Enid in Frinton . . .' She gave her husband a watery smile of apology. 'Oh, Douggie, I'm afraid we're going to have a huge phone bill.'

Quantrill himself rarely used the telephone for social purposes and was given to grumbling over the number and length of his wife's calls, forgetting how much time she had to spend alone because of his job. He was touched and slightly ashamed that, at a time like this, she should feel it necessary to apologize.

He put his arm round her shoulders. 'That's all right, my

dear,' he said gruffly. 'That's what the telephone's for—I'm only sorry that I had to go off and leave you. Have you been to bed?'

'I couldn't, I was too jumpy.' She looked up at him with beseeching eyes. 'You are staying now, aren't you? You haven't got to go out again tonight?'

He gave her shoulder a reassuring pat before taking away his arm. 'There's nothing useful I can do at the moment. I'm simply waiting for information of one sort or another, and I can just as well do that here with you. I need to be off early in the morning, if not before, so I thought I'd have a bath and a shave now.'

'Would you like me to get you something to eat?'

'No, thanks, I had supper.' Molly would hardly approve of his illicit intake of fatty potato chips, and so he made for the stairs before she could ask him to elaborate. 'You go to bed,' he said over his shoulder, 'you've got a telephone there, so there's no point in sitting up.'

Molly was not in bed when he emerged from the bathroom, but she came upstairs almost immediately, carrying a tray of tea. Quantrill had been thinking, in the bath, in terms of sneaking downstairs to quench his thirst with a can of beer, and then tiptoeing to bed for a few hours' sleep, but his wife was obviously in need of his company. He kicked off his slippers, got in beside her and took the cup she offered. She looked more relaxed now; so relieved by his presence that he hadn't the heart to point out that it was after one o'clock in the morning and he'd had a hard day.

'What's this?' he teased her, watching her open a packet of his favorite gingernuts. 'You know you hate crumbs in bed—and besides, I thought I was supposed to be off biscuits.'

She looked slightly sheepish. 'It won't hurt you, just this once.' Then she stared at him anxiously over the rim of her cup. 'What do you honestly think, Douggie? Where would Alison have gone? Will she be all right?'

He said everything he could think of to reassure her, drinking tea and absentmindedly munching half a packet of biscuits while he explained why it was totally unlikely that their daughter would be of any interest to whoever had murdered Jasmine Woods. Murderers, he explained to his wife patiently, were very rarely monsters. Most of the time they turned out to be perfectly ordinary men and women who had lived perfectly ordinary and blameless lives until something temporarily unbalanced them. The chances were that Jasmine Woods's murderer was now in bed at home, sick with guilt and horror over what he had done. The last thing he would want to do would be to add to his wretchedness by harming anyone else.

It sounded so convincing in his own ears that Quantrill might have believed it himself, if it were not for the way this murderer had used his victim.

'But if Alison's all right, why doesn't she get in touch?' objected Molly. 'It's not like her to be so inconsiderate—she's always been more thoughtful than Jennifer in that way; she'd know perfectly well how worried we are. She needn't tell us where she is, as long as she just lets us know that she's all right . . . if she *is* all right . . .'

She began to weep. Quantrill put the tea tray on the floor, hitched himself closer and put his arm round her. 'Of course Alison's all right. Of course she is. It's only natural that she was upset, but I'm sure she's safe and well somewhere.'

Molly leaned against him, rubbing her wet eyes with the heel of her hand.

'It was all my fault,' she mourned. 'I said she'd *have* to talk to you about it, whether she wanted to or not, and that was what really upset her. I can see that now.' Her body tensed. 'I—I was only trying to help, trying to reason with her, but all I did was to drive her away . . .'

Quantrill held his wife more tightly, trying to soothe her. 'No, it wasn't your fault! Good grief, it was mine if it was anybody's—I knew perfectly well how distressed she was, and I should have had more sense than to expect her to be prepared to talk. I should never have mentioned it.'

He felt a dampness against his chest as her tears soaked into his striped pyjama jacket, and he used his free hand to pull a handkerchief from the pocket and mop up a tear that was sliding down her cheek in the same direction. 'Don't cry anymore, Molly-mouse,' he said, reviving a foolish endearment that he hadn't used for years. 'Alison'll be all right, truly. She needs time and quiet to get over the shock, that's all. She's always had an independent streak. Don't you remember that year we went on holiday to Lowestoft—'

He held her close, playing verbal Happy Families: *Do*

you remember, don't you remember, wasn't it funny/awful when we . . . ?

Gradually, Molly began to relax. Her fingers stopped plucking restlessly at the biscuit crumbs on the turned-over top sheet, and she burrowed her head into his shoulder as she used to do years ago. She rested one hand confidingly on his stomach, and he stroked her soft fine hair and traced her profile with the tip of his forefinger. 'We ought to do this more often,' he thought guiltily, wearily; 'we ought to have more togetherness.' It was a sadness he'd observed in his job, the way it could take a tragedy in a family to bring its members together. Except that, please God, Alison's disappearance was no tragedy—

'Hey, do you know what I had for supper?' he boasted lazily. 'A large helping of Cliffie Hammond's fish and chips!'

Molly snuggled even closer. 'Oh, Douggie—' she reprimanded him with a sleepy giggle, 'and you a chief inspector!'

'Even chief inspectors are human,' he murmured, rubbing his cheek against her hair. He would have liked to demonstrate the fact, but he had the wit to know this was the wrong time. The approach was right, though, he remembered; this was how Molly liked it. This same gentle approach, and a happier occasion, and it might once more be possible to get the desired response.

He switched off his bedside light and lay in the dark, feeling her warm and soft against him. He was still a long way from solving the murder, and it seemed that he'd managed to drive his daughter away from home; but it began to look as though he might, with luck, have started a major repair job on his marriage.

22

Later, Quantrill woke with indigestion. He tossed and muttered, then slept heavily, right through the alarm. He got up in a rush, hollered at Peter for being in the bathroom when he wanted to use it, snapped at his wife for not rousing him earlier, and scalded the roof of his mouth with hot tea. It was a bad way to start the morning. But he took time, before he left the house, to give Molly the reassurance she needed; for himself, he found little enough to be optimistic about.

The route from Benidorm Avenue to Divisional Headquarters took him past one of the town's saleyards, where an old, established firm of auctioneers held a livestock market every Tuesday and Friday. The market always included entries of fat cattle, rabbits and poultry, but the biggest attraction, especially on the first Tuesday in every month, was pigs. There would be anything up to a thousand of them, the quality breeding-sows travelling to Breckham in the comparative comfort and exclusiveness of netted trailers, while the young stores and the fat pigs for slaughter were jostled there in three-tiered cattle trucks. By the time Quantrill passed the saleyard that morning it was after nine o'clock and the pigs had long since been unloaded and penned, but the farmers and butchers who converged on Breckham livestock market from all over the region were still arriving.

The Chief Inspector slowed his car, irritated that he had allowed himself to be caught in the traffic that inevitably built up near the entrance. He sat drumming his fingers on the steering wheel, seeing but paying little attention to the people who emerged from the neighbouring car park and walked the twenty yards or so down the road to the saleyard. To find Jasmine Woods's killer, he had to investigate her private life; to do that he needed to talk to her former secretary, Anne. To find Anne, who was staying with her husband-to-be and his parents, he had to remember, or find someone who had been at the party and would remember, the fiancé's name.

It was no great coincidence that he should, in those few minutes while his car was held up, catch sight of the man himself; after all, the fiancé was a farmer. But Quantrill had not expected to see him, and he was too slow to call out to him before the man disappeared. And then, what can you call out with civility to someone whose name you can't remember? Quantrill parked his own car and hurried after him.

Although the man was wearing the uniform of the affluent young farmer, a green Husky jacket and a flat cap set well to the front of his head, he was taller than average and Quantrill was able to pick him out without too much difficulty. He was, however, among a crowd of pig-fanciers on the far side of one of the pens.

'Ah, Wilfred—just the man I want to consult.' Quantrill put a hand on the shoulder of a passing stockyard attendant, a short man in a grubby long white coat who wore his flat cap, unfashionably but practically, well down on the back of his head. His cheerful snub-nosed face was so weather-worn that he might have been any age between thirty and sixty.

'Wheey-up, Mr Quantrill,' cried the stockman, raising the knob of his stick in salute. Some years previously he had provided information that had helped Quantrill, then a sergeant, to trace some stolen heifers, and he had greeted the detective like an old colleague ever since. 'Setting up in farming now, eh? You won't go far wrong with these sows— grand little Welsh cross Large Whites, in pig to a Welsh boar. They'll fetch a hundred quid apiece, and worth every penny.'

'I'll start saving,' promised Quantrill. 'Do you know that man over there, Wilfred? The big dark chap leaning on the rail and looking as though he hates the sight of pigs. I met him not long ago and I'd like a quick word with him now, but I'm hanged if I can remember his name.'

'Why, that's Mr Oliver Buxton. He farms in Norfolk, at Littleover. One of our regulars, just like his father afore him—they keep pigs in a big way. If he wasn't here to buy and sell pigs on the first Tuesday in every month, I'd know the world was coming to an end. Mind you, I daresay he'll be arriving a bit later in the mornings in future. I hear he's getting married at Easter.' The stockman gave Quantrill a wink and a nudge. "Wheey-up! I reckon he'll have picked hisself a goer!'

'I shouldn't be surprised,' Quantrill agreed. Privately, though, from what he could remember of Buxton's fiancée, he doubted it; she had seemed too fine-drawn to have the stamina the stockman evidently envisaged. 'Well, thanks for your help. I only wanted to know where he lived, and I'm in a hurry, so you've saved me from pushing my way round to ask him.' Have one on me when you're in the Crown.'

The stockman pocketed the price of a pint that the Chief

Inspector slipped him. 'Much obliged, Mr Quantrill, sir. I doubt you'd have got a civil reply from him, anyhow. I spoke to him not five minutes ago. "Morning, Mr Buxton," I said, "a grand pen of breeders we've got here," but he walked straight past me with a face as black as your hat. Never a word, and that's not like him at all. But, then, if he's getting married Saturday, I daresay he's got more on his mind than pigs, eh? Wheey-up, eh, Mr Quantrill?'

The stockman gave the Chief Inspector a parting nudge, flourished his stick and moved away to prod some squealing, reluctant baconers into the sale ring. Quantrill lingered for a moment, looking across at Buxton, who was still leaning, dark-browed, on a rail and paying no attention to the sows in front of him. There was nothing at all of the happy prospective bridegroom about his looks and bearing.

But Quantrill found that entirely explicable. Cause and effect, he thought; getting married is, after all, a hell of an undertaking for any young man. He himself had been worried sick. He'd have given anything, in the week beforehand, to call his own wedding off.

If he had the time now, and if the pubs were open, he would have offered to buy Buxton a drink to cheer him up. He could tell him about the things that compensated for the loss of freedom: children, for example . . .

Alison—

He ran for his car. He had been out of contact with Divisional Headquarters for all of ten minutes, and in that time there might well have been some news of her. He was within a quarter of a mile of the office but, too anxious to wait, he radioed through.

There was still no news of his daughter.

Sergeant Tait was on the road early in search of Jasmine Woods's ex-husband, weaving his Citroën through the Suffolk lanes while the sprouting hedgerows looked grey rather than green, and the only other vehicles on the move were mail delivery vans and milk tankers making bulk collections from farms. By seven o'clock he had reached the first of the three addresses provided by the Essex police; but R. J. Potter who lived in the prosperous-looking bungalow was not Robert John but Ronald James, a self-employed long-distance haulier who was, his wife estimated crossly, probably at that moment obliging a belly-dancer in Istanbul while she was stuck in Chelmsford with the kids.

At the second address, a maisonette in Witham, the door was opened by a man who agreed that he was Robert Potter. A pyjama'd and toothless seventy-odd, he was understandably puzzled and indignant at being disturbed so early in the morning. Behind him hovered an equally elderly wife, clutching a teapot to the bosom of her flannel dressing-gown with such protective closeness that Tait concluded that it must contain either life savings or very cool tea. He apologized handsomely for having come to the wrong house, and retreated in a hurry.

By the time he approached the third address, in the breezy blackcurrant and strawberry-growing flatlands north of the Blackwater estuary, he had begun to give up hope of finding his man in Essex. Robert John Potter might well have moved several times in the nine or ten years since his divorce from Jasmine Woods; he might have left the country; he might be dead.

Tait found the address, a small modern detached house in a maze of small modern detached houses that had almost entirely obliterated the Essex village which gave them their identity. His ring was answered by a bespectacled young woman in jeans and a shiny apron that advertised a long-defunct brand of cocoa. She had short straight fair hair, a plain open face and an instantly aggressive manner.

'Robert John Potter—yes, that's my husband. But if you're from his union, you can go to blazes. He voted to call off the strike because he's fed to the teeth with being off work and because we need every penny he can earn, and you needn't think you can talk him into changing his mind. It's outrageous that men who want to work should be prevented from doing so just because a few troublemakers—'

'I'm *not* from any union,' insisted Tait. They both had to raise their voices to be heard above the morning noises from inside the house: children squabbling, excited yelps from a dog, light music and blarneying chat from a radio, and the whirring of a washing machine. 'I'm—'

But as soon as she knew what he was not, her manner softened. 'Phew, that's a relief. I can't be doing with shop stewards on the doorstep at this hour of the morning.' Then she flinched as the crash of something falling or breaking augmented the domestic symphony. 'Oh, Lord—look, come in, whoever you are, while I go and sort somebody out.'

The small metal and glass front porch led straight to an untidy sitting-room, from which rose an open staircase. The room had originally been furnished in young executive style, with teak-look wall units and a low-slung suite upholstered in striped tweed, but it was now shabby after years of being gambolled over by children and pets. It was strikingly different from Jasmine Woods's gracious-life sitting-room at Yeoman's.

'Bob!' bawled his wife up the stairs as she rushed for the kitchen. 'Someone to see you!'

The man who came blundering down was large and blond and healthy, with the chunky, homespun good looks of the men who model sweaters for the covers of knitting patterns. Too unsophisticated to be Jasmine Woods's type, Tait thought—presumably that was one of the factors that had driven them apart—but personable enough to make their marriage understandable. He couldn't have chosen a more different second wife. This one was undoubtedly loyal, but otherwise not even in the same league as Jasmine.

Potter looked at his visitor suspiciously. 'Are you from the union?' he demanded.

'Your wife would never have let a union official in. My name's Tait, I'm a detective sergeant from Breckham Market. I'm investigating—'

He paused. His sharp, restless eyes had noticed, among a litter of children's comics and do-it-yourself magazines on the coffee table, a copy of the previous month's *House and Owner*. He recognized the cover of the issue that Jasmine had shown him when he first visited her.

'You're Jasmine Woods's ex-husband? You've probably heard that she's been murdered.'

Potter nodded, compressing his lips into a straight line.

Tait picked up the magazine and flicked it open. So Potter had recently been brought up to date about his first wife's success; and the article had told him, within a few miles, where she lived. It must have been galling for the man, who was evidently short of money, to read about Jasmine's affluence. It must have been tantalizing for him to see photographs of the strikingly attractive woman he had once been married to.

Potter certainly had a motive, for robbery and for rape if not for murder. And as the DCI was fond of pointing out, violence fuels itself and can turn to murder all too easily.

Tait glanced at one of the photographs in which Jasmine was posed elegantly on the sofa behind which, several weeks later, her body had been found. 'A good-looking woman, wasn't she?' he said, deliberately needling Potter to see how the man would react. 'I knew her well—we were friends. Close friends, you might say.' He smiled reminiscently over the photograph. 'She had a beautiful body . . . but, then, I expect you remember that, don't you?'

An angry, strangled noise rose in Potter's throat. He took a menacing step towards the sergeant and raised his hands. His face was pale, his eyes staring.

Tait backed away, suddenly alarmed by the realization that he had pushed the man too far. *God*, he thought, remembering the violence with which Jasmine had been murdered and measuring himself disadvantageously against her former husband, *what an idiot I was to bait the man when I'm here alone!* He tried to shift unobtrusively towards the door, and at the same time remember what he had learned, and had so far had no opportunity to put into practice, about unarmed combat. Was it better to run, and live to be a prudent chief constable, or to die an heroic sergeant?

Potter made a grab. Tait ducked, dropping the magazine, and vaulted over an armchair, putting it between himself and his assailant. Then he straightened, and took a deep breath. Potter hadn't harmed his wife and family, and the chances were that he wouldn't resort to violence in his own home. Tait decided to arrest him now, and call in the local police immediately for support. He stepped forward resolutely, and put out a hand to make the mandatory arresting contact. 'Robert John Potter—' he began.

But he missed, because Potter was in the process of bending to pick up the magazine, smooth out the pages and replace it on the coffee table.

'I'm sorry,' the man mumbled awkwardly. 'I shouldn't have snatched at the magazine like that. Hell, I've been divorced from her for nearly ten years, so your relationship with her is none of my business.' He moved an Action Man toy from a chair, sat down and blew his nose. His eyes had blurred over with tears, and he wiped them shamefacedly. 'The fact is that I've been distressed by her death, though I tried not to let on to Jill when we saw the news on regional television last night. So when I saw you looking at Jasmine's photographs, and heard you talking about her like that, I felt that I couldn't stand for it. When you know that a woman you once loved has been murdered, you don't want her to be sullied any further.'

Tait's adrenaline had ebbed, leaving him limp. He sat down abruptly opposite Potter. 'If it's any consolation to you, I didn't sully Jasmine,' he confessed. 'I knew her slightly, and I liked her and admired her, but I didn't get anywhere near her. That was only wishful thinking.'

Potter nodded. 'A lot of the men we knew used to indulge in that. It was the same with me, sometimes. She looked a lot sexier than she was.'

They exchanged wry grins, and then two fair chunky little boys rushed in from the kitchen to kiss their father good-bye before they went to school. Potter's face lightened immediately. He tousled their hair, went with them to the front door, meekly accepted his wife's rebuke for messing up their hair just after she had brushed it, and waved them out of sight.

'Come and have some breakfast,' he said to Tait when they had gone. 'If you've driven down from Suffolk, you must be hungry.'

Jill Potter smiled hospitably as the sergeant, embarrassed into silence, entered the kitchen. It was a small room crowded with scuffed electrical appliances on which were piled clothes in various stages of the laundering process. On the Formica-covered table were the remains of the boys' boiled eggs, a tangle of small damp socks and a bulky carton of washing powder. There were just two slices of streaky bacon in the pan that Mrs Potter was holding; she herself appeared to be breakfasting from a mug of coffee.

'Bacon?' she offered. 'Do have this if you'd like it. I can easily cook some more for Bob.'

Tait assured her untruthfully that he had already eaten

on the way down, but he accepted the coffee. Potter made it, with boiling water and a spoonful of a cheap blend of powdered coffee and chicory. 'Milk and sugar?' he enquired, offering Tait a bottle of one and a bag of the other. The men squeezed together side by side on the narrow bench at the table. 'Sergeant Tait came down to tell me about Jasmine,' he explained to his wife.

Jill's face clouded. 'Yes—poor woman, what a terrible thing to happen.' She paused in the act of feeding the washing machine with dirty clothes, and went slightly pink. 'It probably sounds odd, but I've always felt that she was part of the family, in a way. I'm rather proud of the connection. I borrowed a *House and Owner* from a friend last week because there was a feature about Jasmine in it. I was a fan of hers before I met Bob, and I simply couldn't believe that he seriously wanted to marry me after being married to a woman like her...'

Potter looked up from his bacon and gave his wife a fond, totally committed smile. 'Jasmine could never be bothered to learn how to make good Yorkshire pudding,' he said.

'Yes, but still...with her looks and her money...' Jill Potter returned her husband's glance, half questioning, half teasing, steadfastly affectionate. And then her smile vanished and she turned aggressively to Tait.

'*That's* why you're here, isn't it?' she demanded. 'Not to tell Bob that Jasmine is dead, but to find out whether he killed her. He's one of your suspects, isn't he?'

Tait put down his mug. 'We have to make routine enquiries,' he agreed.

'I suppose you do,' said Potter. His wife began to say something indignant, but he interrupted her. 'It's understandable, Jill, and we've got nothing to hide. If you want me to account for my movements, I took young Mark to the dentist yesterday morning, and in the afternoon we went round to Jill's mother's.'

She snatched his empty plate with an angry burst of energy and then stood behind him, pressing the other hand on his shoulder. 'Bob's the last person in the world who would hurt anyone,' she protested. 'It's unthinkable! Oh, you can check what we were doing yesterday, I can give you the addresses, but you'll just be wasting your time.'

'What about the night before?' asked Tait. 'What were you doing on Sunday evening?'

Husband and wife looked at each other uncertainly. Potter scratched his blond head. 'Well . . . nothing I can prove to you. We were here, at home—we haven't any money to spare for outings while I'm on strike. I'd gardened most of the day, and I had a stiff back, so I was glad to put my feet up in the evening. We all watched the children's television serial, and then we had supper and put the boys to bed. Then Mark woke, crying with toothache, and then the dog threw up at the foot of the stairs . . . just a perfectly ordinary family sort of evening.'

Sergeant Tait thanked them for the coffee, and said good-bye to Jill Potter. Her husband accompanied the detective to the front door.

'Am I really under suspicion?' he asked.

'We always keep an open mind until a case is wrapped up, but if your conscience is clear, you needn't lose any sleep over it,' said Tait. 'Tell me, have you seen Jasmine since your divorce? Or kept in touch with her in any way?'

Potter shook his head. 'We'd drifted apart completely long before the divorce came through. We married too young, that was the trouble—we loved each other, but we hadn't enough in common to make a good marriage. I wanted a family, and Jasmine didn't. And then she started writing books, and she began to withdraw from me. In the end I felt that her fiction gave her more satisfaction than I did.' He hesitated. 'Did she marry again?'

'No. I don't think she was really the marrying kind.'

'That was probably our trouble,' Potter agreed. He looked Tait over. 'Are you married yourself?'

'Not yet.' The sergeant's disapproving glance took in the chipped and fingermarked paintwork of the doors, the domestic clutter, the stain on the carpet at the foot of the stairs. His visit to the Potters had reinforced his intention not to marry before he could support a family in a more spacious style; and he certainly intended to find himself a more decorative wife than Bob Potter had settled for.

But Potter, his composure completely regained, was smiling with contentment. 'I can recommend it,' he said.

'There's nothing to beat married life—as long as you can find yourself a wife like Jill rather than Jasmine.'

Looking back at the house as he got into his car, Tait saw that Jill Potter had joined her husband on the front step. They stood for a moment with their arms round each other, and then they turned and went inside and closed the door. Tait, his hand raised in a farewell gesture that they hadn't noticed, had an unaccustomed sensation of being excluded.

23

'Frankly, sir,' said WPC Hopkins firmly, 'if this trip's going to land any more two-year-old dribblers on my lap, I'd rather you took someone else.'

Chief Inspector Quantrill assured her that Oliver Buxton's fiancée was unlikely to have acquired a child of any age during the preceding six weeks. 'But from what little I saw of the girl at Jasmine Woods's party, she seemed very highly strung. She's probably het-up anyway, with her wedding in the offing, and she's bound to be very distressed about the murder. She may be reluctant to talk about her former employer at all, and she'll certainly prefer to talk to another woman rather than to me.'

Patsy Hopkins agreed. It was a sunny, windy morning, and a drive into Norfolk in civilian clothes with Douglas Quantrill was a much pleasanter prospect than a routine patrol round Breckham with spotty young PC Fowler, looking for any trouble that might be brewing in the London overspill estates that circled the old town.

'No news of your daughter?' she asked as they crossed the river boundary between Suffolk and Norfolk.

'None at all,' said Quantrill gloomily. That was one of the reasons why he had sought Patsy Hopkins's company. The relentless optimism that he felt obliged to display to his wife was very wearing, and he needed to be able to talk honestly to someone who was sympathetic but not emotionally involved. 'I'm worried as hell, Patsy, I don't mind telling you.' He rehearsed his fears to her. 'Any suggestions?' he begged. 'Any ideas?'

'I did wonder whether Alison might have got to know someone in Thirling during the time she worked at Yeoman's—someone she liked and might go to if she wanted to hide. For instance, did Jasmine Woods have any domestic help?'

'Yes, a Mrs Fornice Pearce. The boys doing house-to-house enquiries unearthed her—she accounts for a lot of the fingerprints at Yeoman's. Sergeant Tait interviewed her yesterday: a widowed pensioner, rather deaf. She worked three mornings a week at Yeoman's, and was last there on Friday. She wasn't able to give him any useful information as far as the murder's concerned, and I don't recall Alison ever mentioning her, so I doubt she'd go there. But it's worth a try. Anything's worth a try. We'll do another house-to-house at Thirling.' Quantrill was about to radio an instruction to the incident-room when a personal call came through to him from the station sergeant at Divisional Headquarters.

'We've just had some information about your daughter, sir.'

Quantrill did a copy-book emergency stop. 'Yes?'

'A girl answering her description and carrying a small suitcase was picked up by a private hire-car in Breckham market place at about ten last night. She'd rung for the car from a call-box, saying that she wanted to go to Yarchester. The driver said she seemed upset—she hardly spoke on the journey, and he thought that she was crying. She asked him to drop her in Horsefair Street, at the castle end. He asked if she'd be all right, but she seemed to have pulled herself together by that time. She said that she was going to visit a friend, and he saw her go to a public telephone as he was driving off. That would have been at about half-past ten, he thinks.'

Quantrill thanked him, eased his car further into the side of the country road and then sat silent, rubbing his chin. His instinct was to turn the car and head for Yarchester in search of his daughter, but his sense of discipline restrained him. He was, after all, busy with a murder investigation; and if Alison had gone to Yarchester to visit a friend, there was no reason to be concerned for her safety.

'She must be all right, then,' said WPC Hopkins, echoing his thoughts. 'At least you can be sure that there wasn't anyone lurking round your house, trying to silence her. You know for sure that she hasn't been abducted or tried to hitch a lift, and that she hasn't done anything silly like jumping in the river. Panic over, wouldn't you say?'

Quantrill relaxed. He smiled at her. 'You're right, Patsy. I must find her, of course—quite apart from wanting to know where she is, I need to talk to her about what she saw at Yeoman's yesterday morning. But there's no point in my going blundering about looking for her. The Yarchester boys can do that—though if they make as much of a success of it as they have of finding Gilbert Smith . . .'

He turned gloomy again. Smith was still, in default of evidence pointing to anyone else, the number one suspect. If he had any connection with the murder, and if Alison—who might well know where to find him—had gone to Yarchester to join him, thinking of him as a friend, she could be walking right into danger instead of out of it.

The Chief Inspector radioed instructions from his car to Divisional Headquarters. Someone—preferably WPC Beth Knowles—was to visit Mrs Quantrill immediately to tell her that Alison had gone to Yarchester the previous evening to stay with one of her friends; and Mrs Quantrill was to be asked to suggest the names and addresses of anyone she knew, or thought Alison might know, living in or near the city. This information was to be passed straight to Detective Inspector Carrow of the Yarchester division, who would be expecting it. Mrs Quantrill was not, repeat not, on any account to be allowed to think that there was any further anxiety over their daughter's safety.

Quantrill then got through to Yarchester and spoke at some length to John Carrow, with whom he'd once been a sergeant. Afterwards, satisfied that he had done everything he could to find his daughter, he restarted the car. They were in foreign territory and WPC Hopkins sat patiently with her forefinger on an ordnance survey map.

'Right, Patsy. How far to Oliver Buxton's farm?'

'Ten or twelve miles.' She looked about her disparagingly

as they moved off. 'Real prairie farming country round here, isn't it?'

They had left behind the undulating countryside and the woods and hedges of Suffolk and were now in bleaker arable country. The land was flatter and there were fewer trees. The pretty colour-washed plaster and thatch of old Suffolk houses had been replaced by Norfolk brick and flint and pantiles. Being flatter, the land could more easily be worked by machinery; and once the giant machines were in the fields, such hedges and trees as there were became an uneconomic nuisance to progressive farmers, who set about removing them. Farming is, after all, an industry. The countryside is the source of food, not a picturesque leisure area.

'They don't waste an inch of it, do they?' agreed Quantrill, looking about him at the hedgeless, ditchless, almost treeless acres of green winter barley, already ankle-high, growing as close to the sides of the road as the machines could drill it.

The surroundings of the farm he had come to visit were bleak. It was isolated, but clearly visible from its nearest neighbour half a mile away because the intervening hedges had been removed. Spring corn had been sown and the green shoots were beginning to emerge patchily from the drilled lines of brown tilth, giving the fields a threadbare look. The plain, substantial early nineteenth-century brick farmhouse would formerly have been sheltered by an attractive and practical windbreak of oaks or elms, but the erection of prefabricated metal-framed farm buildings close to the house had made natural windbreaks superfluous, and so the trees had been cut down.

The minor road from the nearest village ran within two hundred yards of the farm, which was served by a flat dirt lane. The only objects left standing by the roadside were the telegraph poles, and on the pole next to the lane was nailed a board which read *P.J. Buxton and Son High House Farm No Representatives Except by Written Appointment*.

'Charming,' murmured Patsy Hopkins. 'Imagine what it's like to live here in the middle of winter, when they're up to their knees in mud . . . The girl we're going to see, Anne Downing, is engaged to the son, is that it?'

'Getting married at Easter, so she said when I met her at Jasmine Woods's party.'

'The wedding will be this coming Saturday, then, I suppose. Well, if she's been staying here with his family, at least she knows what she's letting herself in for.'

The car bumped past a long range of windowless sheds that were topped by ventilation cowls. Further progress towards the house was blocked by a high-sided lorry discharging animal feed into a hopper at one end of the shed, and so Quantrill stopped the car and they got out. The stench of pigs was immediately so strong that Patsy clapped her handkerchief over her nose. They hurried towards the house, both of them ducking their heads as though against a storm.

'Good grief,' gasped Patsy, 'rather Anne Downing than me!'

Quantrill raised his head. They had rounded the end of the sheds and were now upwind of the smell, though they could still taste it in the air. 'Oh, I don't know,' he said fairly. 'Buxton seemed to be a very decent sort of fellow. I daresay he'll make her a good husband. And they're not necessarily going to live here after they're married.'

'I should hope not. Honestly—just imagine having *that* beside the lane leading to your front door.'

That was what looked like a deep man-made farmyard pond with a black plastic lining. There were, however, no peacefully paddling ducks. The contents of the pond, almost as black as the lining, glistened and stank.

'It's a slurry pit,' said Quantrill, steering his companion past it. 'There must be a few hundred pigs in those rearing sheds, and their muck has to be hosed into pits for storage until it can be pumped out and sprayed on the land.'

'Yuk!' said WPC Hopkins, a town-bred girl whose father was deputy chief finance officer to the Breckham Market district council.

Quantrill laughed. 'Well, that's modern farming. I can't say that I admire it, but then I lived next to a proper, old-fashioned farm when I was a boy. I loved the place. I used to spend hours round there, getting in the way. The carting was done by horses, and the cows were milked by hand, and the pigs lived in a sty. There was no slurry in those days because all the animals were bedded on straw. There were ricks of straw as high as houses in the yard, and the hens scratched about and laid their eggs wherever they fancied...'

He was silent for a moment, savouring past pleasures: climbing trees, damming the brook, driving the cows to and from their pasture, riding on cart-horses, swinging from beams in the great timbered barn; and forever meddling with the few bits of farm machinery. He recalled with a grin the farmer's threatening bellow when that long-suffering man discovered yet another of young Douglas's misdemeanours: *'Come you out of there, booy, and git on hoom, do I'll tell your faather—'*

'It sounds like a picture-book farm,' said Patsy Hopkins. 'Lovely.'

'Lovely for kids, but not if you had to make a living from it,' said Quantrill. 'All that straw and muck had to be cleared out and heaped in the yard, and then carted to the fields and spread by manpower. It took a lot of men, and their wages were rock-bottom. There wasn't any money in farming then, and the farmers themselves were nearly bankrupt. Thinking back, that farm was a poor, tumbledown place; a hard way of life. But it certainly did look and smell a lot pleasanter than this.'

He glanced sideways at WPC Hopkins, who was wearing a fetching pink raincoat over her uniform shirt and skirt, with a pink and green silk scarf at her throat. 'Not,' he added, 'that it was so very long ago. It's just that there have been big changes in farming in the last thirty years. I'm not *that* old.'

'I never thought you were,' she said.

They had passed the slurry pit, and a shed like an aircraft hangar that contained a good deal of large and expensive agricultural machinery, as well as a pick-up truck, a Rover saloon and a Lotus sports car. Ahead of them was the farmhouse, separated from the yard by a low wall and an area of gravel ornamented by a few tubs of polyanthus. The front door had an unused look about it, and so they followed the cement path round to the side of the house. From there, the view was of fifty acres of emergent sugar beet, drilled almost up to the edge of the cement.

Just as they rounded the corner of the garden wall a black labrador dog rushed up behind them, barking. WPC Hopkins—who was unworried when her police duties required her to cope with disaffected people, but who didn't care for dogs—stepped smartly behind the Chief Inspector.

He turned and saw Oliver Buxton approaching from the piggeries. The farmer could not have spent more than an hour at the saleyard at Breckham Market before returning home, exchanging his shoes for Wellington boots, and getting on with his job.

Buxton called the dog off, but his attitude was as unwelcoming as the labrador's. 'Yes?' he said curtly, striding towards them. 'There's a notice up by the road. If you've come on business—'

'We haven't,' said Quantrill. "I was hoping to have a word with Miss Anne Downing, if she's in. You may not remember me, but we met just after you'd announced your engagement. My name's Quantrill. My daughter Alison took over your fiancée's—'

'No!' Buxton almost shouted the word. He turned away, his face dark with suppressed emotion. 'She's not my fiancée, and she's not here anymore. It's all off.'

Patsy Hopkins was not surprised. Buxton looked, as the Chief Inspector had said, a very decent sort of fellow: quite handsome, in a florid way, with his dark hair breaking out in thick curls behind his ears, below his tipped-forward cap. Presentable, four-square, prosperous. But—she moved closer to verify her first impression—despite the fact that he looked perfectly clean, apart from his boots, it wasn't only the farm that smelled of pigs.

'I'm very sorry to hear that,' said Quantrill, and his sympathy was genuine. He realized now that the fellow-feeling he had imagined with Buxton, when he watched the man in the saleyard, had been completely misplaced.

Buxton's look of dazed delight, at Jasmine Woods's party, had made it clear that he was deeply in love. Instead of the pre-marital depression that Quantrill had projected on him, the farmer was obviously suffering from badly damaged pride and an emotional savaging. Quantrill could see—could smell—Anne Downing's point of view, but his sympathies were undivided. 'Sorry to hear that,' he repeated.

Buxton nodded wretchedly and muttered something inaudible.

'Would you mind telling me where I can find Miss Downing?'

The man hunched his shoulders, burying his hands deep

in the pockets of his jacket. He had the attitude of a cornered bullock, bewildered and angry. 'How should I know? She took herself off, and I haven't heard from her since.'

'Does she have any family?'

'Her parents live abroad. There's an old great-aunt in Bishops Port, a Mrs Alfred Beckett. I suppose she... Anne... may be there.'

'Thanks, I'll try Bishops Port, then. Has she been gone long?'

Buxton's mouth twisted. 'Just a week before our wedding day—' He turned away and whistled to his dog.

'I see. Well, thanks for your help, Mr Buxton. And— er—good luck.'

The Chief Inspector and the policewoman walked silently to their car. 'Bloody women,' growled Quantrill as he switched on the ignition, protesting on behalf of the whole ill-used masculine sex.

WPC Hopkins, who knew better than to take it personally, forbore to comment.

She was map-reading Quantrill from the farm at Littleover towards Bishops Port, when the Chief Inspector was called up on the radio.

A report had come in from the forensic lab. Jasmine Woods's blood group was O, but some of the bloodstains on the carpet near her body belonged to another group, AB.

The bloodstains in Gilbert Smith's flat had also been analysed. Those on the clothes he had abandoned were O. Others, on the door handles and the washbasin, were AB.

24

A wayside pub was in sight, an old house with a brick crowstepped gable, nine miles from nowhere and appropriately named The World's End. It was trying to keep in business by tempting passing motorists with placards offering coffee and snacks rather than beer, and Quantrill pulled on to the deserted forecourt and sent Patsy Hopkins in for refreshments while he held a radio conference.

He was just hanging up the hand-mike when she brought a cup of coffee out to him.

'Thanks, Patsy.' He got out of the driving seat and leaned against the side of the car in the sharp April sunlight, feeling depressed. 'I know the information from forensic sounds useful, but it doesn't really tell us anything we didn't know.'

'Doesn't it? I thought it pointed to the murderer.'

'Possibly, but not necessarily. We know already that Gilbert Smith went up to Jasmine Woods's house before he bolted. It seems reasonable to assume that the AB bloodstains in his flat were his own, and therefore that the AB blood at the scene of the crime was his, too. But that still doesn't indicate whether or not he was the murderer. He might have seen some of Jasmine Woods's valuables on the floor, decided to steal them, and cut himself on the broken glass while he was scrabbling about trying to pick them up. He certainly went into the room where she was murdered, either at the time of the murder or the next morning, because there are some fragments of ivory on the sole of one of the bloodstained sneakers he left behind.'

'Couldn't forensic find anything that would definitely pin it on to Smith?'

'Not so far. What they did find, on the carpet where the body had been lying, were some cotton fibres. Forensic think that the fibres come from denims, cut by broken glass. But there aren't any cuts on the bloodstained jeans that Smith left when he bolted, and anyway the fibres don't match.'

Quantrill drained his cup. 'That doesn't let Smith out, though,' he went on. 'It's possible that he did the murder under the influence of drugs, and hid his blood-soaked clothes the following morning. We've got a couple of men digging up the compost heap at Yeoman's to see if they can find anything.'

Patsy Hopkins took the empty cup and saucer from the roof of the car, where Quantrill had parked them, and returned them to the pub. 'Are we going straight back to Breckham, sir?' she asked briskly.

But the Chief Inspector was still leaning against the car, arms folded. 'I also spoke to Chief Superintendent Mancroft, at Yarchester,' he said. 'He's going to issue a statement to the press, naming Smith as the man we want to interview and releasing a photofit picture. The Yarchester division are going all out to find Smith, so that's out of our hands. I talked to the Chief Super about Alison, too. There's no further news of her, and it begins to seem unlikely that she'll get in touch of her own accord. In view of her discovery of the body, and her connection with Smith, the Chief Super is taking her disappearance seriously. He's going to issue her photograph to the press, and an appeal for her either to telephone home or to contact the nearest police station. I wanted to go to Yarchester to try to find her, but he told me to stay on my own patch and get on with my own job...'

He looked up, desperately worried. 'It's the best thing, I suppose,' he reasoned with himself. 'Molly will be frantic when she sees Alison's photograph on television, but I can't sit at home holding her hand...I'll ring her from the next call-box we come to. There really isn't anything else I can do, except concentrate on this case.'

Patsy Hopkins had been listening patiently. 'Do you still want to talk to Anne Downing? I've been thinking—you said she's highly strung, so she's bound to be in a bad way. She'll have heard about the murder, because it made national news, and that on top of her broken engagement may be almost too much for her to take. If she's hysterical, we'll be wasting our time by going all the way to Bishops Port to try to talk to her.'

Quantrill slid into the driving seat. 'We'll go, anyway,' he said unsympathetically. 'The way I read it, she broke off her engagement herself so she must be pretty strong-minded. And it's months since she worked for Jasmine Woods, so there's no reason why she should be hysterical about that. Besides, I need information from her. I'm sure you'll be able to persuade her to talk to you, Patsy, whether she's upset or not.'

'Thanks a lot, sir,' said WPC Hopkins, resigning herself to a difficult interview. 'By the way,' she added crossly, 'that coffee was 25p a cup.'

'Highway robbery,' agreed the Chief Inspector.

* * *

As the policewoman had anticipated, Anne Downing was in a fragile state. It was with considerable reluctance that she agreed to see them, in the drawing-room of her great-aunt's Edwardian mock-Tudor villa on the outskirts of Bishops Port, overlooking a golf course and the distant estuary.

Quantrill remembered her from the party as slim, attractive and nervily vivacious. In the intervening six weeks she had lost weight, and now she looked much too thin and drawn. Her fair hair had lost its shine, her ringless hands played with each other incessantly, and her eyelids were swollen with crying. Having sympathized entirely with Buxton over the broken engagement, Quantrill could now see that the decision to break it must have cost Anne Downing a good deal. And the news of the murder of her friend and former employer must have distressed her almost as much as it had distressed Alison.

Wanting to play down the police angle, and not expecting the girl to remember him from the party, he used his daughter as a means of introduction.

'My name's Quantrill, and this is Miss Hopkins. You met my daughter Alison a few weeks ago, Miss Downing. She took over your old job at Yeoman's—'

'Oh. Oh, yes.' Anne Downing spoke dully, blinking hard. She turned aside and fumbled in a silver box for a cigarette, lighting it inexpertly. 'I remember her—a shy, dark girl. And I've seen the news item in the *Daily Press*. It said that she—Alison—found . . . found . . .'

She stood for a moment with her back to them, her head down and her shoulders braced in an effort to keep herself from crying. Then she raised her head and said unsteadily, 'How is your daughter?'

'Upset, of course. Very upset. She's gone to stay with some friends for a day or two. That's why I had to come to talk to you, Miss Downing. I'm a police officer, and I'm investigating the case.'

Anne Downing looked at him. Her face was blank, her eyes huge with hurt. 'Why do you want to see me?' she said in a small, lost voice. 'I would never have done anything to harm Jasmine.'

'No, of course not,' agreed Quantrill gently. 'But Alison has been too distressed to talk to me, and I'd be grateful if you can tell me something about your former employer's way of life. How she spent her spare time, the places she went to, the people she knew.'

The girl closed her eyes. 'I can't,' she whispered, shaking her head. 'I can't talk about her. If your daughter's distressed, after a few weeks with her, how do you think—how do you think I—'

Tears began to filter through her eyelashes and fall down her thin cheeks. She swayed, and Patsy Hopkins hurried to her side and guided her to an armchair. Quantrill bent to pick up the cigarette that the girl had dropped on the carpet. He stubbed it out in a marble ashtray and resumed his questioning, kindly but as persistently as his daughter had known he would question her when he found her.

'I'm sorry, Miss Downing, but there are some things I need to know. Men friends, for example. There are a number of names in her address book, but we don't know which ones are the most significant. Can you tell me, please—at the time when you left her employment, in January I believe, did Jasmine Woods have a lover?'

But the girl's precarious composure had already broken. She lay huddled in the big armchair, her voice rising in such anguish that a beagle that had been asleep in a basket near the fireplace woke up and scrambled onto her knee in puzzled sympathy. Anne Downing was drowned so deep in her own tears that she did not even know that the dog was there.

Patsy Hopkins patted the girl's shoulder and murmured reassurance. She gave the Chief Inspector a glare of reproof, but refrained from the obvious comment.

'Sorry, Patsy,' he acknowledged. 'You were right, I shouldn't have tried to push her. But she must know something that would help us. Will you see what you can do?'

Anne Downing's shoulders were still heaving, her voice still rising in hysterical gasps. 'Men...' said WPC Hopkins. 'For goodness' sake go away and leave it to me this time. That's what you brought me for, isn't it?'

'That poor girl,' she said half an hour later as they headed back to Breckham Market. 'She's had a very bad week. She was reluctant to talk about the murder, understandably, but I heard a bit about her engagement after you'd gone. Apparently she'd been doubtful about it for some time—almost as soon as she went to live at High House farm she knew that it was a mistake. Buxton's mother is a semi-invalid, so the couple were expected to live there after their marriage. But Anne obviously isn't suited to life on a farm—not that kind of farm, anyway. And Oliver Buxton is clumsy, she said, a clumsy oaf.'

Quantrill gave a masculine snort of protest.

'Oh, I can believe her,' asserted Patsy Hopkins. 'He may bathe in aftershave to get rid of the smell of pigs, but I can't imagine that he'd have much finesse when it comes to lovemaking. He simply isn't her type, anyone can see that. Anyway, she finally realized that she couldn't face the wedding. She told him that she much preferred living at Yeoman's with Jasmine Woods, and of course they had a row about it. In the end she announced that she was going back to Jasmine's, pulled off his ring and walked out. But even though it was her own choice to break the engagement, it was very upsetting to her. And then, within a couple of days, to hear about Jasmine's death—'

'Did she actually go back to Yeoman's last weekend?'

'I don't think so—she said she hadn't seen Jasmine since the party. She knew that your daughter had taken her old job, so there wouldn't have been much point in going back, would there? She was probably just making an excuse to break the engagement.'

'Did Anne Downing point to anyone who might have wanted to kill Jasmine Woods?'

'No. Any mention of the murder made her hysterical again. But from what she said it sounds as though Jasmine led a very quiet life at Yeoman's, working most of the time and relaxing by pottering about in the garden.'

'She gave some very noisy parties, if the one I went to was a fair sample.'

'I asked about the parties, but apparently Jasmine didn't give more than three or four of them a year. She went to a few writers' dinners and conferences, invited the neighbours in for drinks occasionally, spent the odd weekend with friends in various parts of the country, and took what amounted to working holidays: Anne went with her, and they visited the foreign countries that Jasmine intended to use as settings for her books. It seems to have been a busy, unemotional life. I took Anne through Jasmine's address book, but she didn't seem to know which, if any, of the men in it were lovers or ex-lovers. Or else she wasn't prepared to talk.'

'Do you think she knows something? Is she trying to shield somebody?'

WPC Hopkins considered her answer. 'I think,' she said carefully, 'that if Anne Downing knew for sure who had murdered Jasmine Woods, she'd have told me. She was too fond of the woman and too shocked by the murder to want to conceal the criminal. But she may well suspect someone. I think it'll be worth your while to talk to her again in a few days' time, when she's had a chance to pull herself together.'

'Right, I'll bear that in mind. Perhaps you'd like to come with me to do the talking?'

Patsy Hopkins blushed, afraid that he assumed that she had angled for the invitation. 'I may be quite wrong about that, of course,' she said hurriedly. 'Perhaps Anne really does know nothing—after all, she hadn't been with Jasmine Woods for more than a couple of years. Perhaps Jasmine had a hectic love affair before she came to Suffolk. I asked Anne if she knew anything about her previous life, but she said not. She said that Jasmine was a very private person.'

'So what have we found out between us? Damn all, as far as I can see.'

Quantrill and Tait were in the Chief Inspector's office, refuelling on canteen sandwiches and coffee while they exchanged information. As soon as he had returned from Bishops Port, Quantrill had rung Chief Superintendent Mancroft at Yarchester; but there was no news of either Alison or Gilbert Smith.

The drug squad had, in their searches, uncovered a hitherto unsuspected pusher, a cache of cannabis resin, a very small quantity of impure yellowish-brown Chinese heroin and a variety of hash pipes, roach ends and dirty syringes. Several people had been booked to appear in the magistrate's court, and one girl was in hospital having been found, alone, after taking an overdose. The exercise had apparently given the

Yarchester division some satisfaction, which Quantrill felt unable to share.

'We've done some useful eliminating,' pointed out Tait. 'We know now that it wasn't the ex-husband, and it wasn't Gifford because the girl at the cinema box office confirms his story. And the Harwich customs men took the Belgian dealer, Wouters, and his car to pieces, but they couldn't find any sign of jade or netsuke.'

'That doesn't mean that Hussey is in the clear,' said Quantrill. 'He was the last person to see Jasmine Woods alive, and he was very unhappy about our visit. I've got a feeling that he may know more than he told us, so we'll talk to him again. But first I want to concentrate on Paul Pardoe. He's the one with the big financial motive, and he was near enough to Thirling on Sunday evening to fit a visit to Yeoman's into his pub crawl.'

'But what about the blood?' demanded Tait. 'There was no evidence at Yeoman's that the murderer cleaned himself up before he left, and Pardoe couldn't have gone to another pub with blood on him—or home, for that matter.'

'He might have stopped at a public lavatory somewhere, or gone into the gents at the next pub he visited. But there would be bloodstains in his car, and I want that examined.'

'And what about Jonathan Elliott?'

'What about him? His wife says that he was working at home on Sunday evening, and so does he. We've got no reason to disbelieve them.'

'You didn't see the way he looked at Jasmine at the party. And then there was the argument he had about her with his wife. He could easily have slipped out of his study—'

'I'm not stopping you from using your initiative,' said Quantrill irritably. 'If you've got a good reason for suspecting anybody, follow it up. This obviously isn't a case we're going to solve quickly, so we need to do a thorough check on every story we've heard so far. After that we can start to look further afield. The murderer has to be someone who knew Jasmine Woods, so we'll dig a bit deeper into her past.'

'Talking of digging,' Tait remembered, 'nothing's been found in the compost heap at Yeoman's. So if Gilbert Smith or one of his friends did the murder, he didn't hide the blood-stained clothing there.'

The Chief Inspector frowned. For a few minutes, he had contrived to forget his daughter. Now, it seemed, she was inextricably linked in his mind with Smith; and Smith was still the prime suspect.

'What's the situation at Yeoman's?' he asked.

Tait telephoned the incident-room. 'Nothing's been found in the grounds,' he reported. 'They're still searching the roadside verges and ditches, but getting further away from the gates, so it doesn't look hopeful. But quite apart from the compost heap, there are plenty of newly-dug areas of garden where Smith might have buried the clothing.'

'About an acre of it,' Quantrill agreed, 'if you count all the flower beds and borders as well as the vegetable plots... Well, all right, Martin; you'd better start by going down to Yeoman's and showing the boys where you want them to dig. When they grumble, you can tell them that we've reached the stage where we all have to get down to the nitty-gritty.'

Sergeant Tait winced, and went. Quantrill was about to follow him out of the room when he remembered something, turned back to his desk, and rang his wife.

He had no hope that Molly would have any news about Alison; she would have passed that on to him immediately. And there was nothing that he could tell her, either. In ordinary circumstances he would have thought the call futile, a waste of his time. But Alison's disappearance, and the circumstances of it, had brought him and his wife closer together than they had been for years, and the least he could do was to keep the lines of communication open.

25

When Alison had left home on Monday evening, creeping out of the house with her suitcase while her mother and brother were watching a television comedy, she had no idea of where she was going. All she wanted to do was to get away from the questioning and the suffocating solicitude.

It was nearly nine o'clock, cloudily dark, and the air smelled of a cold, reluctant spring. There was no one in Benidorm Avenue as she left the house. She walked aimlessly for some time, her feet leaden on the pavements and her head heavy with weeping. Presently it began to rain.

She stopped in the doorway of a shop and looked about her. She was near the centre of the town in White Hart Street, the narrow shopping street that had been made into a pedestrian precinct. The shop windows were lighted but the street was dead, apart from one woman in furry hat, calf-length coat and trousers, exercising her dog and fondly encouraging it to foul the pavement.

Alison rubbed her blurred eyes and tried to decide where to go. She knew a good many people in Breckham Market, school friends and the families of school friends, and friends of her own family, but there was no one she could turn to for refuge; no one who would be sympathetic enough to understand her, to accommodate her without question and to allow her to stay without revealing her whereabouts to her parents. She had enough money with her to pay for a night at the Rights of Man, the Georgian-fronted coaching inn turned modern hotel on the corner of the market place and White Hart Street, but her father would soon find her there. Wherever she went in Breckham, he would be bound to find her.

It was nearing 9.30—too late, she knew, in that small town, for either trains or buses. And she had heard enough from her father to make her afraid of trying to hitch a lift. She could neither stay in Breckham Market nor leave it. A feeling of desolation, of loneliness of spirit, seemed to creep up her body from the cold paving stones, contracting her heart into a hard, tight lump that rose and lodged itself in her throat, threatening to choke her.

The woman in the hat disappeared round a corner, although her poodle insisted on lingering at the end of its lead to give a shop front a parting salute. And then the quietness of White Hart Street was broken by a group of youths, shouting and pushing and shoving at each other as they made their way to the next pub on their itinerary. Alison stepped back into the doorway as they passed, but one of them, stopping to light a cigarette, saw her.

''Allo, darling,' he said, identifying himself by his accent as one of the metropolitan immigrants to Suffolk. 'Waiting for me, are you?' He moved closer to her. He was about her own age, tall and thin, wearing a red and blue plaid bomber jacket. His hair hung lank about his face and there was a pustule at one side of his mouth; he smelled beery and imperfectly washed.

Alison found an approximation of her normal voice. 'I'm waiting for my boy-friend,' she asserted.

'Oh, yeh?' He looked round at the street, empty except for his own friends, who had scuffled on. 'Don't look as though he's coming, does it?' He leaned forward and put one hand up against the shop door, blocking her way.

'Yes,' she said, 'of course he's coming.' She tried not to sound nervous; ridiculous that she should have spent eighteen months in London without a single encounter of this kind, only to be cornered in her own home town.

His friends, further up the street, began to shout for him: 'Come on, Keef.'

'Piss off,' bawled Keith over his shoulder, 'I'm busy.' He grinned at Alison, putting out his other hand to touch her hair. 'Big feller, this boy-friend of yours, is he? Bigger 'n me?' His hand moved down and made a grab at her breast.

'Much bigger.' Alison swung her suitcase at him, ducked under his arm and ran. He clutched at his thigh, swore, and then limped menacingly after her. She made for a telephone call-box, halfway down the precinct, and stood in the neon-lit rain, panting, one hand on the door.

'Go away,' she said. 'Leave me alone or I'll—I'll call the police.'

'Oh, yeh?' He approached slowly, rubbing his thigh. 'Not from there you won't, darling. Fixed that 'phone meself, not more than an hour ago, didn't I? Must've expected somefing like this. Whatcher going to do now, then, eh?'

Whether it was his work or not, he was right. Alison could see, from where she stood, that the receiver had been wrenched away from the set.

Her mouth felt dry. 'I'll—I'll scream,' she threatened,

backing away, hoping that he would believe her. The last thing she wanted was to draw attention to herself, to be questioned by helpful citizens—if there were any within earshot—and then to be returned ignominiously to her home and her mother's fussing and her father's interrogation.

'Yah? Well, I might just give you something to scream for,' he said. He made several obscene suggestions. 'You could've damaged me, doing what you did. Really damaged me. You want teaching a lesson, that's what you want.'

Alison turned, dodged round a plane tree, almost slipped on the sloping wet cobblestones that had been set at its base as an additional decorative feature, and ran in the direction of the market place, her suitcase bumping against her leg. She heard the thud of following feet and almost panicked; but then the dignified brick façade of the Rights of Man rose above her, and she slipped thankfully through the doors and into the empty brightly lit foyer.

The receptionist, a cool divorcée who, in common with many hotel staff, considered herself underpaid, badly fed and generally put-upon, was busy with some typing. She had more than enough work to do, and did not invite idle enquiries and interruptions by looking up every time the doors opened. She was telling the truth when she told the policeman who came round later that evening with a photograph of Alison that she had not seen the girl.

Alison had visited the hotel the previous year for a friend's wedding reception, and so she had some idea of its layout. She went straight to the corridor where the public telephone was, and looked up a number in the local directory. Her fingers trembled as they riffled the pages. She felt shaken and sickened by her unpleasant encounter, but at least it had served a purpose. It had reminded her of one person she could turn to, one woman who would give her unquestioning support and refuge.

It was only last week that she had heard Roz Elliott telling Jasmine Woods about the latest women's movement campaign. We need to reclaim the night, Roz had insisted; to make it safe for women to walk through the streets after dark without fear—fear not only of mugging and rape, but of the kind of sexist domination that Alison had just experienced.

They had argued about it, of course, Jasmine and Roz

always argued. Roz believed in national action, although she was usually too much involved with academic and political work in Yarchester to be able to take an active part herself. It was important, she thought, for women to demonstrate their togetherness by gathering in city areas notorious for sexual assault and sexist affront—London's Soho especially, because of its strip clubs and porn shops. Once gathered, the women could set about reclaiming the streets by walking proudly through them with feminist banners and songs.

Jasmine had argued not about the need to alter men's attitudes towards women, and to reclaim the night, but about the method. Gatherings and marches invited confrontations, she had said. Men would jeer, scuffles would start, the police would move in, tempers would give, arrests would be made, violence would erupt. And violent encounters between men and women was precisely what the feminists wanted to end, wasn't it?

One thing was certain, Alison thought as she dialled the Old Rectory number: Roz would never undermine her independence by revealing her whereabouts to her father.

The telephone was answered by Mandy, Roz's pregnant lame duck. 'Oh, Alison—how are you? Wasn't it awful about . . . what? No, sorry, Roz isn't here, she's staying overnight at her flat in Yarchester. The number's 25387. Look, Claire and I were shattered to hear about Jasmine. She was always so nice to us. You must feel absolutely—'

Alison thanked her for her information and dropped the receiver clumsily back on its rest. Mandy was right, she did feel absolutely. She had hoped, if Roz were at home, to be collected from Breckham and taken to Thirling, since it was only a matter of four miles away. But she could hardly expect Roz to drive the seventeen miles from Yarchester to pick her up.

She felt absolutely defeated. If she stayed in the hotel, her father would find her, if she stepped outside, the odious Keith might be waiting.

And then she saw, pinned on to the information board beside the telephone, a card advertising the local taxi firm. She could not make use of it, because she knew that her father knew the proprietor. But also pinned to the board was a hand-written card advertising a private car-hire service.

* * *

As soon as she reached Yarchester, Alison telephoned Roz Elliott. She hardly knew what to say, but Roz's response was immediate: Alison was to stay exactly where she was, and Roz would pick her up.

It was not until Alison had put the receiver down that it occurred to her that she might have rung at a very inconvenient time. She was not sure whether a liberated marriage, like the Elliotts', involved adultery almost as a matter of principle; for all she knew, Roz shared her Yarchester flat with a man.

But if she did, he left no evidence. The flat consisted of a small but well-furnished bed-sitting room with a kitchen and a bathroom, in a modern block near the university. The main room housed a considerable quantity of reading matter: sociological text books and periodicals, and a daunting variety of feminist magazines that Alison had never heard of. The room was dominated by a women's liberation movement wall poster.

Roz Elliott, big and handsome and careless of her appearance, brought two mugs of coffee from the kitchen. Her vigour and her voice were both subdued; she had said very little to Alison, when she picked her up in the centre of Yarchester, but her silence communicated such sympathy that Alison found it easy to tell her everything that had happened, from the time when she had arrived at Yeoman's that morning.

Roz listened, smoked and sipped coffee. 'What are you going to do now?' she asked. 'I don't mean tonight, that's no problem—I can lend you a sleeping-bag. But I'm speaking at a women's conference in Birmingham tomorrow, and I can't very well leave you here. Not that I mind, you understand; you're welcome to stay, but you asked Mandy where to find me and so sooner or later someone will come here looking for you. Whatever else the police are, they're not thick.'

She remembered Alison's father's profession and smiled an apology. 'You know what I mean.'

Alison nodded. 'There are times when I hate policemen—detectives especially. I hate the way their minds work. Oh, I'm fond of Dad, he can be a real old softy; and he usually tries to be fair. But when he's on a case he'll trample on anyone's feelings, even his family's.' She thought about it.

'Mostly his family's,' she added bitterly, on her mother's behalf as well as her own.

Roz Elliott frowned, brushing at her thick fringe with her fingers. 'I tell you where you could go, just for a few days, while you make up your mind about what you're going to do next. My sister Polly lives in a farmhouse about twenty miles away, in the other direction from Breckham Market, so you should be safe from any police visits. It's a sort of commune. I'm not into that kind of squalor myself, but you might find it bearable for a short time. And Polly's a dear, you'll like her, everyone does. Good. I'll take you there first thing tomorrow morning.'

They went to bed, Roz Elliott on her divan and Alison in a sleeping-bag spread against a wall. 'Feeling better?' Roz asked her from across the darkened room.

'Yes.' The duvet made a billowing noise as Roz's big body turned over. 'That goes for me, too.' She paused, and then said, 'I was very fond of Jasmine, you know. It was mutual— you might not have thought it, from the way we argued, but we were very good friends.'

'I realized that. You wouldn't have dropped in so often, otherwise.'

'We enjoyed arguing.' Roz Elliott's voice smiled in the dark. 'We did disagree fundamentally about a lot of things, but to some extent our arguments were just an exercise, a game. And it was a game we particularly enjoyed playing in front of other people. Jasmine and I understood each other; we'd called each other's bluff long ago.'

Alison propped herself up on one elbow. 'Bluff?'

'Yes. You see, we were both, in a sense, public people. We were committed to certain attitudes, Jasmine as a romantic writer, me as a militant feminist. We both wore the appropriate public faces. But in private we both had reservations about our roles, and we understood each other's reservations.'

'What sort of reservations?'

There was another pause. 'Well, take me,' said Roz. 'Only don't for God's sake point this out to any of my supporters, or I'll lose all my credibility. I'm known as an enthusiast for women's liberation: I believe passionately in equality of opportunity for women, and in every woman's right to live as an individual without being forced to play the conventional, supportive, wifely role. I go to meetings all over the country proclaiming these beliefs, and I write articles and books; and I take political action by lobbying Members of Parliament and by encouraging women to band together and join trade unions to fight for their rights.

'But as Jasmine once pointed out to me, I'm a terrible fraud. I've never had to fight for anything. I come from a happy and secure middle-class background, and I was always encouraged to achieve whatever I wanted in life. I've never met with any discrimination on account of being a woman; I'm doing the job I want to do, and I have a sufficiently large private income to allow me to choose whatever lifestyle I prefer. I have something that the vast majority of women, for lack of money, can never have: the luxury of choice. And what have I chosen? Marriage, and not just two but three children!'

'Oh, but yours is a very unusual sort of married life, isn't it?' said Alison.

'Yes, in that I happen to have married an understanding man, and that we're an articulate and reasonably affluent couple. This kind of marriage suits both of us. We love each other, we love our children, and we wouldn't want any other kind of life. So I, the militant feminist, could be described—though I'd flay any journalist who dared to do so—as a happily married mother of three. Whereas Jasmine, the romantic novelist, disliked her experience of married life and simply wasn't interested in children. She was the one who embraced the principle of liberation, and found a very satisfactory alternative to marriage and a family.'

Alison lay on her back with her fingers laced behind her head, staring at the dim outline of the poster on the wall. 'It's something I never thought about,' she admitted. 'But it's true: whatever else happened in Jasmine's books, and whatever independent noises her heroines made, you knew that in the end the girl would marry the hero. It seemed only right and proper. But it obviously wasn't the kind of ending that Jasmine wanted in her own life.'

'No, she knew better than to assume that married couples necessarily live happily ever after. That was something that used to make me cross, because I felt that she was exploiting impressionable girls and giving them a false idea of the realities of life. But last Wednesday I went up to London to a meeting, and afterwards, on the underground train, I happened to be sitting next to a woman of about my own age. She was a West Indian, and she wore a green nylon overall under her coat. She must have been going home from work—I imagine she was a canteen helper or a hospital cleaner or something like that. She looked tired and defeated, her ankles were swollen and her clothes were shoddy, and she was burdened with shopping bags. I doubt if there was anything anyone could tell that woman about the realities of life.

'I felt that I ought to do something to help her—give her some women's movement literature, persuade her that she had a right to a fuller life, encourage her to do something positive for herself instead of meekly accepting a subservient role. But as soon as she sat down she took a women's magazine out of her bag, and flipped through it until she found the serial story. It was from one of Jasmine's novels. I watched her face, and as she read she began to look happier. She obviously loved Jasmine's book, really lapped it up. For ten minutes, as she travelled from a dirty, exhausting, boring job to face the demands of her home and family, she was lost to reality. Jasmine had transported her to another world. And when you think about it, it's quite something, isn't it, to be able to give pleasure like that to thousands of people you've never met?'

'Did you tell Jasmine about the woman?' Alison asked.

'Of course. I told her when Jonathan and I went to Yeoman's for drinks yesterday. But I certainly didn't tell her what I've just told you, that I couldn't help envying her ability to give other people happiness. No, I scolded her for giving opiates to women, for lulling them with romantic trash when they ought to be fighting for their right to self-fulfilment. But Jasmine just smiled and said that fighting wasn't her line, and that it was time I accepted the fact that women have different needs. She said that it was arrogant of me to assume that the woman on the train wanted to be liberated; she might well want nothing more than to devote herself to her family. And she said that I had no right to belittle and badger women who really do find complete fulfilment in being wives and mothers, or to be superior about their tastes in fiction. I think my views must have mellowed since I've known her, because to some extent—and strictly in private—I can see that she was right. I might have said so, if Jonathan hadn't been there. We enjoyed having apparently irreconcilable arguments in front of him.'

'Jonathan used to argue with Jasmine, too,' remembered Alison.

His wife laughed indulgently. 'Oh, that was just a ploy to give him an opportunity to talk to her. Poor man, he did so want to get her into bed with him.'

Alison was surprised. 'But I thought you said that you and Jonathan—'

'That we love each other, yes. But we've agreed that in our kind of marriage, that doesn't preclude sleeping with other people. We're both free individuals. As it happens, though, I'm too busy to want to bother with anyone else, and Jonathan is chased by so many of my students that he's terrified of getting involved with any of them. Jasmine is—was—the only one he really wanted, and he daren't ask her because he's too vain; he won't admit it, but he was afraid she'd reject him. I told him only yesterday that I wished he'd ask her right out, instead of making transparent excuses to talk to her. We had quite an argument about it after we got home from Yeoman's, and he slammed his study door and wouldn't come out for the rest of the day.'

'Would Jasmine have agreed, do you think, if he'd asked her?'

'Good Lord, no!' Roz Elliott floundered into a more comfortable position. 'We'll have to make an early start, so we'd better try to sleep now.'

The girl lay thinking about Jasmine Woods; sadly, but at least about Jasmine alive rather than dead. She was interested in what Roz had said about alternatives to marriage and a family. She herself had always assumed that she would marry and have children. That was what she had hoped would be the outcome of her affair with Gavin Jackson, otherwise she would not have let him make love to her. But Gavin had been a disillusionment, and she had been revolted by the way the youth in Breckham Market had tried to handle her.

'Jasmine was perfectly happy living alone,' she meditated aloud. 'I think that's what I'd like, too. It's ridiculous to imagine, as my mother does, that a woman's life isn't fulfilled unless she's married.'

Roz Elliott muttered something, but it was muffled by the duck-down depths of her duvet.

26

'But I can't descend on your sister without warning,' Alison objected. 'Oughtn't we to ring and ask whether she minds?'

'We can't, she doesn't have a telephone at the farm. That's partly why it's such a good place for you to go to, because they don't let the outside world intrude. They're two miles from the nearest village, and they have no newspapers, no radio, no television—the isolation would drive me mad, but Polly likes it. And don't worry about inconveniencing her, because you won't. She'll be delighted to add you to her family.'

They were travelling briskly from Yarchester into the countryside in Roz Elliott's Mini, which was so permanently dirty that it was easy to overlook the fact that it was only one year old and a 1275 GT model. It was half-past eight on the morning of Tuesday 7 April, the day when Alison's father was pursuing his enquiries in Norfolk and worrying over his daughter's safety. But Alison, feeling relaxed for the first time since her discovery of the murder, and happy in the company of an understanding woman, hardly gave her parents a thought.

'Does Polly have a big family?' she asked.

'Oh, I was using the term loosely, as she does. The commune's her family, and Lord knows how many are in it—I've never attempted to keep track. Polly's a widow. She has five children of her own from two marriages, but they're all away from home now. She and her second husband bought the farm ten years ago, shortly before he died, to restore and use as a weekend and holiday place. He'd turn in his grave if he knew what she'd done with it, but Polly loves kids and enjoys being Mum to everyone.'

Roz turned from the road along a rutted track. There had been a wooden five-bar gate at the entrance to the track but it was now pushed aside and leaning, off its hinges, against a hedge. The name on the gate, Mill Farm, had weathered almost to illegibility. The land immediately surrounding the farmhouse was cultivated only in patches and at first sight it looked virtually derelict. The old sheds and stables, mainly of brick and corrugated iron, black-tarred against the weather, were dilapidated. Ancient pieces of machinery, skeletal with rust, lay dead in corners.

But neglected as it was, the place stirred with life. Spring helped, of course: weeds shouldered aside frost-bitten cement and flourished in the yard; young nettles thrust through the ribs of the abandoned hardware. At one end of the yard a small building rather like a sentry-box—which Alison's father would have identified without hesitation as the privy—had been almost completely overgrown by a bush of honeysuckle, which was just coming into leaf. Each opening leaf resembled a tiny pair of wings, trembling in the sharp air. It looked as though a cloud of pale green butterflies had alighted on the bare twigs of the bush and might at any moment take off again.

The air smelled fresh and damp and earthy, and birds and domestic creatures filled it with their sounds. Two bearded members of the Mill Farm family were in evidence, chopping wood and digging a large vegetable patch with more enthusiasm than skill. They looked up with an amiable 'Hallo' as Roz and Alison passed them on their way to the house, and there were more, and louder, greetings when Roz opened the door and walked into the big kitchen.

The noise, until Alison became accustomed to it, was distracting and almost deafening. A television set or a radio would have been entirely superfluous. The family appeared to consist of about a dozen adults and as many children under the age of five. The children sat at whim at or on a table, using spoons and fingers to attack bowls of porridge. The adults sat at another table, finishing their own breakfast and discussing the tasks for the day, with the exception of one frowning girl whose sole contribution to the discussion was a guitar accompaniment.

There was a certain uniformity of appearance among the members of the family. The children's sex was totally indeterminate, dressed as they all were in homemade dungarees, with their hair fringing their eyes. The adults all wore their hair long, though some of the men held theirs back with a headband. One or two of the women were in long skirts but most of them, like the men, wore frayed jeans and sweaters. There was one older woman at the adults' table, and she rose with a cry of welcome as soon as she saw her sister.

'Roz!'

'Polly dear.'

They embraced with a warmth that surprised Alison, who could not remember having touched her sister Jennifer since they were children. She was even more surprised when Roz introduced her, and Polly insisted on giving her a welcoming hug.

She could hardly hear the conversation that took place between the sisters, but Roz's explanations were minimal. Polly was indifferent to everything except Alison's presence, which seemed to give her genuine pleasure. She put one arm across the girl's shoulders and took her round the room, introducing her to each member of the family; and each one greeted the newcomer with a hug or a friendly kiss. Alison felt almost like a bagatelle ball when, bemused, breathless and liberally smeared with porridge, she fetched up again beside Roz Elliott.

Roz grinned. 'All right? I must go now, or I'll never catch my train. Polly's delighted to have you here, and she's admirably incurious. She doesn't know what's happened— I've simply told her that you want to get away from home for a few days. You can tell her just as much or as little as you like, and stay as long as you want.' She stepped aside to dodge a porridge-encrusted infant that was bent on swarming up her boots. 'Or as long as you can stand it. I shan't tell anyone where you are. You're an independent person, and presumably you'll get in touch with your family when you're ready to do so.'

Polly bustled forward to scoop up the baby, pointing out to her sister with gentle reproof that it was wrong to make children feel in any way rejected. Like Roz, she was a big woman with strong, handsome bones. She was in her middle forties, bulky in jeans and what looked like a hand-woven poncho. Her thick auburn hair, straighter than Roz's, was tied back loosely with a leather thong. She too had a rich warm voice, but a much more relaxed and outgoing personality. She put her free arm round her sister's waist and they walked outside together, with most of the children toddling or crawling after them.

Alison was immediately absorbed into the family. Room was made for her on a bench at the table, between a man with a straggling brown beard who was carving a piece of wood, and a barefooted girl in jeans and a slouch hat, breast-feeding a baby. Someone insisted on providing her with a pottery bowl containing porridge and a pottery mug of warm liquid that looked like tea, although it tasted as though the leaves had been grown considerably nearer to Breckham than to Bombay.

Discussion continued round her while she cautiously swallowed a second breakfast. The family was, apparently, trying to come to a collective decision about the vegetable crops that would be planted that year. As in any family, there was disagreement. Personalities obtruded, points were scored. The sun rose higher, and still the majority of the commune sat round the table, talking rather than doing.

The mounting tension was broken when the girl with the guitar played a loud discord and burst into tears. Immediately, the family reunited. Love and support overflowed, the girl was hugged and talked out of her tears, and the family rose from the table with a sense of harmony and achievement to begin the day's work. It was almost ten o'clock, and the bleating of the goats tethered outside had become piteous.

Alison found herself alone in the kitchen with the family's dirty breakfast dishes. Washing up was not her favourite occupation but she was grateful for the refuge and ready to do her share of the work. She pushed up the sleeves of her sweater and was collecting crockery and scraping up the remains of the porridge when Polly came back, with a different child in her arms.

She gave a rich chuckle when she saw what Alison was

doing. 'Bless your heart, but you needn't. It's Linda's turn for that today, and she'll get round to it eventually.'

'It's the least I can do,' said Alison. 'I mean, it's very good of you—'

'Oh, you'll get your turn, never fear! We all muck in with all the jobs. But Roz tells me that you may not want to stay for long, and there are some things we couldn't expect you to do—the milking, for example, it wouldn't be fair on the goats. So perhaps a bit of extra washing up will even things out. And you'll be glad to hear that this isn't Cold Comfort Farm. We do have hot water and washing-up mops, so you won't need to cletter the porridge dishes with cold water and a twig.'

The allusion was unfamiliar to Alison, but she found the reassurance comforting. Polly worked with her, one-handed because of the child she was carrying, chatting about the commune.

'The family think that they're being simple and unmaterialistic, bless their hearts. It doesn't seem to occur to them that a really simple life doesn't include electricity and plumbing. But I'd find life unbearable without, and so would they—and fortunately I can afford to provide the amenities, so we all continue to take them for granted. But we grow as much of our own food as we can, and sell the surplus, and everyone does some kind of craft work which we sell, too. None of my family goes on social security, that's my one rule. Of course, they're all supported by me to a large extent; real self-sufficiency's a romantic myth. But I enjoy communal living, for part of the year anyway. I cheat, too, I'm afraid. I rent a villa in Spain for a couple of months each winter—don't I, my sweet?' She joggled the gurgling baby against her shoulder, careless of the fact that it was dribbling on her poncho.

'I've never been to a commune before,' said Alison, 'but the man I sat next to at breakfast reminded me of one of my friends. Gil carves, too, and he's into organic gardening and things like that, but he lives alone. I suppose some of your family might know him: Gilbert Smith.'

'Possibly. Does he go to Oxlip Fair?'

'Oh, yes, I've heard him talking about it. He goes every Easter. I've never been myself, but it sounds interesting.'

'It is. We all go from here. Some of the family stay the whole three days, and they'll be going on Friday to set up camp. The rest of us go for odd days. You must come, it's great fun. And you'll probably see your friend there.'

'I'd like that.' Alison had not thought of Gilbert Smith for the past twenty-four hours. Now she did so with affection, wondering what he was doing and how he was coming to terms with the shock of Jasmine's death. He was such a gentle, sensitive man . . . so unlike Alison's ex-lover, and the lout she had encountered in Breckham Market, that the thought of him made her feel more kindly disposed towards men in general.

'Gil's a dear,' she added. 'He does smoke pot, which seems an awful pity—I mean, if you're against using chemicals in the garden, it's a shame if you can't enjoy life without using them on your own mind—but it doesn't stop me from being his friend. My father would go berserk if he knew about the pot. He's a policeman, you see. But fortunately he doesn't know, and I'm certainly not going to tell him. You've got to be loyal to your friends, haven't you?'

That had been one of Jasmine's principles. And more and more, Alison felt an affinity with the murdered woman.

27

PC Ronald Timms, the middle-aged Breckham Market constable with the Kitchener moustache, was passing Chief Inspector Quantrill's office late on Tuesday afternoon when he heard coming from it a woman's voice.

'It was a strange sensation, to be kissed by someone other than Matt,' the woman was saying. 'I hadn't expected it, or wanted it. After Matt died, my senses seemed to atrophy. I'd thought—no, I'd assumed—that they were dead too. But now I began to realize that they weren't.'

The constable raised his eyebrows. Some bird making a statement to the DCI; young, from the sound of her voice, and posh, but definitely sexy. The DCI had all the luck. PC Timms brushed up his moustache and loitered near the door, listening.

The woman drew a deep breath and spoke again. Her voice was low and impassioned. 'I found myself responding to Stephen's kiss. Warily, at first, almost experimentally; but then with an eagerness that took me by surprise. I no longer knew who I was kissing, or cared. I wasn't dead, I was alive! I needed someone to prove it to me conclusively, and any living, breathing man would do. I clung to him fiercely, so blinkered by the intensity of my reawakening that nothing mattered except here and now.'

Ron Timms, eyes bulging, ran a finger round his collar and applied his ear more closely to the door. The woman was alleging rape, presumably. Typical. She'd obviously given this poor sod Stephen a come-on, and now she was going to bleat that she hadn't meant it...

He was totally unprepared for what followed: a derisive snort from the DCI, and a chuckle from the woman herself. 'Phew!' she said, in a lighter, more relaxed voice. 'Thank God that bit's over. I do hate all these refined intimations of sexuality, but my publisher doesn't approve of anything more robust. Just as well for our heroine that Stephen is a gentleman, and will take her at her word when she tells him in the next paragraph to lay off. I must make myself a cup of tea before I do any more, though—heavens, it's ten past six, I'd better ring Heather and tell her I'm behind schedule and can't come to supper this evening.'

There was a slight click as a tape recorder was switched off. PC Timms, realizing that he'd been listening to the recorded voice of the writer who had been murdered, shrugged off his disappointment. But if anyone wanted his opinion—which they wouldn't on account of his being only a poor bloody ordinary copper, not CID—if that was how Jasmine Woods carried on, she'd asked for everything she got.

It was Martin Tait who had remembered Jasmine Woods's tapes. He had begun to play them through without much hope of hearing anything other than the work in progress, but as soon as he realized that her dictation was accompanied by a running commentary on the events of the day—the day of her murder—he had taken the machine to Quantrill's office so that they could listen together.

They had already heard that George Hussey had arrived without warning at lunch-time, just as the Elliotts had left. Jasmine Woods had not been able to get back to work until four o'clock. When she tried to telephone her sister at ten past six, the line had been engaged. She went on working and obviously forgot the telephone call because her next relevant remark was that the door bell was ringing. The detectives could hear it faintly in the background.

'Damn it!' protested Jasmine Woods, in the middle of a cliff-hanger. 'Who on earth's that? I'm not expecting anyone tonight, and anyway—oh, Lord, I never rang Heather and it's after eight already. I must do that as soon as I've got rid of my caller. Don't go away, Ali, I'll be back.'

The recorder blicked off, and the tape hissed to the end of the reel in silence.

'It could have been any one of them,' said Tait. 'Any one of the men we haven't already eliminated.'

'And I'll tell you something else,' said Quantrill slowly. He stood at the window with his hands in his pockets, looking out across the main Yarchester road to the narrow streets of the old town. Just below his first-floor office window was a row of ornamental cherry trees, their reddish branches bumpy with swelling buds. A boy and a girl, he in factory dungarees and she in school skirt and pullover, had run to meet each other under the cherry trees and were kissing with fervour. He couldn't be much more than sixteen, and she looked about fourteen; but, then, as Quantrill had cause to know, the stir of spring takes no account of age.

Spending the afternoon listening to Jasmine Woods's sexy voice dictating a romantic novel hadn't helped, either. It had reminded him of the occasion, back in February, when he had read a page of one of her books in bed, over his wife's shoulder. Molly had been so absorbed in the story that she had become aroused; but her absorption in the fiction had been so total that she had rejected her husband. He could still remember the humiliation of it.

171

He turned from the window. 'We've been working on the assumption that the murderer had to be someone Jasmine Woods knew. But thinking about it, I'm not so sure. After all, her books are best sellers; women lap them up, and a lot of them probably fancy Jasmine Woods's heroes more than they do their own boy-friends or husbands. That's what romantic novels are for, after all, to take women away from reality.'

'They certainly do that,' said Tait. He was contemptuous on principle of formula fiction, but nettled that Jasmine Woods's version of it employed a vocabulary rather larger than his own. There had been a couple of words on her tape that he'd have to look up, as soon as he could get hold of the dictionary that the old man kept in the top drawer of his desk. 'That was something Jasmine's ex-husband said about her: when she started to write her books she began to withdraw from him, and in the end he felt that they gave her more satisfaction than he did.'

'That's just what I mean. As you discovered, though, Potter isn't jealous. But plenty of men are, and there must be quite a few of them who're suffering from frustration on account of Jasmine Woods. There are men who've never set eyes on her who probably feel that they hate her... hundreds of them... thousands... And with that glossy magazine article telling them where she lived—'

The two detectives fell silent, contemplating the possibility that the number of suspects in this case was incalculable.

'Well, we just go on working our way through,' said Quantrill heavily. He looked at his watch and picked up a telephone. 'I'd better have a quick word with my wife. She usually watches the early evening regional news on television, and she'll get into a state when she sees the photograph of Alison on the screen. No, don't go, Martin, this won't take a minute.'

Tait looked through one of the files while the Chief Inspector made reassuring noises into the telephone. A wife like that must be a real drag, the sergeant thought; probably a typical Jasmine Woods fan—and the old man's theory about jealous husbands could be based on more than guesswork...

The internal telephone rang. Tait answered it. There was a call for the Chief Inspector from Inspector Carrow, and Tait hurried next door to his own office to take it.

He burst back into the Chief Inspector's office just as Quantrill finished speaking to his wife.

'That was Yarchester, sir. They've found a girl in a coffee bar, a student friend of Gilbert Smith, who saw him in the city yesterday afternoon. He was wandering round the Earlfield Road area, on his own. He looked strange, she said. Distraught. He wouldn't say what he was doing or where he was going, but he showed her a tiny carved ivory figure that he was carrying in his pocket.'

Quantrill got to his feet. 'He did, did he? The Earlfield Road area... that's near the university, isn't it?'

'Yes. Inspector Carrow said that they'd been concentrating so far on the sleazy side of the city, near the river, where most of the junkies live. But they've switched now to the university area. Not many of the students live there, of course, except for the ones in residence; it's too expensive. But that doesn't mean that Smith hasn't any friends there.'

A telephone rang again. Quantrill answered it, his face at first relieved and then growing anxious. He depressed the rest and held on to the receiver.

'A possible lead on Alison,' he said. 'I sent a man to do another house-to-house in Thirling, making enquiries about her. Apparently there wasn't anyone at home at the Old Rectory when he first called, but he's just been back and interviewed a Miss Mandy Walsh—one of the students we saw there. She knows my daughter. Alison rang her last night, asking for Mrs Elliott—'

'Dr Elliott,' Tait amended. 'Ph.D.,' he explained.

The Chief Inspector stared through him. 'The girl told Alison that the Elliott woman was at her flat in Yarchester, and gave her the number. I've got the address. It's near the university, in Earlfield Crescent...' He put a call through to Inspector Carrow, who promised to send a patrol car straight to Earlfield Crescent and report back.

Douglas Quantrill roamed his office, running his hand through his thick hair. 'That means that Alison and Gilbert Smith were probably both in the same area last night. And he would know the Elliott woman, too, he might have called there... I hope to God we're not too late.'

'I've had a thought about Smith, sir,' said Tait, wanting to get Quantrill out of the role of anxious father and back into his Chief Inspector's cap. 'There's a list in this file of the things that were found in his flat, and one of them was a T-shirt with a blazing sun motif and the legend *A fair field full of folk*. I've been seeing a lot of that about in Breckham lately, on posters and handbills advertising Oxlip Fair.'

'It's the same every year,' said Quantrill absently. 'It seems to be the Oxlip Fair emblem—don't ask me what it means.'

'It's a quote from a medieval poem, Langland's *Piers Plowman*,' Tait supplied. 'Not,' he added modestly, 'that I've ever read it, it's just common knowledge. Anyway,' he went on quickly, evading Quantrill's dirty look, 'I remember Jasmine telling me that she met Gilbert Smith at Oxlip Fair a couple of years ago. If we don't catch up with him before Easter, I should think there's a good chance that we'll find him at the fair.'

Quantrill exploded. 'Good grief, the fair doesn't start until Saturday! We've got to find him before then—we've got to get to him before he finds Alison.'

One of his telephones rang, and he had it in his hand before it had time to give the second half of the initial *brr-brr*.

'Oh,—Molly. Look, not now, my dear, I'm expecting— *what*?... Oh, that's wonderful news! What exactly did she say?... Well, never mind, that's all we need to know. Yes, me too... All right, I'll see you later—no, I don't know when, we're busy... Yes, I'm sure you are. You can relax now, anyway, we both can. Yes... Thank you for letting me know. 'Bye, my dear.'

'Alison's home?' suggested Tait, watching the worry slide off the Chief Inspector's shoulders.

Quantrill sat back in his swivel chair and shook his head, but with relief. 'No—we don't actually know where she is, she wouldn't say. But she rang to let us know that she's perfectly all right and staying with friends—a family in the country—for a couple of days. She apologized for going off without telling us, but I reckon that was forgivable in view of the shock she'd had. She'll be in touch again when she's recovered... Well, she's safe, then. Thank God for that.'

'I'm glad,' said Tait, and meant it. A nice kid, Alison; pretty, and a good figure. When this case was sewn up, he might even take her out one evening. 'About Oxlip Fair, then, sir? If Yarchester can't collar Smith in the meantime, it might be as well if we go there in force. From what I've heard, all the Gilbert Smith types in Eastern England congregate there, and he'll imagine himself safe in the crowds.'

Quantrill was almost lighthearted as he lifted the telephone to tell Inspector Carrow to call off the search for his daughter. 'All right, I agree. If Yarchester can't find our man, we'll all go to the fair.'

28

Douglas Quantrill left his office shortly after ten o'clock that evening. There was nothing to be gained by working any longer, and he needed an early night before setting off for Thaxted. Having depressed himself by the realization that there were potentially as many suspects in this case as there were frustrated husbands and men-friends of Jasmine Woods's readers, he had decided to concentrate his enquiries on the victim's past life. With luck, a visit to the part of Essex where she lived before moving to Thirling might reveal someone with a more substantial motive for murdering him.

There was still Smith to be found, of course, but that he would have to leave to the Yarchester boys. The fact that Smith had been seen wandering in the city in possession of a carved ivory figure certainly hardened the case against him, and the sooner Yarchester got off its collective behind and found the man, the better. It would be a sight easier to pick him out in the city than at Oxlip Fair, where all the men were reputed to wear beards and look half stoned.

Quantrill was thinking hard about Smith as he put his latchkey in his front door. Usually, when he came home so late, he would have to brace himself to meet his wife. Their marriage had almost foundered some years previously, when his irregular hours of work and lack of consideration for her had driven Molly to leave him. Their mutual love for their children had brought them together again, and they had patched their marriage with an unspoken agreement that he would pay more attention to her needs, while she would try not to nag him about his job. And it had worked, after a fashion; he no longer had to come home, tired, to face her outspoken resentment. What he usually had to brace himself against now was her concern, which she habitually expressed in terms of food and drink.

But tonight, he felt, was going to be different. Thinking about Smith had reminded him of Alison; and Alison, thank God, was safe from the man. Tired as he was, he smiled to himself as he opened the front door. And to his pleasure Molly came into the hall to greet him, in frilly housecoat and neat furry slippers, with a look of relief and happiness equal to his own.

He took immediate advantage of it. They were so much accustomed not to touch each other that, when he felt the urge to do so, it was often difficult in daytime to find an appropriate opportunity. And Molly was such a romantic woman, her head so stuffed with the Jasmine Woods-type books she read, that when he eventually did touch her in bed she was liable to accuse him of wanting only one thing. He did want it, of course, but there were times—and this was one of them—when what he wanted more immediately was affection.

He held out his arms, and after a second's hesitation she came into them.

'All right, Molly-mouse?'

'Yes—so relieved, you can't imagine.'

'I can, you know.'

She slid her arms under his jacket and squeezed his large waist. 'Yes, of course you can. But seeing Alison's face on the television screen—oh, Douggie, it was a dreadful experience. I felt so sure that you thought she was either kidnapped or dead...'

'I didn't know what to think. I knew the screening would upset you, but it had to be done. I wished I could have been here with you at the time, though.'

'But you did telephone. You've been very good, Douggie,

176

ringing me so often today. That was the only thing that kept me going.'

'*Good*—my dear love, I'm not just a friend of the family! We're part of each other, aren't we? I may not be the world's most considerate husband and father, but I do care about you all.' He kissed her. 'I care more than you realize... more than I realized myself, I think.'

She returned his kiss and then moved away from him, a little shaken by the strength of her own physical response. 'Well... Would you like something to eat, dear?'

'No thanks, I've been eating on and off all day.' He went into the sitting-room, took off his jacket and loosened his tie. 'What I'd like, though,' he added—forestalling the customary reprimand that it wasn't good for him to live on pies and sandwiches, and wouldn't he like her to make him an omelette and a pot of tea—'is a drink. Nothing to eat, but I'd enjoy a whisky if there's any left.'

Molly looked surprised. Her husband rarely drank spirits. But all she said was, 'I think there's nearly a quarter of a bottle. I'll get you some water.'

'What about you?' called Quantrill, crouching to open the sideboard door and surveying the modest variety of bottles left over from Christmas.

'*Whisky*—ugh, no thanks!'

'Well... cherry brandy?' suggested her husband. 'Or sherry. There's a medium Cyprus—or what about Bristol Cream?'

Molly, returning from the kitchen with water in a small Pyrex measuring-jug, looked pink with pleasurable anticipation; and not merely of the sherry. 'Are we celebrating?' she asked shyly.

'Why not?' He poured her a generous measure of Bristol Cream and splashed some water on his double whisky. 'We've got something to celebrate, haven't we? Here's to—blast! Who the hell's that?'

He strode to the telephone, and watched the happiness ebb from his wife's face as she realized that it was an official call for him. Her cheeks sagged with disappointment, her shoulders slumped. She turned away, and began automatically to tidy the sitting-room, assuming that her husband was being called out and that she would be going to bed as usual with a book.

Quantrill, still watching her while he listened to Inspector Carrow, grieved over the transformation. For a few moments Molly had been young again, glowing and vibrant, warm and beautifully rounded and responsive in his arms. And now she was a disappointed middle-aged housewife, making the best of things. No wonder she sought escape in fiction, where lovers were inexhaustibly ardent and love scenes were never interrupted by anything other than a row of suggestive dots.

Having spent a good part of the afternoon listening to Jasmine Woods's latest book on tape, Quantrill could begin to understand why his wife had become hooked. He wouldn't have admitted it to a soul, but he'd quite enjoyed it; partly on account of the author's frankly sexy voice, of course—he couldn't imagine that she would ever have taken refuge in suggestiveness in her own love-life—but also because it was, quite simply, a rattling good adventure story. Something interesting and unexpected was always happening to Jasmine Woods's heroines. They never had to sit at home and wait, as poor Molly had spent most of her married life doing.

He turned his back to her and concentrated on his telephone call. John Carrow was reporting the discovery in Yarchester of a post-graduate student, a man named Bradley, who admitted to being a friend of Gilbert Smith.

According to Bradley, Smith had arrived at his door the previous evening, looking ill and asking if he could spend the night on the floor of Bradley's bed-sit. He had declined to tell Bradley anything about himself, but he was very jumpy and kept fiddling with a couple of white objects that looked to Bradley like small pieces of bone. They had a meal and rolled a joint together, after which Smith looked more relaxed. He had left the next morning—that morning—at about ten o'clock, without saying where he was going, but he had mentioned during the course of the conversation that he might see Bradley at the weekend, at Oxlip Fair.

'Mind you, I had to put the screws on Bradley to get that much out of him,' said Inspector Carrow with relish. He was a detective who, untypically, enjoyed the exercise of power; he reckoned that, with the city crime-detection rate currently standing at 45°34 percent, and any villain therefore having more than half a chance of getting away with it, the law was entitled to show its teeth occasionally.

'We're holding Bradley on two drugs charges,' he went on, 'possession and supply of cannabis. I've told him that he's likely to get the maximum, fourteen years, for passing a joint to Smith, because that counts as supplying. He won't, of course, particularly as he's a first offender; it's more likely to be a fine and six months suspended; but he's afraid, and that's given me a bit of bargaining power. Trouble is, I think he really has told us all he knows about Smith. Thought I'd let you know, though, in case you want to have a word with him.'

Quantrill thought rapidly. Had Alison still been missing, he would already be on his way to Yarchester. Any connection, however tenuous, with Smith would seem to be a connection with her. He would gladly have spent the whole night with this man Bradley, going over the conversation he had had with Smith in an attempt to find some clue to the man's whereabouts.

But Alison was safe, and he had better things to do. He thanked Inspector Carrow and declined the invitation, watching Molly's face brighten as he did so.

'It's all right, my dear,' he told her, determined to try to go slowly and smoothly and romantically, in the best Jasmine Woods tradition. 'I'm not going to leave you tonight.'

Half an hour later they came jointly to the conclusion that they would be more comfortable in bed. He bolted the door while she put out the lights and then they crept upstairs, arms round each other, exaggeratedly quiet so as not to wake their son.

But in their bedroom, when he took her in his arms as a preliminary to removing the rest of her clothes, Molly sobered.

'It's no good, Douggie,' she said, warding him off with her small hands splayed against his solid chest. 'I can't. You know what'll happen. You're in the middle of a big case, and the phone's bound to ring. It'll be just like that awful time a couple of years ago . . . and I couldn't bear that again, I really couldn't—'

'Don't worry,' said her husband boldly, kissing her again. 'I'll soon fix that!'

For the next hour and thirty-five minutes, Detective Chief Inspector Quantrill's telephone number was unobtainable.

29

The village of Oxlip is in the Breckham Market divisional area, but the policing of the fair had gone far beyond divisional resources. The first fair, six years previously, had attracted a few thousand people to Oxlip. This year, 100,000 were expected.

The traffic police would be out in force to deal with the inevitable jams on the narrow roads that led to the village. The Yarchester drug squad would be there, with additional support from Ipswich. This year, the CID would be there in strength, too. All police leave for the weekend had been cancelled. Oxlip Fair, in police vocabulary, had become two dirty words.

Even the organizers of the fair had, it seemed, had enough. Alarmed by its monstrous growth, they had publicly announced that this fair would be the last. They had described the first one as a spontaneous celebration of spring and the collective joy of individual creation, but the planning required to provide waste-disposal facilities and lavatories for 100,000 people had taken the joy and spontaneity out of it.

They were, however, determined to go out with a bang. This year's fair was going to be the best as well as the biggest. As usual, the theme was medieval. Spuriously, in the sense that everyone involved seemed to equate medieval with simple and uncommercial; apparently it did not occur to them that commerce was the lifeblood of the Middle Ages, as of any other period, and that medieval workers made leather hats and pottery not for the joy of creation, but because there was a demand for them.

The participants, however—because Oxlip Fair was essentially a join-in rather than a spectator event—loved what they thought of as the medieval flavour. The fair provided an annual opportunity for those who had opted out of conventional living to meet together and reaffirm their purpose, and for the more cowardly—or more prudent—who had stuck to their salaries and mortgages, to taste an alternative way of life. At Oxlip they could identify with each other by wearing medieval costume. All stallholders and their assistants were required to wear it, and visitors were given an incentive to do so in the form of reduced admission charges.

Chief Inspector Quantrill, passing the entrance on a preliminary tour of the site, was mildly amused by the haggling that went on between visitors and those on gate duty as to whether everyday long skirts, or jeans crossgartered with string, could be counted as medieval costume. Like the man who was given the allegedly simple job of separating the green apples from the red ones, the people on gate duty found themselves having to take decisions every time.

It was Quantrill's first visit to Oxlip Fair. He had never before had reason to attend on duty, and like any other native East Anglian, he would not have thought of going there for pleasure.

Oxlip Fair was for outsiders. The organizers said that one of the motives in setting up the fair was to provide an opportunity for East Anglian craftsmen to meet and sell their wares, but local people disowned it. Oxlip Fair, in their opinion, was for townspeople playing at country life: for all the professional people and potters and painters and poets who had come flocking to the region during the past ten years to take advantage of the comparative cheapness of property. The only East Anglian accents to be heard were those of some of the police.

It had always been police policy, at the fair, to keep a low profile. The only real problem was with the traffic, and there were uniformed men in the road that ran past the site, at crossroads on the outskirts of the village, and on motor cycles further afield, trying to keep vehicles moving. There was usually little trouble on the site itself. A police caravan was parked just inside, near the entrance, and a couple of uniformed officers stood by it, looking tolerant and amused, available if required to look after lost children or deal with emergencies, but interfering with no one's pleasure.

At the back of the fairground site, however, behind a convenient hedge, was a mobile control-room with more uniformed police standing by. The drug squad also operated from here. It was not that the people who smoked cannabis at the fair gave any trouble. But they were knowingly breaking the law, and members of the drug squad, matey in jeans and longish hair, wandered round among the crowds, looking for the tell-tale sharing of pipes and hand-rolled cigarettes.

This year however, the policing of Oxlip Fair was far more serious. The profile was still low, but there were an unusual number of police cars parked out of sight beside the control room. Chief Inspector Quantrill had called a briefing for 9.30 on the morning of Easter Saturday, the opening day of the fair, and a dozen CID men and officers in plain clothes attended it.

Most of the briefing was done by Sergeant Tait, unusually scruffy in faded jeans and an old leather jerkin that he'd borrowed for the job. He described the man who was wanted in connection with the murder of Jasmine Woods, and passed round photofit pictures. Tait had already spent two days at Oxlip under cover, purporting to lend a hand with the setting up of the fair, and he had chatted to the organizers and helpers who had been camped for the past fortnight in a field opposite the site.

'They're not people who read newspapers or watch television,' he explained. 'They know nothing about the murder, or the fact that we're looking for Smith. His name didn't mean anything to them, so we can assume that he isn't in any way connected with the running of the fair. I got a look at the lists of stall-holders and entertainers, and Smith's name isn't among them either.

'But if he comes to the fair, I don't think it will be as a day visitor. The visitors are mostly people who are in conventional jobs. They put on homespun as a lark, and they come in their own transport because that's the only way they can get here. But Smith ditched his motor bike on the day the murder was discovered. He can't come unless someone gives him a lift, and anyone who does so is likely to be as committed as Smith himself to unconventional living. Jasmine Woods, the murdered woman, met him here last year when he was trying to sell leather. I think that's where we're likely to find him this weekend, at one of the stalls.'

A young detective constable pointed out that Tait had said that Smith's name wasn't on the list of stallholders.

'Right. But this isn't a conventional market, it's a weekend sleep-in as well. The stallholders don't have to camp across the road, they're allowed to sleep on the site to keep an eye on their wares. They bring their families and friends and animals with them, and they live in shelters that they put up behind their stalls. And as there are over 300 stalls, it's rather like a medieval town, huddled and unhygienic. One carrier of typhoid at a food stall and there'll be a major epidemic...'

Martin Tait had suffered, during the past two days. He had hated living in the discomfort of a pup tent that one of the police cadets had lent him. He had forced himself to be useful and friendly, fetching and carrying and knocking in nails and helping to hoist a maypole, eating curious stews, drinking home-brewed beer from homemade mugs, and listening to half-baked philosophy. But the longer he stayed, the more the ethos of the fair irritated him.

Most of the participants were about his own age—he'd recognized a couple of contemporaries from his schooldays at Framlingham—but he found it impossible to identify with them. The only son of a strong-minded, ambitious widow, he had nothing in common with people who wanted to reject the values of contemporary society. The idea of being poor by choice, of spending his time growing vegetables or playing a flute or doing leatherwork appalled him. He deplored the fact that the skills and hard work he had seen going into the creation of the fair were not put to regular, socially acceptable use.

'And since the fairground is rather like a town,' he continued, raising his voice above the muttered disenchantment of the assembled police officers, 'that's how I suggest we treat it. I've made a map of the site—' he passed round photostat copies '—not guaranteed accurate, but near enough. And I've divided it into beats, so that each of us can concentrate on getting to know the resident population of our area. Without, of course, letting them know that we're their friendly neighbourhood coppers. Most of them like to think they're anti-fuzz, though they'll scream for us soon enough if they're in any trouble.'

The policemen cheered up at the thought of having something definite to work on, and began to study their maps. Quantrill left Tait to finish the briefing and went outside. The fair was not yet officially open, but the site already looked crowded and the traffic police were working their arms as busily as bookmakers at a race meeting.

Cars were converging on Oxlip from all over the region. The fields beyond the site had been designated as official car-parks, at 25p a time, but as usual a good many motorists, intent on being medieval and simplistically equating that with individual freedom, preferred to try to avoid paying by parking on the roadside verges. The road that ran past the site had already been reduced to half its width, and a police motor cyclist reported a tailback as far as Bungay.

As soon as the cars stopped, their drivers and passengers tried to abandon the twentieth century. Nearly all of them got out wearing homemade costumes of some kind: tights dyed to make men's hose, Hessian jerkins, unisex surtouts in various colours and materials. Some men were dressed as monks or friars, beggars or Robin Hoods. Many of the girls were in long dresses, and pointed hats of the kind recommended for wear by fifteenth-century damsels imprisoned in castle turrets.

Quantrill felt uncomfortably conspicuous as he stood watching the visitors enter the site. He had dressed casually, in an old pair of tweed trousers and his fishing sweater, but he knew that his hair was too neatly cut and his chin too closely shaven. He was conscious of looking both unacceptably orthodox, and, at forty-six, older than almost anyone else on the site apart from one or two other coppers. The majority of men were about Gilbert Smith's age. Nearly all of them were bearded, and half the beards in sight were as thin and medium brown as Tait had described Gilbert Smith's.

'Trouble with these buggers is, they all look the same.' PC Ronald Timms, trying to be inconspicuous in dark-grey flannel trousers and navy-blue anorak, but every inch a policeman behind his lugubrious moustache, had come up behind the Chief Inspector.

Quantrill agreed, and began to move on. Together, he

and Ron Timms were a dead giveaway. 'Hope you've got a good beat, Ron,' he said pointedly.

Unexpectedly, PC Timms chuckled. 'I hear it includes the beer tent...' He gave his moustache an anticipatory wipe with the knuckle of his forefinger.

'I'll know where to come at lunch-time, then,' Quantrill told him. He walked away, climbing a grassy hill to view the site from the highest point.

The fifteen-acre meadow where the fair was held was too small now for the numbers involved, but otherwise ideal. It was glebe land, and a footpath ran across it from the village to the church, which provided an appropriately medieval backdrop. The church was small, fourteenth century without any later external additions, and built of flint with a characteristically East Anglian round tower and a thatched roof. The rough grass of the surrounding churchyard was bright with primroses and daffodils that had sprung up among the leaning, lichened gravestones like a renewed promise of resurrection.

Part of the meadow, between the village and the churchyard, was level but the rest of the site undulated, rising to the hillock on which Quantrill was standing. Trees and bushes grew here and there in the meadow and a chestnut crowned the top of the hill, thrusting its pale fuzzy opening leaves into the clear blue of the sky. All round the meadow were hedges, some white with blackthorn blossom, some purple with trailing brambles, some yellow with willow, some bursting into green.

But the colours of spring, lit palely by the sun, were eclipsed by the colours of the fair. Spuriously medieval or not, Oxlip Fair had a look of joy and gaiety. Poles had been hoisted aloft, and from them streamed ribbons and flags and banners contrived from old sheets and army surplus parachute silk dyed in brilliant colours. In the centre of the meadow was a great maypole, nearly seventy feet tall, garlanded with blossoms and greenery. Giant kites, bird-shaped, flew towards the sun.

And then there was the sound of music, coming nearer as a costumed procession entered the meadow led by a drum and a fiddle and a tambourine. Someone read a proclamation at the foot of the maypole. A wicker basket was thrown open and a flock of pigeons exploded into the air, vying for height with the banners, the maypole, the church tower, the chestnut tree, the kites and eventually the skylarks before setting course for their lofts. Oxlip Fair had begun.

There was colour and movement everywhere, but not the mechanical movement and neon-lit garishness of a modern fairground. Informal entertainment was provided by clowns and tumblers, by jugglers and minstrels and an early music consort, by puppeteers and morris dancers and anyone else who felt sufficiently extrovert to have a go. Stages had been set up in different parts of the meadow for drama and music, and fir poles planted beside each stage were lively with banners. Silken dragons flapped over one, a castle painted on tarpaulin towered behind another, a third was sited in the gaping mouth of a bamboo dragon whose cardboard scales were held together by orange baler twine.

'All very jolly,' said Quantrill to his sergeant, who had climbed the hill to join him. It was the first time they had met since Wednesday, when they had found that there were no traces of blood in Paul Pardoe's car, and that they could get no further information from either Jonathan Elliott or George Hussey. Digging operations at Yeoman's had uncovered nothing, but the scene-of-crime team was still searching the house and grounds. In the absence of any new leads, Quantrill had since been making enquiries about Jasmine Woods in her previous home at Thaxted, while Tait had come to set up the Oxlip operation.

'Or it would be jolly,' Quantrill amended, 'if we weren't on a murder investigation. That was a good briefing you did, Martin. I like your idea of treating the place as a town. Trying to spot one man among 100,000 would be hopeless otherwise.'

'Let's hope it works,' said Tait.

'It had better. We've got to find Smith.'

'Did you get any useful information about him from Alison, sir?'

Quantrill chewed his lower lip. Then, 'I haven't seen her,' he said abruptly. 'We haven't heard anything more since that telephone call on Tuesday.'

'*What?* But I thought—'

'I know. That's what I thought, that she'd be home within a couple of days—or at least that she'd ring again. It's not just fatherly concern, though there's that, too, God knows, but we *need* her. We need her evidence. I haven't so far found anything significant about Jasmine Woods at Thaxted, and Patsy Hopkins hasn't yet been able to get anything coherent out of the ex-secretary, Anne Downing—so we must talk to Alison. And we want to know in detail what she saw when she went into the room where the woman was murdered, so that we can compare it with what we found ourselves. We know that Smith took at least two netsuke, but we don't know whether that was on the night of the murder or the next morning, after Alison found the body. So her evidence is going to be vital—and Smith knows that as well as we do.'

'There may be a perfectly simple explanation,' said Tait. 'Perhaps she just wanted to stay on with her friends over the holiday weekend.' He thought about it. 'Wouldn't she be likely to come here, to Oxlip?'

Quantrill shook his head impatiently. 'No. Alison isn't interested in this kind of caper, she's a sensible girl. That's why I can't understand why we've heard nothing more from her. I know she was upset over the murder, it stands to reason. But she must have got over the shock by now. And she's alert, she reads the papers and watches the television news, so she'll know we want information about Smith. She's usually very considerate. I'm sure she wouldn't go on keeping us in suspense, not of her own free will...'

The phrase lingered on the air as Quantrill and Tait avoided each other's eyes, conscious of its corollary.

30

Alison had begun to grow more accustomed to life at Mill Farm. Despite occasional tensions the atmosphere was friendly; she would have found it relaxing if it were not for the physical contact in which the family indulged. Everyone touched and hugged and kissed everyone else with casual affection, and Alison found it alien and embarrassing. She tightened up instinctively when any adult members of the family came anywhere near her. It was not easy for her to identify with any of the other women, since she was not into yoga or vegetarianism or spinning, but she was glad to spend the time helping with the children and the animals.

When her conscience had nagged her to walk up to the village on Tuesday and telephone her mother, she had fully intended to ring home again in a couple of days; but the days drifted by and she let them go. The thought of home, and of the inevitable questioning that awaited her, brought so much stress that, having done her duty, she deliberately tried to put home out of her mind. She pulled a shutter down over it, as she had pulled a shutter over her discovery of the murder.

But although she refused to think of that morning when she had found Jasmine's body, she could not forget the fact of her friend's death. It was too recent, too raw. There would be occasions when it slipped from her memory and she could feel, for a few moments, almost happy; but then it would come back, hitting her like a physical blow, stopping her in the middle of what she was doing while her body clenched with pain. At other times the misery would creep up on her slowly, like cold dark water rising in a lock. She would carry on mechanically with her tasks, but she would be unable to stop the tears from rolling down her cheeks while she worked. And all the time, in Quantrill family tradition, she kept her emotions to herself.

It was one of the children who began the process of breaking down her habitual reticence. 'Alison's crying *again*,' he reported to Polly, who was in the studio she had converted from a cowshed, generously slapping oil paint onto canvas.

'Is she? Well, that's good, isn't it? We all need to cry sometimes.' She shooed the child away and went in search of Alison. 'No, don't stop crying,' she told her. 'It's therapeutic. Only don't keep your sorrows to yourself—it really does help if you share them.'

And so Alison had begun, haltingly, to tell Polly what she had told Roz. But whereas Roz's reaction had been practical and intellectual, her sister's was characteristically physical and emotional. Appalled by Alison's story, Polly swept the girl into her motherly arms. 'Oh, my poor sweet child—you poor lamb . . .'

Alison felt so weakened that after a moment's hesitation she clung to her and gave way to a long slow flood of grief. Securely held as she had not been held since she was a child, she felt able to abandon herself to emotion and tell Polly everything.

When the tears eventually began to lessen, Polly spoke, her cheek pressed warmly against the girl's. 'I never met Jasmine, but I heard about her from Roz. Of course you're shattered—no, don't move. It's all right, relax... Go on holding me, we all need other people to hold on to. And not just in times of grief—we ought to show warmth and affection, too. Our families and friends are precious, and they should be told so. That's the way we live here at Mill Farm, and that's how we're bringing up the children.'

It was not a way of life that Alison felt tempted to adopt, but Polly had been both comforting and enlightening. Alison hoped to be able to pass on some of that comfort to Gilbert Smith when she saw him, because she knew how grieved he must be over Jasmine's death. She began to look forward to the weekend, and to the probability of meeting him at Oxlip Fair.

The Mill Farm family talked of little else but the fair while she was with them. An advance party went off on Good Friday to set up the stall and the camp site, travelling in a farm cart drawn by the family horse. On Saturday morning everyone else was up early, and Polly provided a ferry service to Oxlip in her old car, taking Alison and the older children last.

The fair was well under way by the time they arrived, and the children shrieked with pleasure at the sight. The air was filled with the sound of excitement, of guitars and flutes and folk songs. From a group of food stalls came the sizzle of cooking and appetizing smells of curry, kebabs and fried chicken. Woodsmoke drifted everywhere, faint but pervasive, a genuine breath of pre-industrial living.

Polly was cheerfully irreverent as they wandered through the fairground, pointing out with relish all the anachronisms. One Robin Hood smelled of aftershave. A family group with a very rough encampment, dressed in grubby sacking and looking decidedly Early English, was trying to sell orange squash from a plastic container. A monk was cooking corn on the cob, and serving it with butter from Danish foil packs; and a man frying chicken quarters on a barbecue, wearing a very short jerkin over his hose, had prudently protected himself from the hot fat with a PVC apron advertising Colman's mustard.

They made their way through the higgledy-piggledy rows of stalls that formed the streets of the temporary town, exchanging the smells of cooking for those of leather and incense. It was supposed to be an Oxlip rule that nothing offered for sale should be commercially mass-produced. As a consequence, there was nothing offered for sale that anyone actually needed. But the visitors were determined to join in, and so they bought pendants and candles and nettle shampoos and corn dollies and the Papal indulgences and joss sticks and Oxlip Fair T-shirts and tarot cards and medieval love potions ('Satisfaction guaranteed' called the manufacturer, 'or your money back next year!').

Alison enjoyed it, catching the gaiety of Polly, who wandered round with a grin on her face. She felt so happy that for a short time she forgot that only five days ago she had found her friend and employer lying murdered. She lingered beside one of the stalls, watching a woman at work on a loom while Polly took the children to an adventure playground among the trees on the side of the hill. And then she saw Gilbert Smith.

A large number of plain-clothes policemen discovered, at about 12.30, that the beer tent was on their beat. Real ale was being served from casks set up along the back wall of the marquee, and there were so many clamouring customers that the barman found it simplest to tap the beer into plastic watering cans and fill the mugs from those.

The mugs were plastic, too. It would spoil the taste of the Adnams, thought Quantrill, but with such a heaving press of customers it would be unreasonable to hope for glasses. He nodded amiably to a group of policemen as he pushed past them to down his drink in the open air. They had nothing significant to report, but the fair at least provided them with some entertainment: '. . . *and this feller, cheeky bastard, is carrying a placard reading "We're following the drug squad, follow us." There's a couple of dozen people trailing after*

*him, and Lenny Rundle, in uniform of course, tagging along
behind red in the face with his notebook out . . .' 'There's this
stall, more of a homemade tent really, with a notice on it
saying "Medieval Massage." "How much?" I asked the girl.
"That depends what you want," she says, perfectly serious,
"it's hands 45p, feet 60p, neck 75p, and 90p for the body" . . .'*

Quantrill stood with his drink, watching a crowd gathering to watch a circle of costumed adults dancing round the
maypole. Among the crowd was a girl he thought he knew; so
pregnant that he rapidly identified her as one of the students
he had met at the Old Rectory at Thirling. She was with a girl
of her own age, and two men. All of them wore costumes and
appeared to be enjoying themselves thoroughly. They were
accompanied by two children, a small curly-haired boy carrying a painted cardboard shield and a wooden sword, and a
girl of about ten in a long yellow robe.

Quantrill recognized the children as the two youngest
Elliotts, Vanessa and Toby. Neither of them seemed happy.
Toby was being advanced upon by an adult dragon-headed
figure with red hose; he looked apprehensive, as though not
knowing whether to hit it with his sword or run. Vanessa,
prim and neat, appeared to be trying to disassociate herself
from the proceedings. 'Personally,' Quantrill heard her say in
her high, clear voice, 'I think the whole thing is stupid.'

The Chief Inspector joined Tait, who was soberly drinking bitter lemon from a bottle. 'It's going to be more difficult
than I thought, Martin,' Quantrill said. 'I didn't realize that
all the stalls and shelters were homemade. I thought they'd
be proper market stalls and tents, not hovels botched up out
of wood and tarpaulin and sacking. You can't possibly see
what's going on inside them, or how many people are quietly
sleeping off booze or pot. If Smith keeps his head down, he
could stay here all weekend without being spotted.'

'But he's got to come out sometime,' said Tait practically.
He pointed to the urinal, a system of troughing protected
from public view by a long canvas banner painted with male
torsos in medieval garb. Strategically sited in an open part of
the meadow near the beer tent, it formed part of the general
entertainment; a woman was happily taking a photograph of
the banner, with visiting heads and shoulders projecting
above it and knees and feet below. 'If the beat coppers are

doing their job, they'll catch Smith when he comes down here.'

'*If* he comes down here.' Quantrill, having a longer acquaintance with human nature than his sergeant, was ever more practical. 'It's a long way to come, and I reckon a lot of the people on the stalls are making use of the rectory shrubbery, up at the back there. Smith could just dodge through the stalls and nip over the fence—that's what most of the others seem to be doing.'

'Dirty pigs,' said PC Timms, overhearing them. 'I went along by that fence an hour ago, and it was starting to sniff even then.'

'That'll make it authentically medieval, anyway,' muttered Tait. 'All right, I'll put someone on obbo up by the fence—'

'Not me,' said Timms promptly, 'I've got my work cut out watching this beer tent.' He turned to the Chief Inspector. 'Is Mrs Quantrill here, at the fair, sir?'

'Good grief, no!'

'Oh.' Timms looked slightly offended. 'Well, I only asked on account of seeing your daughter.'

'My *daughter*? Alison? Are you sure?'

'Of course I'm sure. I wasn't near enough to speak to her, but it was definitely Alison. I ought to know her, she and my Paula were at school together—'

'When was this? When did you see her?'

'Oh . . . half an hour ago . . . three-quarters . . .'

Quantrill seized him by the shoulder. 'My God, man, why didn't you say so! You know we're looking for her—she's our key witness in this case.'

'But you'd found her, sir,' objected PC Timms. 'I know she disappeared, but then she rang you and you called off the search. I didn't know you were still looking for her—'

He protested himself into silence. The DCI's face was grim and his grip was so tight as to be painful. 'Where exactly did you see her?' he was saying. 'Come on, man. Who was she with? What was she wearing?'

Alison saw Gilbert Smith a few moments before he saw her. He was walking slowly between the stalls, his shoulders hunched, his hands crammed into the pockets of his ragged jeans, his bearded head held down. She ran to him immediately, stopping to block his path.

'Gilbert!' she said. 'Gil, dear—'

She had intended to show that she was fond of him. She had intended to hug him—or at least to touch his arm or his hand, as a way of acknowledging their mutual bereavement and her gratitude for the way he had coped with all the practicalities on that dreadful Monday morning. But as soon as he raised his head she realized that he was not the vague, kind, amiable man she had known. His face was white and set and his eyes seemed to be staring at some horrifying inner vision. It was Gilbert Smith, but he had become a stranger.

She stepped back, suddenly afraid. 'Gil?' she faltered.

He blinked. 'What—?' He shook the long hair out of his eyes and made an effort to focus on her face. 'Alison . . . Oh, God, and I thought no one would find me here! What are you doing? This isn't your scene. I thought this was one place where I could be among people of my own kind. No one asks questions at Oxlip, no one hassles us, we can just blow our minds in peace—and that's what I've got to do. I've got to forget, don't you see? I can't live with it, I've got to shut it out. But now you've found me, and your father's the fuzz. There'll be questions, and more questions, and I can't bear it—I can't bear to think of it—'

His long legs folded, almost in slow motion, until he was crouching close to the earth, shivering as though he had a fever.

Alison forgot her fear. She couldn't bring herself to touch him, but she felt a strengthening of their friendship. She crouched beside him on the grass underneath a black-budded ash tree, regardless of and unregarded by the stallholders, shouting their wares above her head, and the passersby.

'But my father's not here, Gil! I haven't seen him for days—I can't bear to see him, because I can't face any questions either. I've left home and I'm here with some friends from a commune. I'm trying to forget, too. You can trust me, Gil, you know you can. I wouldn't tell my father about my friends—I've always known that you smoke pot, but I've never told Dad about it.'

He nodded a vague acknowledgement. 'I had to have them,' he said, more to himself than to her. 'They were so

beautiful. And I could appreciate their beauty so much more
than Jasmine could. Oh, she thought she could, but she'd
never smoked, she'd never had windows opened in her
mind... We used to argue about it sometimes.' He looked
up, his eyes dark with horror. 'But I wouldn't have harmed
her. It was just that I had to have them. I can't show them to
you because I've buried them. I'm staying with some friends,
acid heads, they've rented a cottage out in the country.
They're good friends, but if they knew I'd got the netsuke
they'd want to sell them to buy acid. Then there'd be more
violence, and I couldn't bear that, I couldn't bear any more
blood...'

He rose to his feet, stiffly, like an elderly man. 'I came
out to get a pizza for us—' He gestured towards the huddle of
stalls that climbed the side of the hill. 'But I'll come back to
talk to you. It's a relief to be able to talk. Don't go away,
Alison, please.'

She got up slowly, using the grey trunk of the tree as a
support, and watched him shambling away. She was appalled
at what he had done. She felt white and she knew that she
was trembling. But she thought that she could understand
him; sickened as she was, she believed that she could follow
the fuddled reasoning that made him take the netsuke when
he went up to Yeoman's on Monday morning and found
Jasmine dead.

She knew that she couldn't stay and talk to Gilbert, not
after what he had done. She couldn't remain the friend of a
man whose sense of beauty was stronger than his sense of
compassion, of decency. How *could* he see Jasmine's mutilated body and think only in terms of picking the scattered
netsuke off the blood-stained carpet...?

But what was she to do? Go and talk to one of the
uniformed policemen by the gate? But she'd told Gilbert he
could trust her, and she couldn't betray that trust. Besides, if
she made herself known to the police, that would be the end
of her peace. There would be questions, and more questions.

The only thing for her to do was to rejoin Polly and the
children, to run back to the sanctuary of the Mill Farm
family. She turned, poised for flight, and found herself face to
face with Martin Tait.

*　　*　　*

Tait had decided on a soft approach. Obviously the girl's parents had dealt with her tactlessly after her discovery of the murder; that was why she had run, and why she had stayed away for so long. She wouldn't want to be badgered or questioned, or told brisk instructions. Then he stepped out of the shelter of the stall, into the lane.

Alison had just seen Gilbert Smith. She took two steps backwards away from him, turned as if to run, and then saw Tait.

She looked back over her shoulder. 'Gil!' she shouted. 'Gil—I'm sorry! Run!'

But Tait was already moving, fast. Smith had heard the shouts and stopped; now, seeing Tait heading straight for him, he dropped his pizza and tried to go back the way he had come.

He hadn't a chance. He wasn't used to running. Tait, pushing spectators aside like rugby opponents, got him with a flying tackle.

Chief Inspector Quantrill, gasping as much with relief as with the exertion of getting there, put his arms round his daughter.

'It's all right, sweetheart,' he said, using an endearment he hadn't ventured to use since she was eight years old. 'It's all right, we've got him. You needn't worry anymore. Come on, I'll take you home.'

31

'But I've told you. I've told you four or five times already.'

'We're in no hurry. We're not going anywhere, and neither are you. So tell us again: when did you last see Jasmine Woods?'

Gilbert Smith, looking white and sick, was sitting slumped

at a table in an interview room at Breckham Market police station. He gave a long, shuddering, sigh.

'On Sunday morning,' he repeated tonelessly. 'I got up late—I don't know what time—and then I went up to Jasmine's for coffee.'

'Had she invited you?'

'No. She didn't give me invitations, I just dropped in. We were good friends.'

'Close friends?'

'No. It was an easy, casual relationship. She always had a pot of coffee on the go, and whenever I called she told me to help myself.'

'And what did you talk about, on Sunday morning?'

'We didn't. Her head was full of her book—she'd been working, and she always found it difficult to switch off. She told me that the Elliotts were coming in for drinks, and she got ready for them while I drank coffee in the kitchen. She asked me to stay, but I didn't want to. I said hallo to them when they came, then I finished my coffee and went. That was the last time I saw her.'

'Did you ask her for money?'

'No! I told you—she paid me to do her garden, and I lived rent free on her property. I didn't need money. And if I had, I certainly wouldn't have asked her for it. She was good to me, and I wouldn't have done anything to upset our relationship.'

'And how did you spend the rest of the day?'

He sighed again, and began a recital. 'I worked in the garden, then I went to my flat and made something to eat. Then it was dark, and I spent the evening reading and listening to tapes and drinking. I didn't go out and I didn't see anybody and I didn't hear anything. I smoked some hash, and later on I took some dexies as well. I got stoned. The next thing I knew, somebody was hammering on my door. I didn't do anything about it at first, but then I went to see who it was. I don't know the time, but it was daylight so it must have been Monday. Alison was at the door, saying something about Jasmine being dead. She was incoherent, and I wasn't feeling too good, so it took me a long time to think what to do. But then I went up to the house, and through the front door and into the sitting-room, and found Jasmine. She'd obviously been murdered.'

Quantrill and Tait sat watching him, saying nothing. Smith swallowed, and wiped his bearded mouth with the back of his hand. 'It was horrible,' he said in a hoarse whisper, 'horrible . . .'

After a few moments he added, toneless again, 'And there they were, you see. Two of her netsuke, lying in a pool of her blood. Whoever killed her must have dropped them in his hurry to get away. And I couldn't just leave them there, lying in her blood. I mean, they were no good to poor Jasmine. I wasn't doing any harm to her by taking them. They were such beautiful things, I had to have them. I don't think Jasmine would have minded. But I knew that the fuzz wouldn't understand. I got her blood on my hands and clothes when I picked the netsuke up, and I cut my own finger on some of the broken glass. If you saw the blood on me, you might even think that I'd killed her. So I went back to my flat and washed and changed and packed my gear. With Jasmine dead I'd have had to leave anyway, so there was no point in hanging about. But I could hear Alison crying, and I couldn't desert her. So when I was ready I went back to the house and dialled 999 from the office. Then I left. That's all, except that I can show you where I hid the netsuke. One of my friends in Yarchester told me that the fuzz were after me, and on Tuesday he took me to stay with some people in the country until the heat was off. I buried the netsuke in the university park before I left.'

'And what do you know about the murder?' Quantrill asked.

'Nothing at all. I swear it, nothing at all!'

'But on your own admission you were stoned on Sunday night. You smoked cannabis, you drank, you took amphetamines. You got yourself into such a state that you didn't know which day of the week it was, or whether it was night or morning. You said you took some dexies, and the next thing you knew someone was hammering on your door. *The next thing you knew* . . . that was something like twelve hours later!'

'And you coveted her netsuke,' said Tait. 'All right, perhaps you didn't need the money. Perhaps you didn't want them because of their value. But on your own admission, you coveted them for their beauty. I think you went up to her house on Sunday evening, not necessarily to steal them but perhaps to look at them. That would be the best time to look at them, wouldn't it, when you were drugged to reality and your perceptions were at their height? But if you were in that condition, I doubt if Jasmine would have wanted you in her house. You had to use violence on her—'

'And once you started,' said Quantrill, 'you couldn't stop, could you? You went on beating her on the head until the bottle broke—'

Smith's arms curled protectively over his own head, as though warding off physical blows. 'I didn't,' he grieved, 'I didn't.'

There was a knock on the door and the station sergeant beckoned Quantrill out into the corridor. The Chief Inspector scowled and went.

'Your daughter's in the front office, sir. She says she wants to speak to you urgently about Smith.'

Quantrill followed him. Alison was standing in the entrance hall, looking pale and resolute. Her father wanted to take her to his office, but she refused.

'Are you trying to charge Gilbert with Jasmine's murder?' she demanded. 'Because if so, you've got the wrong man. Gilbert stole some of her netsuke when he went up to the house on Monday morning, I know that, he told me. It was a horrible thing to do, but it doesn't make him a murderer. He's really very gentle. He liked Jasmine, he wouldn't have done anything to harm her.'

The Chief Inspector suppressed a sigh. Alison had had a very rough week, poor girl. He knew that he had to go very gently with her; all the same, he couldn't have her interfering with a murder case, and particularly not in the front office.

He put an arm round her shoulder and turned her towards the door. 'Well, I'm glad to hear your opinion. And I'm sure you're right to some extent—druggies aren't by nature violent people. But drugs do frightening things. They can bring out aggressions that are usually buried too deep for anyone to suspect, least of all the user.'

Alison pulled away from his arm. 'I can't argue about that. I don't want to argue about it. But I'm sure that Gilbert didn't do the murder because I think I know the man who did.'

Her father stared at her. 'Who?' he demanded. 'And where's your evidence? Look, we can't talk here—come to my office.'

She shook her head. 'I haven't really got any evidence. It's just intuition, I suppose. Oh, but there is something I've remembered about Jasmine's sitting-room, something that makes me sure I've got the right man. Only—the thing is, I don't want to talk to you about it. I'm sorry, Dad, but I think I'd find it easier to talk to Martin Tait.'

'To me? I didn't think I'd be *persona grata* with your daughter, after the way I conned her this afternoon at Oxlip.'

Quantrill tried not to look as hurt as he felt. 'Don't ask me how her mind works, just find out what she knows. But she doesn't want to see you here, she wants to keep it informal. So take her out into the town, Martin, and buy her a cup of tea or something. And be kind to her, or I'll pin your ears to the noticeboard.'

Alison refused the offer of tea. They walked in silence, several feet apart, across the main road and down into the town. They went down Market Street, along White Hart Street, past the Rights of Man and so to the narrow river Dodman. It was a feature of the town centre, with a paved walk on one side opening on to a pedestrian shopping precinct, and gardens on the other. There were seats on the paved walk, looking out over the river towards flower-beds yellow and white with spring.

It was quiet by the river. The shops had just closed, after the busyness of Easter Saturday, and the precinct had an exhausted, wind-blown, littered look. It was too cool for sitting about. Nearly everyone had gone home to tea. People would return later, when the pubs and the Chinese takeaway opened and the dog owners emerged for their evening walks, but for the moment Alison and Tait had the area to themselves.

She tucked her hands into the pockets of her velvet jacket. 'This is going to be a bit difficult to explain,' she said, keeping her voice distant. 'I can't tell Dad because he's emotionally involved with me. He'd be all upset. Anyway, his generation is so prejudiced. That's one reason why I thought it would be easier to talk to you, because we're the same generation.'

She turned to him, her cheeks flaring. 'That doesn't mean that I've forgiven you for the way you set me up this afternoon,' she said vigorously. 'I think it was despicable. Oh, I know, you're a detective and this is a murder investigation and so your job comes before everything. I know all about that, I've heard about it all my life. But I won't stand for being *used*—particularly when you're not even after the right man.'

She walked on. 'The point is, though, that I think I can talk to you. It's always easiest to talk to someone you're not emotionally involved with, and that's certainly true of us. We don't need ever to see each other again after today. So I don't mind telling you why I'm sure you've got the wrong man, because you can think what you like, it won't worry me in the least.'

'Right,' agreed Tait peaceably. He couldn't imagine that she had anything significant to reveal, but he was prepared to indulge her. Smith was in custody and they could hold him on a charge of stealing the netsuke, so there was no need to rush the questioning about the murder. He felt pleased with the way the Oxlip Fair operation had gone. The world looked good to him on that spring evening. So did Alison. He glanced with amusement at her determined profile, thinking how much more attractive her guileless personality became when she was fired with indignation.

They had reached the part of the walk directly opposite the small shopping precinct, where the river Dodman, on its way to the Ouse, was joined by the even smaller river Dunnock. The confluence was spanned by an elegant modern triple footbridge. Alison walked halfway across it and leaned on the rail, looking down at the water.

Tait joined her. He could sense that she was searching for words, and he had the wisdom to keep quiet.

She straightened and looked at him. 'Would you say I was normal?' she demanded, holding her head high and her voice steady.

Tait shrugged. 'What's normal?' he asked, trying to sound idle rather than wary. He peered down into the river. Shoals of tiddlers hovered and darted just under the surface, above the thick ribbons of weed that streamed with the flow of the current. As the weed moved, he thought that he could glimpse a shining object beneath it, a kind of metal grille.

Alison went on looking at him. 'Hetero,' she said.

Tait smiled at her, relieved and slightly amused. He had been half-afraid that she had been about to disclose some terminal disease, or imagined psychosis. 'I've never thought of doubting it. Why?' he added tolerantly. 'Aren't you?'

'Yes, of course I am! At least, I've always taken it for granted. I've had boy-friends ever since I was sixteen.' She spoke as though sixteen was three centuries rather than three years ago. 'But now I'm not so sure. I didn't think about it until this week—I wouldn't let myself think about it—but I was so upset about Jasmine—'

Her voice rose, wavered and broke. She bent again over the handrail of the bridge to conceal her tears, and Tait waited patiently beside her. He slewed his head to look at the object in the river from a different angle, and finally identified it as part of a shopping trolley, almost buried in mud and weed. The manager of the Fine Fare supermarket had complained to the police that he lost on average five trolleys a month, so here was at least one of them.

'Anyway.' Alison scrubbed at her eyes and recovered her voice. 'Since then I've been talking to Roz Elliott and her sister Polly, and I can see why I've been so upset. I've understood it, and admitted it to myself. I was falling in love with Jasmine.'

'Well, that's perfectly understandable,' said Tait easily. He could remember being a lonely new thirteen-year-old boarder at public school and falling in love with the captain of the rugby team. It hadn't been reciprocated, it hadn't lasted more than a term, and it certainly hadn't affected him permanently. It was a fact of life, a phase that most adolescents went through; but he could remember how painful it was, and how shaming. He would have died rather than let his mother know, and so he could understand Alison's unwillingness to talk to her father.

'Jasmine was an attractive woman,' he went on, 'and she'd made a name for herself. She had a strong personality. She was helpful and friendly to you, and so you became infatuated. Naturally, you're more upset about her death than you would otherwise have been. But there's no reason why you should worry about it, or think that it has changed your orientation.'

Alison's reply was iced with contempt. 'I'm not an adolescent, Martin. I do know what I'm talking about. I've been in love several times, and I wanted—I thought I wanted—to marry the man I had an affair with before I came back to Breckham. What I felt for Jasmine wasn't infatuation.'

'Yes, all right.' Tait tried to soothe her. 'I'm not doubting the strength of your feelings. But I don't see what this has to do with Jasmine's murder. I mean, you're surely not trying to tell me that she felt the same way about you?'

'No . . . at least, she never gave me any reason to think so, but . . . oh, it's all intuition, but I believe she might have done if we'd been together longer—if she'd lived . . .'

Tait tried to go on being patient. It wasn't only that the girl's father had told him to be kind; he felt too protective towards her to want to say or do anything that would give her feelings any more of a battering. But he knew that she was talking nonsense.

'Oh, come on, Alison—' He put a friendly hand on her shoulder. 'Jasmine was very fond of you, I'm sure of that. She couldn't help but be fond of you, you're a very sweet girl. But she was no lesbian. After all, she was a romantic novelist. She spent her life describing passionate love affairs between men and women.'

Alison pulled away from his hand. 'What's that got to do with it?' she said coolly. 'Jasmine was a professional writer. She wrote fiction, not autobiography.'

'But Jasmine liked men,' insisted Tait. 'And this time *I* know what I'm talking about. If it hadn't been for her friend Smith and his drugs, I'd have been after her myself. She was keen enough, I can tell you that.'

'You think so?'

Tait glowered.

'There's no need to feel offended,' Alison went on kindly. 'You see, I knew Jasmine a good deal better than you did. Not that she discussed her private life with me, but I know how she felt about men. Yes, she liked them as friends, and she found them useful for her books. She enjoyed knowing that some of them were after her. But I've realized, this week, that she happened to prefer women.'

'How do you know that?'

The girl hesitated. 'Intuition again, I suppose. But you were the one who brought it to my notice, when you told me that Anne Downing had broken off her engagement. Do you know when that happened, by the way?'

'Last weekend, I think.'

'Yes, that fits . . . You couldn't have known it, but Jasmine was very fond of Anne. They were very close—Anne lived at Yeoman's, and they did everything together. I don't know what broke them up, Jasmine didn't talk about it, but I gathered that they had a quarrel and Anne went off. That was a few weeks before the party that you took me to. And after you'd left the party, Anne turned up with her fiancé—did you know that?'

'Your father mentioned it.'

'Yes, that's the odd thing. Dad saw exactly what I saw at the party, but he couldn't ever put it together for himself because, like you, he thought of Jasmine only as a romantic novelist. What we thought we saw was Jasmine's ex-secretary calling in to say that she'd become engaged. I can remember how flushed Anne looked, and how bright her eyes were. I put it down to happiness, and so did Dad I suppose, and everybody else. But what I now think we were seeing was Anne coming back in triumph to her ex-lover, and saying in effect that she could do without her.'

'You mean that Anne was using Buxton as a way of getting even with Jasmine after their quarrel?'

'It's possible. It didn't occur to me at the time, of course, but I've been doing a lot of thinking in the past few days. I know that at the party her fiancé looked as though he couldn't believe what had happened to him. He was overjoyed. But once she'd made her point to Jasmine, Anne would have had to come to terms with the fact that she'd agreed to marry the man. She must have decided that she couldn't go through with it, and I suppose she had a row with him. She must have let him know about Jasmine—perhaps she even taunted him . . . I don't know. I don't *know* any of this, but it's possible, isn't it? It does make sense?'

Tait was thinking hard. 'Oh, it makes sense all right. It

makes very good sense. But it's only intuition, and I can't go to your father with that.'

'I don't want you to,' she said, alarmed. 'I don't want you to tell him how I felt about Jasmine, he's too old-fashioned to take it. I love him, and I don't want to hurt him. But there is just one fact I can tell you. I've been trying, ever since I found—ever since Monday morning, *not* to think about what I saw at Yeoman's. It was too dreadful. But this morning, when Gilbert was telling me how he stole the netsuke, I did think about what I saw. And I remembered quite clearly that just as I turned from opening the window curtains, I noticed that a photograph was missing. It had always stood in the same place, on a writing desk. It was a photograph of Jasmine and Anne, standing close together and looking very happy. And I can think of only one person who would want to get rid of that.'

32

At High House Farm, Oliver Buxton had given his pigman Easter Saturday off. Instead of getting married, Buxton had spent the day in the farrowing shed. He was crossing the yard in working jeans and Wellington boots, combat hat and jacket, on his way to the house for supper, when three cars came roaring up the approach road. The first was unmarked, the others were police cars. Buxton stood motionless beside the slurry pit, his eyes on the ground, as the cars stopped and their occupants approached him. He said nothing at all, until Quantrill asked him what he had done the previous Sunday evening.

Buxton looked up. He needed a shave, and a bath. It was not a factor that Quantrill was crass enough to hold against a hard-working man, but it did strengthen the theory

that Tait had put to him on the basis of the photograph that
Alison believed to be missing.

The relationship that Tait had postulated between Jasmine Woods and Anne Downing might or might not be true, but Quantrill could see and smell for himself that life at High House Farm would have been a good deal less pleasant for the girl than life at Yeoman's. Whatever the fundamental reason for the broken engagement, there was—as Tait had said—only one person who would have wanted to get rid of the photograph of the two women.

'Sunday?' said Buxton gruffly. 'I went out for a drink. A pub crawl. I had a good reason for getting drunk, so I did.'

'Was that the day Anne Downing broke off your engagement?' asked Quantrill.

Buxton nodded.

'Did you go out on your own?'

'Yes.'

'Did you go to Norfolk? Did you go to Thirling?'

Buxton said nothing.

'That's where I would have been tempted to go,' suggested Tait, needling the man deliberately. 'I can understand your wanting to hurt Jasmine Woods. Any man would loathe a woman who had an affair with the girl he wanted to marry.'

Buxton's healthy face became a darker red. The muscles at the sides of his jaw tightened with suppressed fury, but he said nothing.

'We shall be able to trace the man who killed Jasmine Woods,' said Quantrill quietly, 'because of the blood. It spurts, doesn't it, when a major blood vessel is ruptured— you're a farmer, you deal with animals, so you know about that. Even though he'll have cleaned his car, there's bound to be a speck left and we'll find it. And then there are the clothes he wore—it's not easy to get rid of clothes, and we'll find some trace of them somewhere. The valuables, too, the jade and netsuke that he took to try to give the impression that they were the reason for the murder. And the photograph, of course. The photograph of Jasmine Woods with your fiancée... What did you do with that, I wonder?'

Buxton made no reply, but the police did not need one. They watched his eyes instead and saw—with satisfaction or squeamishness, according to rank and the follow-up action they anticipated—that he glanced involuntarily at the slurry pit.

33

Douglas Quantrill looked at his digital watch, converted the figures to nearly a quarter-past eight, and drained his cup.

'I'll be back just after eleven, to take Alison to catch her train,' he informed his wife.

Molly turned a page of her newly-arrived *Woman's Weekly*. 'You needn't bother, dear,' she said absently, looking at an article on Spring Brides. 'Martin Tait's coming to do that.'

'Oh, is he? Does Alison know?'

'Not yet.' Molly placidly finished her toast and marmalade. 'He wanted to surprise her. He's been trying to talk to her for the past two weeks, ever since you caught that man who murdered Jasmine Woods. He's telephoned nearly every day, but she won't speak to him. Apparently he wants to apologize to her for something that happened at Oxlip Fair.' She looked up. 'What did happen at Oxlip, Douggie?'

'Damned if I know,' said Quantrill. 'Nobody ever tells me anything.'

'Well, this will be a good opportunity for the two of them to sort it out.'

'Huh!' He felt fiercely disappointed that he would not be able to see his daughter safely on the train. She was sleeping late—if she could sleep through the thumps and bangs made by Peter in process of getting up, late for school as usual—and so he wouldn't even be able to say good-bye. 'If Alison doesn't want to see Martin, I'm not having him forcing his attentions on her.'

'Oh, don't be so old-fashioned! It'll do no harm if Martin gives her a lift to the station. With Alison going back to work in London, there's no need for her to see him again if she doesn't want to. But if she changes her mind about him, well, she's coming down again at the end of April for Paula Timms's wedding—'

Quantrill nearly commented that his wife read too much romantic fiction, but thought better of it. He went into the hall, with Molly following, and picked up his tweed hat. 'You'd better say good-bye to her for me, then,' he said sadly. 'Tell her to take care, and to keep in touch.' He went to the front door.

'Douggie—' prompted his wife, hurt that his reawakened interest in her should be waning already.

'Oh—sorry, dear.' He smiled at her a little guiltily, but his kiss was affectionate as well as dutiful.

Molly accepted it, and brushed a crumb of toast from his lapel. 'And don't you forget to keep in touch with me, Doug Quantrill,' she reminded him.

Alison stopped dead in the front path when she saw Martin Tait's Citroën parked at the gate. He got out, said a cheerful good-morning, and began to load her cases. 'Your father sends his apologies,' he explained. 'He was tied up, so he asked me to come instead.'

Alison reluctantly took her seat beside him. 'Why do detectives always have to be such liars?' she said.

They drove in silence through the town and out along the Saintsbury Road, past the industrial estate.

'I suppose it's no use saying I'm sorry about Oxlip?' he offered, as the railway bridge came into sight.

'Not really. What's the point? It doesn't matter what we think of each other, does it?'

'I know you think badly of me,' he said, 'but I certainly don't of you.'

'Not after what I told you? About my feelings for Jasmine—'

'Good Lord, no.' In fact, Tait had discovered, her confession had made Alison rather more interesting. He had thought about her a good deal in the past fourteen days, and he could see that her unhappy love affair in London might well have led, temporarily, to a revulsion from men. He could understand how she had come to focus her emotions on Jasmine Woods. But that was all over; she needed now to return to

207

normality, and he felt challenged to make sure that she did so as soon as possible. That was why he had persisted in his attempts to see her.

She was, too, he decided, every bit as attractive as he had thought her that day on the bridge over the river. And now she was going back to live in London... He cursed himself for having been so slow off the mark when he first met her, misled by Jasmine's assured good looks into dismissing Alison as immature and unworthy of his attention.

'Well, I am sorry about Oxlip anyway,' he said. 'But we had to catch Smith—after all, it was possible that he was the murderer.'

'What'll happen to Gilbert?'

'Nothing very alarming. A suspended sentence, probably, with attendance at a drug clinic as one of the conditions. They'll try to help him rather than punish him—though whether he wants to be helped is another matter. Druggies often don't, that's their problem. They may have a heightened perception of beauty when they're on drugs, but that can mean that ordinary life becomes intolerable for them when they come off. He'll miss Jasmine, of course, she must have helped him tremendously.'

Tait drove over the coal sidings, parked his car and carried Allison's cases up on to the open platform. It was a bright, cool day and the wind from across the fields disordered her dark hair, and the gauzy scarf that was as green as her eyes. She looked understandably sad, though whether because of Jasmine Woods or because of leaving home, he couldn't decide. Something of both, perhaps.

'Supposing I hadn't told you what I did,' she said. 'Would you have charged Gilbert with Jasmine's murder?'

'No, we hadn't any evidence. All we were able to prove was what he'd told us, that he took the netsuke when he went up to the house next morning. But we'd have gone on questioning him for days, so you saved him from a lot of hassle. And you saved us—your father and me—a lot of work. I'm very grateful for your help. We'd have got the same result in the end, of course; we'd have caught Buxton ourselves, as soon as we started digging about in Jasmine's past life and putting facts together. It might have taken some time, but

ooner or later we'd have unearthed something that would
ave told us what we learned from you.'

Alison shivered. 'Then I'm glad I told you myself,' she
aid proudly. 'It took a lot of courage, but it was worth it.
'oor Jasmine . . . at least some part of her life has been left
ndisturbed.'

Tait felt too protective towards her to tell her that the
onfession had been unnecessary. All she'd needed to do was
o tell him about the missing photograph. He could have
vorked out Buxton's involvement for himself.

He changed the subject. He wanted to talk to her about
erself, not about the Jasmine Woods case. 'What are you
oing to do when you get back to London?' he asked. The
latform near the booking office was becoming crowded and
o he steered her up towards the end, his fingers touching
er elbow so lightly that she didn't notice.

'Oh, I'll probably do temporary secretarial work, until I
an find something more interesting. I'm not exactly sure
vhat I want to do, except that I don't want to spend the rest
f my life being a secretary. But I need time to look round, so
'll stick to typing for a bit. I'm going to stay with my sister at
irst, but I shall try to find a share in a flat as soon as I can.
'hat's what I had before.'

Tait didn't like the sound of a shared flat. If that was the
et-up she'd lived in before, when she'd had an affair with the
vretched man who treated her badly, he would prefer her to
ive with her sister. There were altogether too many spare
nen in London. The DCI must be out of his mind to let a
ice girl like Alison go back to a place like that with the idea
f fending for herself.

He debated the possibility of putting in some kind of
id. Normally he'd find it easy. If you put a girl on a train,
ou naturally kissed her good-bye, and a kiss was a useful
tart to further negotiations.

But he couldn't attempt to kiss Alison just yet. Not
ecause she'd told him she didn't like him; that was merely
art of the challenge. He couldn't attempt to kiss her because
e didn't want her to think him brash or crude or insincere.
Ie didn't want to risk putting her off.

She pushed a blown strand of hair out of her eyes. 'I've
got to get away from home and the family,' she explained

earnestly, 'so that I can sort myself out. After all, it comes as
shock when you realize that you aren't like most other girl
Oh, perhaps I am, of course. Perhaps the way I felt abou
Jasmine was just a temporary reaction. I suppose I may car
on typing, get married, have two or three children and
part-time job and be completely happy. But at the moment
don't know what lifestyle I want. I've seen so many altern
tives. I do know that I don't want to join a commune, and
certainly don't feel militantly women's lib. I'd hate to be a
unmarried mother, and I don't think I want to be lik
Jasmine. I don't know what I want, except an emotion
breathing space. I need time to come to terms with mysel
After what's happened to me here, I feel...ambiguous.'

She looked delightful, thought Tait. He liked the wa
her nose tilted, and the way strands of hair blew across he
face and clung to her full, moist lower lip until she brushe
them away. And the seriousness with which she talked non
sense was oddly endearing.

A signal bell rang. He went on looking at her, trying t
fix her image in his mind, but she glanced up the railwa
track in the direction of Yarchester. The lines were straight fe
nearly two miles, and she could just see at the far end th
pinhead that would materialize into a train.

'Martin,' she said.

'Mm?'

'Will you do something for me?'

'Of course, if I can.'

She took a deep breath. 'Will you kiss me?' she said.
'*What?*'

'Please. You see, I hate being ambiguous. I don't want t
go back to London not knowing whether I'm turned on t
men or to women. And I can ask you to do it because we'r
not emotionally involved. We don't even like each othe
much. It'll be a perfectly objective exercise, but I think I'
know right away whether I'm still off men. You don't mind, d
you?'

He was too dazed to reply. Alison had closed her eye
and lifted her face, like a child waiting with resignation for
farewell kiss from her least favourite uncle.

He felt absurdly nervous. He put his hands on he
shoulders and found that he was shaking slightly. He gave he

a gentle, tentative kiss, first on the cheek and then on the mouth. She didn't move. He felt his confidence returning, and applied a little more pressure.

Gradually, experimentally, her lips gave way. He held her more tightly, tasted her tongue, and immediately felt the world cartwheeling round him. For the first time since he was seventeen, he knew that he was in danger of falling seriously in love. He had to restrain himself from clutching her to him and babbling about letters, about telephone calls, about going up to London to see her.

Alison broke away from him and stood back. 'Thank you,' she said.

Tait blinked and tried to steady his breathing. 'Well,' he said, hoping that he sounded nonchalant. 'I imagine that's resolved your ambiguity for you, hasn't it?'

She said nothing, but looked grave and a little judicial, as though she had been asked to pronounce on the quality of a wine.

'Hasn't it?' he appealed.

Her reply was lost in the chunter and throb of the diesel engine as the London train came in.

ABOUT THE AUTHOR

SHEILA RADLEY is a well-known British writer of romantic thrillers as well as mysteries. She holds a degree in history from the University of London. For nearly two decades she has helped run a village store and post office in East Anglia, England.

Kinsey Millhone is . . .

"The best new private eye."   —The Detroit News

"A tough-cookie with a soft center."   —Newsweek

"A stand-out specimen of the new female operatives."
                                        —Philadelphia Inquirer

Sue Grafton is . . .

The Shamus and Anthony Award winning creator of Kinsey
Millhone and quite simply one of the hottest new mystery
writers around.

Bantam is . . .

The proud publisher of Sue Grafton's Kinsey Millhone
mysteries:

    ☐ 26563 "A" IS FOR ALIBI $3.50
    ☐ 26061 "B" IS FOR BURGLAR $3.50
    ☐ 26468 "C" IS FOR CORPSE $3.50